Eleven Kinds of Loneliness

Eleven Kinds of Loneliness

SHORT STORIES BY Richard Yates

GREENWOOD PRESS, PUBLISHERS
WESTPORT, CONNECTICUT

The Library of Congress has catalogued this publication as follows:

Library of Congress Cataloging in Publication Data

Yates, Richard, 1926–
  Eleven kinds of loneliness.

    CONTENTS: Doctor Jack-o'-lantern.--The best of
everything.--Jody rolled the bones. [etc.]
    I. Title.
[PZ4.Y335El7] [PS3575.A83]   813'.5'4   72–603
ISBN 0-8371-5727-7

Some of these stories were first published in *Atlantic, Charm, Cosmopolitan,* and *Esquire.*
The following stories are reprinted with the permission of Charles Scribner's Sons from SHORT STORY 1, *The Best of Everything* by Richard Yates: "Fun with a Stranger" (Copyright 1955 Richard Yates); "The Best of Everything" (Copyright 1954 Richard Yates); "Jody Rolled the Bones" (Copyright 1953 Richard Yates); "A Really Good Jazz Piano" (Copyright © 1958 Richard Yates).
The author is grateful to Mills Music, Inc., for permission to quote a modified version of the following lines from "Sweet Lorraine," words by Mitchell Parish, music by Cliff Burwell:

> "A pair of eyes
> That are bluer than the summer skies
> When you see them you will realize
> Why I love my sweet Lorraine."

Copyright 1928 Mills Music, Inc. Used by permission of the copyright owner.
The author is grateful to Irving Berlin Music Corporation for permission to quote (with a change of spelling from "fellow" to "fella") the lyrics from "Easter Parade" by Irving Berlin on page 26.
Copyright 1933 Irving Berlin. Copyright Renewed. Reprinted by Permission of Irving Berlin Music Corporation.

Originally published in 1962 by Little, Brown and Company, Boston, in association with Atlantic Monthly Press

Reprinted with the permission of Richard Yates

Reprinted in 1972 by Greenwood Press, a division of Congressional Information Service, Inc. 88 Post Road West, Westport, Connecticut 06881

Library of Congress catalog card number 72-603
ISBN 0-8371-5727-7

Printed in the United States of America

10 9 8 7 6 5 4 3

To

Sharon Elizabeth

and

Monica Jane

Contents

Doctor Jack-o'-lantern

ALL Miss Price had been told about the new boy was that he'd spent most of his life in some kind of orphanage, and that the gray-haired "aunt and uncle" with whom he now lived were really foster parents, paid by the Welfare Department of the City of New York. A less dedicated or less imaginative teacher might have pressed for more details, but Miss Price was content with the rough outline. It was enough, in fact, to fill her with a sense of mission that shone from her eyes, as plain as love, from the first morning he joined the fourth grade.

He arrived early and sat in the back row — his spine very straight, his ankles crossed precisely under the desk and his hands folded on the very center of its top, as if symmetry might make him less conspicuous — and while the other children were filing in and settling down, he received a long, expressionless stare from each of them.

"We have a new classmate this morning," Miss Price said, laboring the obvious in a way that made everybody want to giggle. "His name is Vincent Sabella and he comes from New York City. I know we'll all do our best to make him feel at home."

This time they all swung around to stare at once, which caused him to duck his head slightly and shift his weight from one buttock to the other. Ordinarily, the fact of someone's coming from New York might have held a certain prestige, for to most of the children the city was an awesome, adult place that swallowed up their fathers every day, and which they themselves were permitted to visit only rarely, in their best clothes, as a treat. But anyone could see at a glance that Vincent Sabella had nothing whatever to do with skyscrapers. Even if you could ignore his tangled black hair and gray skin, his clothes would have given him away: absurdly new corduroys, absurdly old sneakers and a yellow sweatshirt, much too small, with the shredded remains of a Mickey Mouse design stamped on its chest. Clearly, he was from the part of New York that you had to pass through on the train to Grand Central — the part where people hung bedding over their windowsills and leaned out on it all day in a trance of boredom, and where you got vistas of straight, deep streets, one after another, all alike in the clutter of their sidewalks and all swarming with gray boys at play in some desperate kind of ball game.

The girls decided that he wasn't very nice and turned away, but the boys lingered in their scrutiny, looking him up and down with faint smiles. This was the kind of kid they were accustomed to thinking of as "tough," the kind whose stares had made all of them uncomfortable at one time or another in unfamiliar neighborhoods; here was a unique chance for retaliation.

"What would you like us to call you, Vincent?" Miss Price inquired. "I mean, do you prefer Vincent, or Vince, or — or what?" (It was purely an academic question; even Miss Price knew that the boys would call him "Sabella" and that the girls wouldn't call him anything at all.)

"Vinny's okay," he said in a strange, croaking voice that had evidently yelled itself hoarse down the ugly streets of his home.

"I'm afraid I didn't hear you," she said, craning her pretty head forward and to one side so that a heavy lock of hair swung free of one shoulder. "Did you say 'Vince'?"

"Vinny, I said," he said again, squirming.

"Vincent, is it? All right, then, Vincent." A few of the class giggled, but nobody bothered to correct her; it would be more fun to let the mistake continue.

"I won't take time to introduce you to everyone by name, Vincent," Miss Price went on, "because I think it would be simpler just to let you learn the names as we go along, don't you? Now, we won't expect you to take any real part in the work for the first day or so; just take your time, and if there's anything you don't understand, why, don't be afraid to ask."

He made an unintelligible croak and smiled fleetingly, just enough to show that the roots of his teeth were green.

"Now then," Miss Price said, getting down to business. "This is Monday morning, and so the first thing on the program is reports. Who'd like to start off?"

Vincent Sabella was momentarily forgotten as six or seven hands went up, and Miss Price drew back in mock confusion. "Goodness, we do have a lot of reports this morning," she said. The idea of the reports — a fifteen-minute period every Monday in which the children were encouraged to relate their experiences over the weekend — was Miss Price's own, and she took a pardonable pride in it. The principal had commended her on it at a recent staff meeting, pointing out that it made a splendid bridge between the worlds of school and home, and that it was a fine way for children to learn poise and assurance. It called for intelligent supervision — the shy children had to be drawn out and the show-offs curbed — but in general, as Miss Price had assured the principal, it was fun for everyone. She particularly hoped it would be fun today, to help put Vincent Sabella at ease, and that was why she chose Nancy Parker to start off; there was nobody like Nancy for holding an audience.

The others fell silent as Nancy moved gracefully to the head of the room; even the two or three girls who secretly despised her had to feign enthrallment when she spoke (she was that popular), and every boy in the class, who at recess liked nothing better than to push her shrieking into the mud, was unable to watch her without an idiotically tremulous smile.

"Well —" she began, and then she clapped a hand over her mouth while everyone laughed.

"Oh, *Nancy,*" Miss Price said. "You *know* the rule about starting a report with 'well.' "

Nancy knew the rule; she had only broken it to get the laugh. Now she let her fit of giggles subside, ran her fragile forefingers down the side seams of her skirt, and began again in the proper way. "On Friday my whole family went for a ride in my brother's new car. My brother bought this new Pontiac last week, and he wanted to take us all for a ride — you know, to try it out and everything? So we went into White Plains and had dinner in a restaurant there, and then we all wanted to go see this movie, 'Doctor Jekyll and Mr. Hyde,' but my brother said it was too horrible and everything, and I wasn't old enough to enjoy it — oh, he made me so mad! And then, let's see. On Saturday I stayed home all day and helped my mother make my sister's wedding dress. My sister's engaged to be married, you see, and my mother's making this wedding dress for her? So we did that, and then on Sunday this friend of my brother's came over for dinner, and then they both had to get back to college that night, and I was allowed to stay up late and say goodbye to them and everything, and I guess that's all." She always had a sure instinct for keeping her performance brief — or rather, for making it seem briefer than it really was.

"Very good, Nancy," Miss Price said. "Now, who's next?"

Warren Berg was next, elaborately hitching up his pants as he made his way down the aisle. "On Saturday I went over to Bill Stringer's house for lunch," he began in his direct, man-to-man style, and Bill Stringer wriggled bashfully in the front row. Warren Berg and Bill Stringer were great friends, and their reports often overlapped. "And then after lunch we went into White Plains, on our bikes. Only we *saw* 'Doctor Jekyll and Mr. Hyde.' " Here he nodded his head in Nancy's direction, and Nancy got another laugh by making a little whimper of envy. "It was real good, too," he went on, with mounting excitement. "It's all about this guy who —"

"About *a man* who," Miss Price corrected.

"About a man who mixes up this chemical, like, that he drinks? And whenever he drinks this chemical, he changes into this real monster, like? You see him drink this chemical, and then you see his hands start to get all scales all over them, like a reptile and everything, and then you see his face start to change into this real horrible-looking face — with fangs and all? Sticking out of his mouth?"

All the girls shuddered in pleasure. "Well," Miss Price said, "I think Nancy's brother was probably wise in not wanting her to see it. What did you do *after* the movie, Warren?"

There was a general "Aw-w-w!" of disappointment — everyone wanted to hear more about the scales and fangs — but Miss Price never liked to let the reports degenerate into accounts of movies. Warren continued without much enthusiasm: all they had done after the movie was fool around Bill Stringer's yard until suppertime. "And then on Sunday," he said, brightening again, "Bill Stringer came over to *my* house, and my dad helped us rig up this old tire on this long rope? From a tree? There's this steep hill down behind my house, you see — this ravine, like? — and we hung this tire so that what you do is, you take the tire and run a little ways and then lift your feet, and you go swinging way, way out over the ravine and back again."

"That sounds like fun," Miss Price said, glancing at her watch.

"Oh, it's *fun*, all right," Warren conceded. But then he hitched up his pants again and added, with a puckering of his forehead, " 'Course, it's pretty dangerous. You let go of that tire or anything, you'd get a bad fall. Hit a rock or anything, you'd probably break your leg, or your spine. But my dad said he trusted us both to look out for our own safety."

"Well, I'm afraid that's all we'll have time for, Warren,"

Miss Price said. "Now, there's just time for one more report. Who's ready? Arthur Cross?"

There was a soft groan, because Arthur Cross was the biggest dope in class and his reports were always a bore. This time it turned out to be something tedious about going to visit his uncle on Long Island. At one point he made a slip — he said "botormoat" instead of "motorboat" — and everyone laughed with the particular edge of scorn they reserved for Arthur Cross. But the laughter died abruptly when it was joined by a harsh, dry croaking from the back of the room. Vincent Sabella was laughing too, green teeth and all, and they all had to glare at him until he stopped.

When the reports were over, everyone settled down for school. It was recess time before any of the children thought much about Vincent Sabella again, and then they thought of him only to make sure he was left out of everything. He wasn't in the group of boys that clustered around the horizontal bar to take turns at skinning-the-cat, or the group that whispered in a far corner of the playground, hatching a plot to push Nancy Parker in the mud. Nor was he in the larger group, of which even Arthur Cross was a member, that chased itself in circles in a frantic variation of the game of tag. He couldn't join the girls, of course, or the boys from other classes, and so he joined nobody. He stayed on the apron of the playground, close to school, and for the first part of the recess he pretended to be very busy with the laces of his sneakers. He would squat to undo and retie them, straighten up and take a few experimental steps in a springy, athletic way, and then get down and go to work on them again. After five minutes of this he gave it up, picked up a handful of pebbles and began shying them at an invisible target several yards away. That was good for another five minutes, but then there were still five minutes left, and he could think of nothing to do but stand there, first with his hands in his pockets, then with his hands on his hips, and then with his arms folded in a manly way across his chest.

Miss Price stood watching all this from the doorway, and she spent the full recess wondering if she ought to go out and do something about it. She guessed it would be better not to.

She managed to control the same impulse at recess the next day, and every other day that week, though every day it grew more difficult. But one thing she could not control was a tendency to let her anxiety show in class. All Vincent Sabella's errors in schoolwork were publicly excused, even those having nothing to do with his newness, and all his accomplishments were singled out for special mention. Her campaign to build him up was painfully obvious, and never more so than when she tried to make it subtle; once, for instance, in explaining an arithmetic problem, she said, "Now, suppose Warren Berg and Vincent Sabella went to the store with fifteen cents each, and candy bars cost ten cents. How many candy bars would each boy have?" By the end of the week he was well on the way to becoming the worst possible kind of teacher's pet, a victim of the teacher's pity.

On Friday she decided the best thing to do would be to speak to him privately, and try to draw him out. She could say something about the pictures he had painted in art class — that would do for an opening — and she decided to do it at lunchtime.

The only trouble was that lunchtime, next to recess, was the most trying part of Vincent Sabella's day. Instead of going home for an hour as the other children did, he brought his lunch to school in a wrinkled paper bag and ate it in the classroom, which always made for a certain amount of awkwardness. The last children to leave would see him still seated apologetically at his desk, holding his paper bag, and anyone who happened to straggle back later for a forgotten hat or sweater would surprise him in the middle of his meal — perhaps shielding a hard-boiled egg from view or wiping mayonnaise from his mouth with a furtive hand. It was a situation that Miss Price did not improve by walking up to him while the room was still half full of children and sitting prettily on the edge of the desk beside his, making it clear that she was cutting her own lunch hour short in order to be with him.

"Vincent," she began, "I've been meaning to tell you how much I enjoyed those pictures of yours. They're really very good."

He mumbled something and shifted his eyes to the cluster of departing children at the door. She went right on talking and smiling, elaborating on her praise of the pictures; and finally, after the door had closed behind the last child, he was able to give her his attention. He did so tentatively at first; but the more she talked, the more he seemed to relax, until she realized she was putting him at ease. It was as simple and as gratifying as stroking a cat. She had finished with the pictures now and moved on, triumphantly, to broader fields of praise. "It's never easy," she was saying, "to come to a new school and adjust yourself to the — well, the new work, and new working methods, and I think you've done a splendid job so far. I really do. But tell me, do you think you're going to like it here?"

He looked at the floor just long enough to make his reply — "It's awright" — and then his eyes stared into hers again.

"I'm so glad. Please don't let me interfere with your lunch, Vincent. Do go ahead and eat, that is, if you don't mind my sitting here with you." But it was now abundantly clear that he didn't mind at all, and he began to unwrap a bologna sandwich with what she felt sure was the best appetite he'd had all week. It wouldn't even have mattered very much now if someone from the class had come in and watched, though it was probably just as well that no one did.

Miss Price sat back more comfortably on the desk top, crossed her legs and allowed one slim stockinged foot to slip part of the way out of its moccasin. "Of course," she went on, "it always does take a little time to sort of get your bearings in a new school. For one thing, well, it's never too easy for the new member of the class to make friends with the other members. What I mean is, you mustn't mind if the others seem a little rude to you at first. Actually, they're just as anxious to make friends as you are, but they're shy. All it takes is a little time, and a little effort on your part as well as theirs. Not too much, of course, but a little. Now for instance, these reports we have Monday mornings — they're a fine way for people to get to know one another. A person never feels he has to make a report; it's just a thing he can do if he wants to. And that's only one way of helping others to know the kind of person you are; there are lots and lots of ways. The main thing to remember is that making friends is the most natural thing in the world, and it's only a question of time until you have all the friends you want. And in the meantime, Vincent, I hope you'll consider *me* your friend, and feel free to call on me for whatever advice or anything you might need. Will you do that?"

He nodded, swallowing.

"Good." She stood up and smoothed her skirt over her long thighs. "Now I must go or I'll be late for *my* lunch. But I'm glad we had this little talk, Vincent, and I hope we'll have others."

It was probably a lucky thing that she stood up when she did, for if she'd stayed on that desk a minute longer Vincent Sabella would have thrown his arms around her and buried his face in the warm gray flannel of her lap, and that might have been enough to confuse the most dedicated and imaginative of teachers.

At report time on Monday morning, nobody was more surprised than Miss Price when Vincent Sabella's smudged hand was among the first and most eager to rise. Apprehensively she considered letting someone else start off, but then, for fear of hurting his feelings, she said, "All right, Vincent," in as matter-of-fact a way as she could manage.

There was a suggestion of muffled titters from the class as he walked confidently to the head of the room and turned to face his audience. He looked, if anything, too confident: there were signs, in the way he held his shoulders and the way his eyes shone, of the terrible poise of panic.

"Saturday I seen that pitcha," he announced.

"Saw, Vincent," Miss Price corrected gently.

"That's what I mean," he said; "I sore that pitcha. 'Doctor Jack-o'-lantern and Mr. Hide.' "

There was a burst of wild, delighted laughter and a chorus of correction: "Doctor *Jekyll!*"

He was unable to speak over the noise. Miss Price was on her feet, furious. "It's a *perfectly natural mistake!*" she was saying. "There's no reason for any of you to be so rude. Go on, Vincent, and please excuse this very silly interruption." The laughter subsided, but the class continued to shake their heads derisively from side to side. It hadn't, of course, been a perfectly natural mistake at all; for one thing it proved that he was a hopeless dope, and for another it proved that he was lying.

"That's what I mean," he continued. " 'Doctor Jackal and Mr. Hide.' I got it a little mixed up. Anyways, I seen all about where his teet' start comin' outa his mout' and all like that, and I thought it was very good. And then on Sunday my mudda and fodda come out to see me in this car they got. This Buick. My fodda siz, 'Vinny, wanna go for a little ride?' I siz, 'Sure, where yiz goin'?' He siz, 'Anyplace ya like.' So I siz, 'Let's go out in the country a ways, get on one of them big roads and make some time.' So we go out — oh, I guess fifty, sixty miles — and we're cruisin' along this highway, when this cop starts tailin' us? My fodda siz, 'Don't worry, we'll shake him,' and he steps on it, see? My mudda's gettin' pretty scared, but my fodda siz, 'Don't worry, dear.' He's tryin' to make this turn, see, so he can get off the highway and shake the cop? But just when he's makin' the turn, the cop opens up and starts shootin', see?"

By this time the few members of the class who could bear to look at him at all were doing so with heads on one side and mouths partly open, the way you look at a broken arm or a circus freak.

"We just barely made it," Vincent went on, his eyes gleaming, "and this one bullet got my fodda in the shoulder. Didn't hurt him bad — just grazed him, like — so my mudda bandaged it up for him and all, but he couldn't do no more drivin' after that, and we had to get him to a doctor, see? So my fodda siz, 'Vinny, think you can drive a ways?' I siz, 'Sure, if you show me how.' So he showed me how to work the gas and the brake, and all like that, and I drove to the doctor. My mudda siz, 'I'm prouda you, Vinny, drivin' all by yourself.' So anyways, we got to the doctor, got my fodda fixed up and all, and then he drove us back home." He was breathless. After an uncertain pause he said, "And that's all." Then he walked quickly back to his desk, his stiff new corduroy pants whistling faintly with each step.

"Well, that was very — entertaining, Vincent," Miss Price said, trying to act as if nothing had happened. "Now, who's next?" But nobody raised a hand.

Recess was worse than usual for him that day; at least it was until he found a place to hide — a narrow concrete alley, blind except for several closed fire-exit doors, that cut between two sections of the school building. It was reassuringly dismal and cool in there — he could stand with his back to the wall and his eyes guarding the entrance, and the noises of recess were as remote as the sunshine. But when the bell rang he had to go back to class, and in another hour it was lunchtime.

Miss Price left him alone until her own meal was finished. Then, after standing with one hand on the doorknob for a full minute to gather courage, she went in and sat beside him for another little talk, just as he was trying to swallow the last of a pimento-cheese sandwich.

"Vincent," she began, "we all enjoyed your report this morning, but I think we would have enjoyed it more—a great deal more — if you'd told us something about your real life instead. I mean," she hurried on, "for instance, I noticed you were wearing a nice new windbreaker this morning. It *is* new, isn't it? And did your aunt buy it for you over the weekend?"

He did not deny it.

"Well then, why couldn't you have told us about going to the store with your aunt, and buying the windbreaker, and whatever you did afterwards. That would have made a perfectly good report." She paused, and for the first time looked steadily into his eyes. "You do understand what I'm trying to say, don't you, Vincent?"

He wiped crumbs of bread from his lips, looked at the floor, and nodded.

"And you'll remember next time, won't you?"

He nodded again. "Please may I be excused, Miss Price?"

"Of course you may."

He went to the boys' lavatory and vomited. Afterwards he washed his face and drank a little water, and then he returned to the classroom. Miss Price was busy at her desk now, and didn't look up. To avoid getting involved with her again, he wandered out to the cloakroom and sat on one of the long benches, where he picked up someone's discarded overshoe and turned it over and over in his hands. In a little while he heard the chatter of returning children, and to avoid being discovered there, he got up and went to the fire-exit door. Pushing it open, he found that it gave onto the alley he had hidden in that morning, and he slipped outside. For a minute or two he just stood there, looking at the blankness of the concrete wall; then he found a piece of chalk in his pocket and wrote out all the dirty words he could think of, in block letters a foot high. He had put down four words and was trying to remember a fifth when he heard a shuffling at the door behind him. Arthur Cross was there, holding the door open and reading the words with wide eyes. "Boy," he said in an awed half-whisper. "Boy, you're gonna get it. You're really gonna *get* it."

Startled, and then suddenly calm, Vincent Sabella palmed his chalk, hooked his thumbs in his belt and turned on Arthur

Cross with a menacing look. "Yeah?" he inquired. "Who's gonna squeal on me?"

"Well, nobody's gonna *squeal* on you," Arthur Cross said uneasily, "but you shouldn't go around writing —"

"Arright," Vincent said, advancing a step. His shoulders were slumped, his head thrust forward and his eyes narrowed, like Edward G. Robinson. "Arright. That's all I wanna know. I don't like squealers, unnastand?"

While he was saying this, Warren Berg and Bill Stringer appeared in the doorway — just in time to hear it and to see the words on the wall before Vincent turned on them. "And that goes fa you too, unnastand?" he said. "Both a yiz."

And the remarkable thing was that both their faces fell into the same foolish, defensive smile that Arthur Cross was wearing. It wasn't until they had glanced at each other that they were able to meet his eyes with the proper degree of contempt, and by then it was too late. "Think you're pretty smart, don'tcha, Sabella?" Bill Stringer said.

"Never mind what I think," Vincent told him. "You heard what I said. Now let's get back inside."

And they could do nothing but move aside to make way for him, and follow him dumfounded into the cloakroom.

It was Nancy Parker who squealed — although, of course, with someone like Nancy Parker you didn't think of it as squealing. She had heard everything from the cloakroom; as soon as the boys came in she peeked into the alley, saw the words and, setting her face in a prim frown, went straight to Miss Price. Miss Price was just about to call the class to order for the afternoon when Nancy came up and whispered in her ear. They both disappeared into the cloakroom — from which, after a moment, came the sound of the fire-exit door being abruptly slammed — and when they returned to class Nancy was flushed with righteousness, Miss Price very pale. No announcement was made. Classes proceeded in the ordinary way all afternoon, though it was clear that Miss Price was upset, and it wasn't until she was dismissing the children at three o'clock that she brought the thing into the open. "Will Vincent Sabella please remain seated?" She nodded at the rest of the class. "That's all."

While the room was clearing out she sat at her desk, closed her eyes and massaged the frail bridge of her nose with thumb and forefinger, sorting out half-remembered fragments of a book she had once read on the subject of seriously disturbed children. Perhaps, after all, she should never have undertaken the responsibility of Vincent Sabella's loneliness. Perhaps the whole thing called for the attention of a specialist. She took a deep breath.

"Come over here and sit beside me, Vincent," she said, and when he had settled himself, she looked at him. "I want you to tell me the truth. Did you write those words on the wall outside?"

He stared at the floor.

"Look at me," she said, and he looked at her. She had never looked prettier: her cheeks slightly flushed, her eyes shining and her sweet mouth pressed into a self-conscious frown. "First of all," she said, handing him a small enameled basin streaked with poster paint, "I want you to take this to the boys' room and fill it with hot water and soap."

He did as he was told, and when he came back, carrying the basin carefully to keep the suds from spilling, she was sorting out some old rags in the bottom drawer of her desk. "Here," she said, selecting one and shutting the drawer in a businesslike way. "This will do. Soak this up." She led him back to the fire exit and stood in the alley watching him, silently, while he washed off all the words.

When the job had been done, and the rag and basin put away, they sat down at Miss Price's desk again. "I suppose you think I'm angry with you, Vincent," she said. "Well, I'm not. I almost wish I could be angry — that would make it much easier — but instead I'm hurt. I've tried to be a good friend to you, and I thought you wanted to be my friend too. But this kind of thing — well, it's very hard to be friendly with a person who'd do a thing like that."

She saw, gratefully, that there were tears in his eyes. "Vincent, perhaps I understand some things better than you think. Perhaps I understand that sometimes, when a person does a thing like that, it isn't really because he wants to hurt anyone, but only because he's unhappy. He knows it isn't a good thing to do, and he even knows it isn't going to make him any happier afterwards, but he goes ahead and does it anyway. Then when he finds he's lost a friend, he's terribly sorry, but it's too late. The thing is done."

She allowed this somber note to reverberate in the silence of the room for a little while before she spoke again. "I won't be able to forget this, Vincent. But perhaps, just this once, we can still be friends — as long as I understand that you didn't mean to hurt me. But you must promise me that you won't forget it either. Never forget that when you do a thing like that, you're going to hurt people who want very much to like you, and in that way you're going to hurt yourself. Will you promise me to remember that, dear?"

The "dear" was as involuntary as the slender hand that reached out and held the shoulder of his sweatshirt; both made his head hang lower than before.

"All right," she said. "You may go now."

He got his windbreaker out of the cloakroom and left, avoiding the tired uncertainty of her eyes. The corridors were deserted, and dead silent except for the hollow, rhythmic knocking of a janitor's push-broom against some distant wall. His own rubber-soled tread only added to the silence; so did the lonely little noise made by the zipping-up of his windbreaker, and so did the faint mechanical sigh of the heavy front door. The silence made it all the more startling when he found, several yards down the concrete walk outside, that two boys were walking beside him: Warren Berg and Bill Stringer. They were both smiling at him in an eager, almost friendly way.

"What'd she do to ya, anyway?" Bill Stringer asked.

Caught off guard, Vincent barely managed to put on his Edward G. Robinson face in time. "Nunnya business," he said, and walked faster.

"No, listen — wait up, hey," Warren Berg said, as they trotted to keep up with him. "What'd she do, anyway? She bawl ya out, or what? Wait up, hey, Vinny."

The name made him tremble all over. He had to jam his hands in his windbreaker pockets and force himself to keep on walking; he had to force his voice to be steady when he said "Nunnya *business*, I told ya. Lea' me alone."

But they were right in step with him now. "Boy, she must of given you the works," Warren Berg persisted. "What'd she say, anyway? C'mon, tell us, Vinny."

This time the name was too much for him. It overwhelmed his resistance and made his softening knees slow down to a slack, conversational stroll. "She din say nothin'" he said at last; and then after a dramatic pause he added, "She let the ruler do her talkin' for her."

"The *ruler?* Ya mean she used a *ruler* on ya?" Their faces were stunned, either with disbelief or admiration, and it began to look more and more like admiration as they listened.

"On the knuckles," Vincent said through tightening lips. "Five times on each hand. She siz, 'Make a fist. Lay it out here on the desk.' Then she takes the ruler and *Whop! Whop! Whop!* Five times. Ya think that don't hurt, you're crazy."

Miss Price, buttoning her polo coat as the front door whispered shut behind her, could scarcely believe her eyes. This couldn't be Vincent Sabella — this perfectly normal, perfectly happy boy on the sidewalk ahead of her, flanked by attentive friends. But it was, and the scene made her want to laugh aloud with pleasure and relief. He was going to be all right, after all. For all her well-intentioned groping in the shadows she could never have predicted a scene like this, and certainly could never have caused it to happen. But it was happening, and it just proved, once again, that she would never understand the ways of children.

She quickened her graceful stride and overtook them, turning to smile down at them as she passed. "Goodnight, boys," she called, intending it as a kind of cheerful benediction; and then, embarrassed by their three startled faces, she smiled even wider and said, "Goodness, it *is* getting colder, isn't it? That windbreaker of yours looks nice and warm, Vincent. I envy you." Finally they nodded bashfully at her; she called goodnight again, turned, and continued on her way to the bus stop.

She left a profound silence in her wake. Staring after her, Warren Berg and Bill Stringer waited until she had disappeared around the corner before they turned on Vincent Sabella.

"Ruler, my eye!" Bill Stringer said. "Ruler, my eye!" He gave Vincent a disgusted shove that sent him stumbling against Warren Berg, who shoved him back.

"Jeez, you lie about *everything*, don'tcha, Sabella? You lie about *everything!*"

Jostled off balance, keeping his hands tight in the windbreaker pockets, Vincent tried in vain to retain his dignity. "Think *I* care if yiz believe me?" he said, and then because he couldn't think of anything else to say, he said it again. "Think *I* care if yiz believe me?"

But he was walking alone. Warren Berg and Bill Stringer were drifting away across the street, walking backwards in order to look back on him with furious contempt. "Just like the lies you told about the policeman shooting your father," Bill Stringer called.

"Even *movies* he lies about," Warren Berg put in; and suddenly doubling up with artificial laughter he cupped both hands to his mouth and yelled, "Hey, Doctor Jack-o'-lantern!"

It wasn't a very good nickname, but it had an authentic ring to it — the kind of a name that might spread around, catch on quickly, and stick. Nudging each other, they both took up the cry:

"What's the matter, Doctor Jack-o'-lantern?"

"Why don'tcha run on home with Miss Price, Doctor Jack-o'-lantern?"

"So long, Doctor Jack-o'-lantern!"

Vincent Sabella went on walking, ignoring them, waiting until they were out of sight. Then he turned and retraced his steps all the way back to school, around through the playground and back to the alley, where the wall was still dark in spots from the circular scrubbing of his wet rag.

Choosing a dry place, he got out his chalk and began to draw a head with great care, in profile, making the hair long and rich and taking his time over the face, erasing it with moist fingers and reworking it until it was the most beautiful face he had ever drawn: a delicate nose, slightly parted lips, an eye with lashes that curved as gracefully as a bird's wing. He paused to admire it with a lover's solemnity; then from the lips he drew a line that connected with a big speech balloon, and in the balloon he wrote, so angrily that the chalk kept breaking in his fingers, every one of the words he had written that noon. Returning to the head, he gave it a slender neck and gently sloping shoulders, and then, with bold strikes, he gave it the body of a naked woman: great breasts with hard little nipples, a trim waist, a dot for a navel, wide hips and thighs that flared around a triangle of fiercely scribbled pubic hair. Beneath the picture he printed its title: "Miss Price."

He stood there looking at it for a little while, breathing hard, and then he went home.

— 1954

The Best of Everything

Nobody expected Grace to do any work the Friday before her wedding. In fact, nobody would let her, whether she wanted to or not.

A gardenia corsage lay in a cellophane box beside her typewriter — from Mr. Atwood, her boss — and tucked inside the envelope that came with it was a ten-dollar gift certificate from Bloomingdale's. Mr. Atwood had treated her with a special shy courtliness ever since the time she necked with him at the office Christmas party, and now when she went in to thank him he was all hunched over, rattling desk drawers, blushing and grinning and barely meeting her eyes.

"Aw, now, don't mention it, Grace," he said. "Pleasure's all mine. Here, you need a pin to put that gadget on with?"

"There's a pin that came with it," she said, holding up the corsage. "See? A nice white one."

Beaming, he watched her pin the flowers high on the lapel of her suit. Then he cleared his throat importantly and pulled out the writing panel of his desk, ready to give the morning's dictation. But it turned out there were only two short letters, and it wasn't until an hour later, when she caught him handing over a pile of Dictaphone cylinders to Central Typing, that she realized he had done her a favor.

"That's very sweet of you, Mr. Atwood," she said, "but I do

think you ought to give me all your work today, just like any oth—"

"Aw, now, Grace," he said. "You only get married once."

The girls all made a fuss over her too, crowding around her desk and giggling, asking again and again to see Ralph's photograph ("Oh, he's *cute!*"), while the office manager looked on nervously, reluctant to be a spoilsport but anxious to point out that it was, after all, a working day.

Then at lunch there was the traditional little party at Schrafft's — nine women and girls, giddy on their unfamiliar cocktails, letting their chicken à la king grow cold while they pummeled her with old times and good wishes. There were more flowers and another gift — a silver candy dish for which all the girls had whisperingly chipped in.

Grace said "Thank you" and "I certainly do appreciate it" and "I don't know what to say" until her head rang with the words and the corners of her mouth ached from smiling, and she thought the afternoon would never end.

Ralph called up about four o'clock, exuberant. "How ya doin', honey?" he asked, and before she could answer he said, "Listen. Guess what I got?"

"I don't know. A present or something? What?" She tried to sound excited, but it wasn't easy.

"A bonus. Fifty dollars." She could almost see the flattening of his lips as he said "fifty dollars" with the particular earnestness he reserved for pronouncing sums of money.

"Why, that's lovely, Ralph," she said, and if there was any tiredness in her voice he didn't notice it.

"Lovely, huh?" he said with a laugh, mocking the girlishness of the word. "Ya *like* that, huh Gracie? No, but I mean I was really surprised, ya know it? The boss siz, 'Here, Ralph,' and he hands me this envelope. He don't even crack a smile or nothin', and I'm wonderin', what's the deal here? I'm getting fired here, or what? He siz, 'G'ahead, Ralph, open it.' So I open it, and then I look at the boss and he's grinning a mile wide." He chuckled and sighed. "Well, so listen, honey. What time ya want me to come over tonight?"

"Oh, I don't know. Soon as you can, I guess."

"Well listen, I gotta go over to Eddie's house and pick up that bag he's gonna loan me, so I might as well do that, go on home and eat, and then come over to your place around eight-thirty, nine o'clock. Okay?"

"All right," she said. "I'll see you then, darling." She had been calling him "darling" for only a short time — since it had become irrevocably clear that she was, after all, going to marry him — and the word still had an alien sound. As she straightened the stacks of stationery in her desk (because there was nothing else to do), a familiar little panic gripped her: she couldn't marry him — she hardly even *knew* him. Sometimes it occurred to her differently, that she couldn't marry him because she knew him too well, and either way it left her badly shaken, vulnerable to all the things that Martha, her roommate, had said from the very beginning.

"Isn't he funny?" Martha had said after their first date. "He says 'terlet.' I didn't know people really said 'terlet.'" And Grace had giggled, ready enough to agree that it *was* funny. That was a time when she had been ready to agree with Martha on practically anything — when it often seemed, in fact, that finding a girl like Martha from an ad in the *Times* was just about the luckiest thing that had ever happened to her.

But Ralph had persisted all through the summer, and by fall she had begun standing up for him. "What don't you *like* about him, Martha? He's perfectly nice."

"Oh, everybody's perfectly nice, Grace," Martha would say in her college voice, making perfectly nice a faintly absurd thing to be, and then she'd look up crossly from the careful painting of her fingernails. "It's just that he's such a little — a little *white worm*. Can't you see that?"

"Well, I certainly don't see what his *complexion* has to do with —"

"Oh God, *you* know what I mean. Can't you see what I *mean?* Oh, and all those friends of his, his Eddie and his Marty and his George with their mean, ratty little clerks' lives and their mean, ratty little. . . . It's just that they're all *alike*, those people. All they ever say is 'Hey, wha' happen t'ya Giants?' and 'Hey, wha' happen t'ya Yankees?' and they all live way out in Sunnyside or Woodhaven or some awful place, and their mothers have those damn little china elephants on the mantelpiece." And Martha would frown over her nail polish again, making it clear that the subject was closed.

All that fall and winter she was confused. For a while she tried going out only with Martha's kind of men — the kind that used words like "amusing" all the time and wore small-shouldered flannel suits like a uniform; and for a while she tried going out with no men at all. She even tried that crazy business with Mr. Atwood at the office Christmas party. And all the time Ralph kept calling up, hanging around, waiting for her to make up her mind. Once she took him home to meet her parents in Pennsylvania (where she never would have dreamed of taking Martha), but it wasn't until Easter time that she finally gave in.

They had gone to a dance somewhere in Queens, one of the big American Legion dances that Ralph's crowd was always going to, and when the band played "Easter Parade" he held her very close, hardly moving, and sang to her in a faint, whispering tenor. It was the kind of thing she'd never have expected Ralph to do — a sweet, gentle thing — and it probably wasn't just then that she decided to marry him, but it always seemed so afterwards. It always seemed she had decided that minute, swaying to the music with his husky voice in her hair:

> "*I'll be all in clover*
> *And when they look you over*
> *I'll be the proudest fella*
> *In the Easter Parade. . . .*"

That night she had told Martha, and she could still see the look on Martha's face. "Oh, Grace, you're not — surely you're not *serious*. I mean, I thought he was more or less of a *joke* — you can't really mean you want to —"

"Shut up! You just shut up, Martha!" And she'd cried all night. Even now she hated Martha for it; even as she stared blindly at a row of filing cabinets along the office wall, half sick with fear that Martha was right.

The noise of giggles swept over her, and she saw with a start that two of the girls — Irene and Rose — were grinning over their typewriters and pointing at her. "*We* saw ya!" Irene sang. "*We* saw ya! Mooning again, huh Grace?" Then Rose did a burlesque of mooning, heaving her meager breasts and batting her eyes, and they both collapsed in laughter.

With an effort of will Grace resumed the guileless, open smile of a bride. The thing to do was concentrate on plans.

Tomorrow morning, "bright and early," as her mother would say, she would meet Ralph at Penn Station for the trip home. They'd arrive about one, and her parents would meet the train. "Good t'see ya, Ralph!" her father would say, and her mother would probably kiss him. A warm, homely love filled her: *they* wouldn't call him a white worm; *they* didn't have any ideas about Princeton men and "interesting" men and all the other kinds of men Martha was so stuck-up about. Then her father would probably take Ralph out for a beer and show him the paper mill where he worked (and at least Ralph wouldn't be snobby about a person working in a paper mill, either), and then Ralph's family and friends would come down from New York in the evening.

She'd have time for a long talk with her mother that night, and the next morning, "bright and early" (her eyes stung at the thought of her mother's plain, happy face), they would start getting dressed for the wedding. Then the church and the ceremony, and then the reception (Would her father get drunk? Would Muriel Ketchel sulk about not being a bridesmaid?), and finally the train to Atlantic City, and the hotel. But from the hotel on she couldn't plan any more. A door would lock behind her and there would be a wild, fantastic silence, and nobody in all the world but Ralph to lead the way.

"Well, Grace," Mr. Atwood was saying, "I want to wish you every happiness." He was standing at her desk with his hat and coat on, and all around here were the chattering and scraping-back of chairs that meant it was five o'clock.

"Thank you, Mr. Atwood." She got to her feet, suddenly surrounded by all the girls in a bedlam of farewell.

"All the luck in the world, Grace."

"Drop us a card, huh Grace? From Atlantic City?"

"So long, Grace."

"G'night, Grace, and listen: the best of everything."

Finally she was free of them all, out of the elevator, out of the building, hurrying through the crowds to the subway.

When she got home Martha was standing in the door of the kitchenette, looking very svelte in a crisp new dress.

"Hi, Grace. I bet they ate you alive today, didn't they?"

"Oh no," Grace said. "Everybody was — real nice." She sat down, exhausted, and dropped the flowers and the wrapped candy dish on a table. Then she noticed that the whole apartment was swept and dusted, and the dinner was cooking in the kitchenette. "Gee, everything looks wonderful," she said. "What'd you do all this for?"

"Oh, well, I got home early anyway," Martha said. Then she smiled, and it was one of the few times Grace had ever seen her look shy. "I just thought it might be nice to have the place looking decent for a change, when Ralph comes over."

"Well," Grace said, "it certainly was nice of you."

The way Martha looked now was even more surprising: she looked awkward. She was turning a greasy spatula in her fingers, holding it delicately away from her dress and examining it, as if she had something difficult to say. "Look, Grace," she began.

"You do understand why I can't come to the wedding, don't you?"

"Oh, sure," Grace said, although in fact she didn't, exactly. It was something about having to go up to Harvard to see her brother before he went into the Army, but it had sounded like a lie from the beginning.

"It's just that I'd hate you to think I — well, anyway, I'm glad if you do understand. And the other thing I wanted to say is more important."

"What?"

"Well, just that I'm sorry for all the awful things I used to say about Ralph. I never had a right to talk to you that way. He's a very sweet boy and I — well, I'm sorry, that's all."

It wasn't easy for Grace to hide a rush of gratitude and relief when she said, "Why, that's all right, Martha, I —"

"The chops are on fire!" Martha bolted for the kitchenette. "It's all right," she called back. "They're edible." And when she came out to serve dinner all her old composure was restored. "I'll have to eat and run," she said as they sat down. "My train leaves in forty minutes."

"I thought it was *tomorrow* you were going."

"Well, it was, actually," Martha said, "but I decided to go tonight. Because you see, Grace, another thing — if you can stand one more apology — another thing I'm sorry for is that I've hardly ever given you and Ralph a chance to be alone here. So tonight I'm going to clear out." She hesitated. "It'll be a sort of wedding gift from· me, okay?" And then she smiled, not shyly this time but in a way that was more in character — the eyes subtly averted after a flicker of special meaning. It was a smile that Grace — through stages of suspicion, bewilderment, awe, and practiced imitation — had long ago come to associate with the word "sophisticated."

"Well, that's very sweet of you," Grace said, but she didn't really get the point just then. It wasn't until long after the meal was over and the dishes washed, until Martha had left for her train in a whirl of cosmetics and luggage and quick goodbyes, that she began to understand.

She took a deep, voluptuous bath and spent a long time drying herself, posing in the mirror, filled with a strange, slow excitement. In her bedroom, from the rustling tissues of an expensive white box, she drew the prizes of her trousseau — a sheer nightgown of white nylon and a matching negligee — put them on, and went to the mirror again. She had never worn anything like this before, or felt like this, and the thought of letting Ralph see her like this sent her into the kitchenette for a glass of the special dry sherry Martha kept for cocktail parties. Then she turned out all the lights but one and, carrying her glass, went to the sofa and arranged herself there to wait for him. After a while she got up and brought the sherry bottle over to the coffee table, where she set it on a tray with another glass.

When Ralph left the office he felt vaguely let down. Somehow, he'd expected more of the Friday before his wedding. The bonus check had been all right (though secretly he'd been counting on twice that amount), and the boys had bought him a drink at lunch and kidded around in the appropriate way ("Ah, don't feel too bad, Ralph — worse things could happen"), but still, there ought to have been a real party. Not just the boys in the office, but Eddie, and *all* his friends. Instead there would only be meeting Eddie at the White Rose like every other night of the year, and riding home to borrow Eddie's suitcase and to eat, and then having to ride all the way back to Manhattan just to see Gracie for an hour or two. Eddie wasn't in the bar when he arrived, which sharpened the edge of his loneliness. Morosely he drank a beer, waiting.

Eddie was his best friend, and an ideal best man because he'd been in on the courtship of Gracie from the start. It was in this very bar, in fact, that Ralph had told him about their first date last summer: "Ooh, Eddie — what a paira *knockers!*"

And Eddie had grinned. "Yeah? So what's the roommate like?"

"Ah, you don't want the roommate, Eddie. The roommate's a dog. A snob, too, I think. No, but this *other* one, this little *Gracie* — boy, I mean, she is *stacked*."

Half the fun of every date — even more than half — had been telling Eddie about it afterwards, exaggerating a little here and there, asking Eddie's advice on tactics. But after today, like so many other pleasures, it would all be left behind. Gracie had promised him at least one night off a week to spend with the boys, after they were married, but even so it would never be the same. Girls never understood a thing like friendship.

There was a ball game on the bar's television screen and he watched it idly, his throat swelling in a sentimental pain of loss. Nearly all his life had been devoted to the friendship of boys and men, to trying to be a good guy, and now the best of it was over.

Finally Eddie's stiff finger jabbed the seat of his pants in greeting. "Whaddya say, sport?"

Ralph narrowed his eyes to indolent contempt and slowly turned around. "Wha' happen ta you, wise guy? Get lost?"

"Whaddya — in a hurry a somethin'?" Eddie barely moved his lips when he spoke. "Can't wait two minutes?" He slouched on a stool and slid a quarter at the bartender. "Draw one, there, Jack."

They drank in silence for a while, staring at the television. "Got a little bonus today," Ralph said. "Fifty dollars."

"Yeah?" Eddie said. "Good."

A batter struck out; the inning was over and the commercial came on. "So?" Eddie said, rocking the beer around in his glass. "Still gonna get married?"

"Why not?" Ralph said with a shrug. "Listen, finish that, willya? I wanna get a move on."

"Wait awhile, wait awhile. What's ya hurry?"

"C'mon, willya?" Ralph stepped impatiently away from the bar. "I wanna go pick up ya bag."

"Ah, bag schmagg."

Ralph moved up close again and glowered at him. "Look, wise guy. Nobody's gonna *make* ya loan me the goddamn bag, ya know. I don't wanna break ya *heart* or nothin' —"

"Arright, arright, arright. You'll getcha bag. Don't worry so much." He finished the beer and wiped his mouth. "Let's go."

Having to borrow a bag for his wedding trip was a sore point with Ralph; he'd much rather have bought one of his own. There was a fine one displayed in the window of a luggage shop they passed every night on their way to the subway — a big, tawny Gladstone with a zippered compartment on the side, at thirty-nine ninety-five — and Ralph had had his eye on it ever since Easter time. "Think I'll buy that," he'd told Eddie, in the same offhand way that a day or so before he had announced his engagement ("Think I'll marry the girl"). Eddie's response to both remarks had been the same: "Whaddya — crazy?" Both times Ralph had said, "Why not?" and in defense of the bag he had added, "Gonna get married, I'll *need* somethin' like that." From then on it was as if the bag, almost as much as Gracie herself, had become a symbol of the new and richer life he sought. But after the ring and the new clothes and all the other expenses, he'd found at last that he couldn't afford it; he had settled for the loan of Eddie's, which was similar but cheaper and worn, and without the zippered compartment.

Now as they passed the luggage shop he stopped, caught in the grip of a reckless idea. "Hey wait awhile, Eddie. Know what I think I'll do with that fifty-dollar bonus? I think I'll buy that bag right now." He felt breathless.

"Whaddya — crazy? Forty bucks for a bag you'll use maybe one time a year? Ya crazy, Ralph. C'mon."

"Ah — I dunno. Ya think so?"

"Listen, you better *keep* ya money, boy. You're gonna *need* it."

"Ah — yeah," Ralph said at last. "I guess ya right." And he fell in step with Eddie again, heading for the subway. This was the way things usually turned out in his life; he could never own a bag like that until he made a better salary, and he accepted it — just as he'd accepted without question, after the first thin sigh, the knowledge that he'd never possess his bride until after the wedding.

The subway swallowed them, rattled and banged them along in a rocking, mindless trance for half an hour, and disgorged them at last into the cool early evening of Queens.

Removing their coats and loosening their ties, they let the breeze dry their sweated shirts as they walked. "So what's the deal?" Eddie asked. "What time we supposed to show up in this Pennsylvania burg tomorra?"

"Ah, suit yourself," Ralph said. "Any time in the evening's okay."

"So whadda we do then? What the hell can ya *do* in a hill-billy town like that, anyway?"

"Ah, I dunno," Ralph said defensively. "Sit around and talk, I guess; drink beer with Gracie's old man or somethin'; I dunno."

"Jesus," Eddie said. "Some weekend. Big, big deal."

Ralph stopped on the sidewalk, suddenly enraged, his damp coat wadded in his fist. "Look, you bastid. Nobody's gonna *make* ya come, ya know — you or Marty or George or any a the rest of 'em. Get that straight. You're not doin' *me* no favors, unna-stand?"

"Whatsa matta?" Eddie inquired. "Whatsa matta? Can'tcha take a joke?"

"Joke," Ralph said. "You're fulla jokes." And plodding sullenly in Eddie's wake, he felt close to tears.

They turned off into the block where they both lived, a double row of neat, identical houses bordering the street where they'd fought and loafed and played stickball all their lives. Eddie pushed open the front door of his house and ushered Ralph into the vestibule, with its homely smell of cauliflower and over-shoes. "G'wan in," he said, jerking a thumb at the closed living-room door, and he hung back to let Ralph go first.

Ralph opened the door and took three steps inside before it hit him like a sock on the jaw. The room, dead silent, was packed deep with grinning, red-faced men — Marty, George, the boys from the block, the boys from the office — everybody, all his friends, all on their feet and poised motionless in a solid mass. Skinny Maguire was crouched at the upright piano, his spread fingers high over the keys, and when he struck the first rollicking chords they all roared into song, beating time with their fists, their enormous grins distorting the words:

> "*Fa he's a jally guh fella*
> *Fa he's a jally guh fella*
> *Fa he's a jally guh fell-ah*
> *That nobody can deny!*"

Weakly Ralph retreated a step on the carpet and stood there wide-eyed, swallowing, holding his coat. "*That nobody can deny!*" they sang, "*That nobody can deny!*" And as they swung into the second chorus Eddie's father appeared through the dining-room curtains, bald and beaming, in full song, with a great glass pitcher of beer in either hand. At last Skinny hammered out the final line:

"*That—no—bod—dee—can—dee—nye!*"

And they all surged forward cheering, grabbing Ralph's hand, pounding his arms and his back while he stood trembling, his own voice lost under the noise. "Gee, fellas — thanks. I — don't know what to — thanks, fellas. . . ."

Then the crowd cleaved in half, and Eddie made his way slowly down the middle. His eyes gleamed in a smile of love, and from his bashful hand hung the suitcase — not his own, but a new one: the big, tawny Gladstone with the zippered compartment on the side.

"*Speech!*" they were yelling. "*Speech! Speech!*"

But Ralph couldn't speak and couldn't smile. He could hardly even see.

At ten o'clock Grace began walking around the apartment and biting her lip. What if he wasn't coming? But of course he was coming. She sat down again and carefully smoothed the billows of nylon around her thighs, forcing herself to be calm. The whole thing would be ruined if she was nervous.

The noise of the doorbell was like an electric shock. She was halfway to the door before she stopped, breathing hard, and composed herself again. Then she pressed the buzzer and opened the door a crack to watch for him on the stairs.

When she saw he was carrying a suitcase, and saw the pale seriousness of his face as he mounted the stairs, she thought at first that he knew; he had come prepared to lock the door and take her in his arms. "Hello, darling," she said softly, and opened the door wider.

"Hi, baby." He brushed past her and walked inside. "Guess I'm late, huh? You in bed?"

"No." She closed the door and leaned against it with both hands holding the doorknob at the small of her back, the way heroines close doors in the movies. "I was just — waiting for you."

He wasn't looking at her. He went to the sofa and sat down, holding the suitcase on his lap and running his fingers over its surface. "Gracie," he·said, barely above a whisper. "Look at this."

She looked at it, and then into his tragic eyes.

"Remember," he said, "I told you about that bag I wanted to buy? Forty dollars?" He stopped and looked around. "Hey, where's Martha? She in bed?"

"She's gone, darling," Grace said, moving slowly toward the sofa. "She's gone for the whole weekend." She sat down beside him, leaned close, and gave him Martha's special smile.

"Oh yeah?" he said. "Well anyway, listen. I said I was gonna borrow Eddie's bag instead, remember?"

"Yes."

"Well, so tonight at the White Rose I siz, 'C'mon, Eddie, let's go home pick up ya bag.' He siz, 'Ah, bag schmagg.' I siz, 'Whatsa matta?' but he don't say nothin', see? So we go home to his place and the living-room door's shut, see?"

She squirmed closer and put her head on his chest. Automatically he raised an arm and dropped it around her shoulders, still talking. "He siz, 'G'ahead, Ralph, open the door.' I siz, 'Whatsa deal?' He siz 'Never mind, Ralph, open the door.' So I open the door, and oh Jesus." His fingers gripped her shoulder with such intensity that she looked up at him in alarm.

"They was all there, Gracie," he said. "All the fellas. Playin' the piana, singin', cheerin' —" His voice wavered and his eyelids fluttered shut, their lashes wet. "A big surprise party," he said, trying to smile. "Fa me. Can ya beat that, Gracie? And then — and then Eddie comes out and — Eddie comes out and hands me this. The very same bag I been lookin' at all this time. He bought it with his own money and he didn't say nothin', just to give me a surprise. 'Here, Ralph,' he siz. 'Just to let ya know you're the greatest guy in the world.' " His fingers tightened again, trembling. "I cried, Gracie," he whispered. "I couldn't help it. I don't think the fellas saw it or anything, but I was cryin'." He turned his face away and worked his lips in a tremendous effort to hold back the tears.

"Would you like a drink, darling?" she asked tenderly.

"Nah, that's all right, Gracie. I'm all right." Gently he set the suitcase on the carpet. "Only, gimme a cigarette, huh?"

She got one from the coffee table, put it in his lips and lit it. "Let me get you a drink," she said.

He frowned through the smoke. "Whaddya got, that sherry wine? Nah, I don't like that stuff. Anyway, I'm fulla beer." He leaned back and closed his eyes. "And then Eddie's mother feeds us this terrific meal," he went on, and his voice was almost normal now. "We had *steaks*; we had French-fried *po-tatas*" — his head rolled on the sofa-back with each item of the menu — "lettuce-and-tomata *salad, pickles, bread, butter —* everything. The works."

"Well," she said. "Wasn't that nice."

"And afterwards we had ice cream and coffee," he said, "and all the beer we could drink. I mean, it was a real spread."

Grace ran her hands over her lap, partly to smooth the nylon and partly to dry the moisture on her palms. "Well, that certainly was nice of them," she said. They sat there silent for what seemed a long time.

"I can only stay a minute, Gracie," Ralph said at last. "I promised 'em I'd be back."

Her heart thumped under the nylon. "Ralph, do you — do you like this?"

"What, honey?"

"My negligee. You weren't supposed to see it until — after the wedding, but I thought I'd —"

"Nice," he said, feeling the flimsy material between thumb and index finger, like a merchant. "Very nice. Wudga pay fa this, honey?"

"Oh — I don't know. But do you like it?"

He kissed her and began, at last, to stroke her with his hands. "Nice," he kept saying. "Nice. Hey, I like this." His hand hesitated at the low neckline, slipped inside and held her breast.

"I do love you, Ralph," she whispered. "You know that, don't you?"

His fingers pinched her nipple, once, and slid quickly out again. The policy of restraint, the habit of months was too strong to break. "Sure," he said. "And I love you, baby. Now you be a good girl and get ya beauty sleep, and I'll see ya in the morning. Okay?"

"Oh, Ralph. Don't go. Stay."

"Ah, I promised the fellas, Gracie." He stood up and straightened his clothes. "They're waitin' fa me, out home."

She blazed to her feet, but the cry that was meant for a woman's appeal came out, through her tightening lips, as the whine of a wife: "Can't they wait?"

"Whaddya — *crazy?*" He backed away, eyes round with righteousness. She would *have* to understand. If this was the way she acted before the wedding, how the hell was it going to be afterwards? "Have a *heart,* willya? Keep the fellas waitin' *tonight?* After all they done fa *me?*"

After a second or two, during which her face became less pretty than he had ever seen it before, she was able to smile. "Of course not, darling. You're right."

He came forward again and gently brushed the tip of her chin with his fist, smiling, a husband reassured. " 'At's more like it," he said. "So I'll see ya, Penn Station, nine o'clock tomorra. Right, Gracie? Only, before I go —" he winked and slapped his belly. "I'm fulla beer. Mind if I use ya terlet?"

When he came out of the bathroom she was waiting to say goodnight, standing with her arms folded across her chest, as if for warmth. Lovingly he hefted the new suitcase and joined her at the door. "Okay, then, baby," he said, and kissed her. "Nine o'clock. Don't forget, now."

She smiled tiredly and opened the door for him. "Don't worry, Ralph," she said. "I'll be there."

— 1952

Jody Rolled the Bones

Sᴇʀɢᴇᴀɴᴛ Rᴇᴇᴄᴇ was a slim, quiet Tennessean who always managed to look neat in fatigues, and he wasn't exactly what we'd expected an infantry platoon sergeant to be. We learned soon enough that he was typical — almost a prototype — of the men who had drifted into the Regular Army in the thirties and stayed to form the cadres of the great wartime training centers, but at the time he surprised us. We were pretty naïve, and I think we'd all expected more of a Victor McLaglen — burly, roaring and tough, but lovable, in the Hollywood tradition. Reece was tough, all right, but he never roared and we didn't love him.

He alienated us on the first day by butchering our names. We were all from New York, and most of our names did require a little effort, but Reece made a great show of being defeated by them. His thin features puckered over the roster, his little mustache twitching at each unfamiliar syllable. "Dee—Dee Alice —" he stammered. "Dee Alice—"

"Here," D'Allessandro said, and it went like that with almost every name. At one point, after he'd grappled with Schacht, Scoglio, and Sizscovicz, he came to Smith. "Hey, Smith," he said, looking up with a slow, unengaging grin. "What the hell *yew* doin' heah 'mong all these gorillas?" Nobody thought it was funny. At last he finished and tucked the clipboard under his arm. "All right," he told us. "My name's Sahjint Reece and

I'm your platoon sahjint. That means when I say do somethin',
do it." He gave us a long, appraising glare. "P'toon!" he snapped,
making his diaphragm jump. "Tetch—*hut!*" And his tyranny began. By the end of that day and for many days thereafter we
had him firmly fixed in our minds as, to use D'Allessandro's
phrase, a dumb Rebel bastard.

I had better point out here that we were probably not very
lovable either. We were all eighteen, a confused, platoon-
sized bunch of city kids determined to be unenthusiastic about
Basic Training. Apathy in boys of that age may be unusual —
it is certainly unattractive — but this was 1944, the war was no
longer new, and bitterness was the fashionable mood. To throw
yourself into Army life with gusto only meant you were a kid
who didn't know the score, and nobody wanted to be that.
Secretly we may have yearned for battle, or at least for ribbons,
but on the surface we were shameless little wise guys about
everything. Trying to make us soldiers must have been a staggering job, and Reece bore the brunt of it.

But of course that side of the thing didn't occur to us, at first.
All we knew was that he rode us hard and we hated his guts.
We saw very little of our lieutenant, a plump collegiate youth
who showed up periodically to insist that if we played ball with
him, he would play ball with us, and even less of our company
commander (I hardly remember what he looked like, except
that he wore glasses). But Reece was always there, calm and contemptuous, never speaking except to give orders and never smiling except in cruelty. And we could tell by observing the other
platoons that he was exceptionally strict; he had, for instance,
his own method of rationing water.

It was summer, and the camp lay flat under the blistering
Texas sun. A generous supply of salt tablets was all that kept
us conscious until nightfall; our fatigues were always streaked
white from the salt of our sweat and we were always thirsty, but
the camp's supply of drinking water had to be transported from
a spring many miles away, so there was a standing order to go

easy on it. Most noncoms were thirsty enough themselves to construe the regulation loosely, but Reece took it to heart. "If yew men don't learn nothin' else about soldierin'," he would say, "you're gonna learn water discipline." The water hung in Lister bags, fat canvas udders placed at intervals along the roads, and although it was warm and acrid with chemicals, the high point of every morning and every afternoon was the moment when we were authorized a break to fill our canteens with it. Most platoons would attack a Lister bag in a jostling wallowing rush, working its little steel teats until the bag hung limp and wrinkled, and a dark stain of waste lay spreading in the dust beneath it. Not us. Reece felt that half a canteenful at a time was enough for any man, and he would stand by the Lister bag in grim supervision, letting us at it in an orderly column of twos. When a man held his canteen too long under the bag, Reece would stop everything, pull the man out of line, and say, "Pour that out. All of it."

"I'll be *God damned* if I will!" D'Allessandro shot back at him one day, and we all stood fascinated, watching them glare at each other in the dazzling heat. D'Allessandro was a husky boy with fierce black eyes who had in a few weeks become our spokesman; I guess he was the only one brave enough to stage a scene like this. "Whaddya think I am," he shouted, "a God damn *camel*, like you?" We giggled.

Reece demanded silence from the rest of us, got it, and turned back to D'Allessandro, squinting and licking his dry lips. "All right," he said quietly, "drink it. All of it. The resta yew men keep away from that bag, keep your hands off your canteens. I want y'all to watch this. Go on, drink it."

D'Allessandro gave us a grin of nervous triumph and began to drink, pausing only to catch his breath with the water dribbling on his chest. "Drink it," Reece would snap each time he stopped. It made us desperately thirsty to watch him, but we were beginning to get the idea. When the canteen was empty Reece told him to fill it up again. He did, still smiling but looking a little worried. "Now drink that," Reece said. "Fast. Faster." And when he was finished, gasping, with the empty canteen in his hand, Reece said, "Now get your helmet and rifle. See that barracks over there?" A white building shimmered in the distance, a couple of hundred yards away. "You're gonna proceed on the double to that barracks, go around it and come back on the double. Meantime your buddies're gonna be waitin' here; ain't none of 'em gonna get nothin' to drink till yew get back. All right, now, move. *Move*. On the *double*."

In loyalty to D'Allessandro none of us laughed, but he did look absurd trotting heavily out across the drill field, his helmet wobbling. Before he reached the barracks we saw him stop, crouch, and vomit up the water. Then he staggered on, a tiny figure in the faraway dust, disappeared around the building, and finally emerged at the other side to begin the long trip back. At last he arrived and fell exhausted on the ground. "Now," Reece said softly. "Had enough to drink?" Only then were the rest of us allowed to use the Lister bag, two at a time. When we were all through, Reece squatted nimbly and drew half a canteen for himself without spilling a drop.

That was the kind of thing he did, every day, and if anyone had suggested he was only doing his job, our response would have been a long and unanimous Bronx cheer.

I think our first brief easing of hostility toward him occurred quite early in the training cycle, one morning when one of the instructors, a strapping first lieutenant, was trying to teach us the bayonet. We felt pretty sure that in the big, modern kind of war for which we were bound we probably would not be called on to fight with bayonets (and that if we ever were it wouldn't make a hell of a lot of difference whether we'd mastered the finer points of parry and thrust), and so our lassitude that morning was even purer than usual. We let the instructor talk to us, then got up and fumbled through the various positions he had outlined.

The other platoons looked as bad as we did, and faced with

such dreary incompetence on a company scale the instructor rubbed his mouth. "No," he said. "No, no, you men haven't got the idea at all. Fall back to your places and sit down. Sergeant Reece front and center, please."

Reece had been sitting with the other platoon sergeants in their customary bored little circle, aloof from the lecture, but he rose promptly and came forward.

"Sergeant, I'd like you to show these people what a bayonet is all about," the instructor said. And from the moment Reece hefted a bayoneted rifle in his hands we knew, grudgingly or not, that we were going to see something. It was the feeling you get at a ball game when a heavy hitter selects a bat. At the instructor's commands he whipped smartly into each of the positions, freezing into a slim statue while the officer crouched and weaved around him, talking, pointing out the distribution of his weight and the angles of his limbs, explaining that this was how it should be done. Then, to climax the performance, the instructor sent Reece alone through the bayonet course. He went through it fast, never off balance and never wasting a motion, smashing blocks of wood off their wooden shoulders with his rifle butt, driving his blade deep into a shuddering torso of bundled sticks and ripping it out to bear down on the next one. He looked good. It would be too much to say that he kindled our admiration, but there is an automatic pleasure in watching a thing done well. The other platoons were clearly impressed, and although nobody in our platoon said anything, I think we were a little proud of him.

But the next period that day was close-order drill, at which the platoon sergeants had full command, and within half an hour Reece had nagged us into open resentment again. "What the hell's he think," Schacht muttered in the ranks, "he's some kind of a big deal now, just because he's a hotshot with that stupid bayonet?" And the rest of us felt a vague shame that we had so nearly been taken in.

When we eventually did change our minds about him, it did

not seem due, specifically, to any act of his, but to an experience that changed our minds about the Army in general, and about ourselves. This was the rifle range, the only part of our training we thoroughly enjoyed. After so many hours of drill and calisthenics, of droning lectures in the sun and training films run off in sweltering clapboard buildings, the prospect of actually going out and shooting held considerable promise, and when the time came it proved to be fun. There was a keen pleasure in sprawling prone on the embankment of the firing line with a rifle stock nestled at your cheek and the oily, gleaming clips of ammunition close at hand; in squinting out across a great expanse of earth at your target and waiting for the signal from a measured voice on the loud-speaker. "Ready on the right. Ready on the left. Ready on the firing line. . . . The flag is up. The flag is waving. The flag is down. Commence — *fire!*" There would be a blast of many rifles in your ears, a breathless moment as you squeezed the trigger, and a sharp jolt as you fired. Then you'd relax and watch the target slide down in the distance, controlled by unseen hands in the pit beneath it. When it reappeared a moment later a colored disk would be thrust up with it, waved and withdrawn, signaling your score. The man kneeling behind you with the score card would mutter, "Nice going" or "Tough," and you'd squirm in the sand and take aim again. Like nothing else we had found in the Army, this was something to rouse a competitive instinct, and when it took the form of wanting our platoon to make a better showing than the others, it brought us as close to a genuine *esprit de corps* as anything could.

We spent a week or so on the range, leaving early every morning and staying all day, taking our noon meal from a field kitchen that was in itself a refreshing change from the mess hall. Another good feature — at first it seemed the best of all — was that the range gave us a respite from Sergeant Reece. He marched us out there and back, and he supervised the cleaning of our rifles in the barracks, but for the bulk of the day he turned us over to the range staff, an impersonal, kindly crowd, much less concerned with petty discipline than with marksmanship.

Still, Reece had ample opportunity to bully us in the hours when he was in charge, but after a few days on the range we found he was easing up. When we counted cadence on the road now, for instance, he no longer made us do it over and over, louder each time, until our dry throats burned from yelling, "HUT, WHO, REEP, HOE!" He would quit after one or two counts like the other platoon sergeants, and at first we didn't know what to make of it. "What's the deal?" we asked each other, baffled, and I guess the deal was simply that we'd begun to do it right the first time, loud enough and in perfect unison. We were marching well, and this was Reece's way of letting us know it.

The trip to the range was several miles, and a good share of it was through the part of camp where marching at attention was required — we were never given route step until after we'd cleared the last of the company streets and buildings. But with our new efficiency at marching we got so that we almost enjoyed it, and even responded with enthusiasm to Reece's marching chant. It had always been his habit, after making us count cadence, to go through one of those traditional singsong chants calling for traditional shouts of reply, and we'd always resented it before. But now the chant seemed uniquely stirring, an authentic piece of folklore from older armies and older wars, with roots deep in the life we were just beginning to understand. He would begin by expanding his ordinary nasal "Left . . . left . . . left" into a mournful little tune: "Oh yew *had* a good *home* and yew *left* —" to which we would answer, "RIGHT!" as our right feet fell. We would go through several variations on this theme:

"Oh yew had a good job and yew left —"
"RIGHT!"
"Oh yew had a good gal and yew left —"

"RIGHT!"

And then he'd vary the tune a little: "Oh Jody rolled the bones when yew left —"

"RIGHT!" we'd yell in soldierly accord, and none of us had to wonder what the words meant. Jody was your faithless friend, the soft civilian to whom the dice-throw of chance had given everything you held dear; and the next verses, a series of taunting couplets, made it clear that he would always have the last laugh. You might march and shoot and learn to perfection your creed of disciplined force, but Jody was a force beyond control, and the fact had been faced by generations of proud, lonely men like this one, this splendid soldier who swung along beside our ranks in the sun and bawled the words from a twisted mouth: "Ain't no use in goin' home — Jody's got your gal and gone. Sound off —"

"HUT, WHO!"

"Sound off —"

"REEP, HOE!"

"Ever' time yew stand Retreat, Jody gets a piece of meat. Sound off —"

"HUT, WHO!"

"Sound off —"

"REEP, HOE!" It was almost a disappointment when he gave us route step on the outskirts of camp and we became individuals again, cocking back our helmets and slouching along out of step, with the fine unanimity of the chant left behind. When we returned from the range dusty and tired, our ears numb from the noise of fire, it was somehow bracing to swing into formal cadence again for the last leg of the journey, heads up, backs straight, and split the cooling air with our roars of response.

A good part of our evenings, after chow, would be spent cleaning our rifles with the painstaking care that Reece demanded. The barracks would fill with the sharp, good smells of bore cleaner and oil as we worked, and when the job had been done to

Reece's satisfaction we would usually drift out to the front steps for a smoke while we waited our turns at the showers. One night a group of us lingered there more quietly than usual, finding, I think, that the customary small talk of injustice and complaint was inadequate, unsuited to the strange well-being we had all begun to feel these last few days. Finally Fogarty put the mood into words. He was a small, serious boy, the runt of the platoon and something of a butt of jokes, and I guess he had nothing much to lose by letting his guard down. "Ah, I dunno," he said, leaning back against the doorjamb with a sigh, "I dunno about you guys, but I like this — going out to the range, marching and all. Makes you feel like you're really soldiering, you know what I mean?"

It was a dangerously naïve thing to say — "soldiering" was Reece's favorite word — and we looked at him uncertainly for a second. But then D'Allessandro glanced dead-pan around the group, defying anyone to laugh, and we relaxed. The idea of soldiering had become respectable, and because the idea as well as the word was inseparable in our minds from Sergeant Reece, he became respectable too.

Soon the change had come over the whole platoon. We were working with Reece now, instead of against him, trying instead of pretending to try. We wanted to be soldiers. The intensity of our effort must sometimes have been ludicrous, and might have caused a lesser man to suspect we were kidding — I remember earnest little choruses of "Okay, Sergeant" whenever he dispatched an order — but Reece took it all straight-faced, with that air of unlimited self-assurance that is the first requisite of good leadership. And he was as fair as he was strict, which must surely be the second requisite. In appointing provisional squad leaders, for example, he coolly passed over several men who had all but licked his shoes for recognition, and picked those he knew could hold our respect — D'Allessandro was one, and the others were equally well chosen. The rest of his formula was classically simple: he led by being excellent, at everything from cleaning a rifle to rolling a pair of socks, and we followed by trying to emulate him.

But if excellence is easy to admire it is hard to like, and Reece refused to make himself likable. It was his only failing, but it was a big one, for respect without affection can't last long — not, at least, where the sentimentality of adolescent minds is involved. Reece rationed kindness the way he rationed water: we might cherish each drop out of all proportion to its worth, but we never got enough or anything like enough to slake our thirst. We were delighted when he suddenly began to get our names right at roll call and when we noticed that he was taking the edge of insult off most of his reprimands, for we knew these signs to be acknowledgments of our growth as soldiers, but somehow we felt a right to expect more.

We were delighted too at the discovery that our plump lieutenant was afraid of him; we could barely hide our pleasure at the condescending look that came over Reece's face whenever the lieutenant appeared, or at the tone of the young officer's voice — uneasy, almost apologetic — when he said, "All right, Sergeant." It made us feel close to Reece in a proud soldierly alliance, and once or twice he granted us the keen compliment of a wink behind the lieutenant's back, but only once or twice. We might imitate his walk and his squinting stare, get the shirts of our suntans tailored skintight like his and even adopt some of his habits of speech, Southern accent and all, but we could never quite consider him a Good Joe. He just wasn't the type. Formal obedience, in working hours, was all he wanted, and we hardly knew him at all.

On the rare evenings when he stayed on the post he would sit either alone or in the unapproachable company of one or two other cadremen as taciturn as himself, drinking beer in the PX. Most nights and all weekends he disappeared into town. I'm sure none of us expected him to spend his free time with us — the thought would never have occurred to us, in fact — but the smallest glimpse into his personal life would have helped. If he had ever reminisced with us about his home, for instance, or related the conversations of his PX friends, or told us of a bar he liked in town, I think we would all have been touchingly grateful, but he never did. And what made it worse was that, unlike him, we had no real life outside the day's routine. The town was a small, dusty maze of clapboard and neon, crawling with soldiers, and to most of us it yielded only loneliness, however we may have swaggered down its avenues. There wasn't enough town to go around; whatever delights it held remained the secrets of those who had found them first, and if you were young, shy, and not precisely sure what you were looking for anyway, it was a dreary place. You could hang around the USO and perhaps get to dance with a girl long hardened against a callow advance; you could settle for the insipid pleasures of watermelon stands and penny arcades, or you could prowl aimlessly in groups through the dark back streets, where all you met as a rule were other groups of soldiers on the aimless prowl. "So whaddya wanna *do?*" we would ask each other impatiently, and the only answer was, "Ah, I dunno. Cruise around awhile, I guess." Usually we'd drink enough beer to be drunk, or sick, on the bus back to camp, grateful for the promise of an orderly new day.

It was probably not surprising, then, that our emotional life became ingrown. Like frustrated suburban wives we fed on each other's discontent; we became divided into mean little cliques and subdivided into jealously shifting pairs of buddies, and we pieced out our idleness with gossip. Most of the gossip was self-contained; for news from the extraplatoon world we relied largely on the company clerk, a friendly, sedentary man who liked to dispense rumors over a carefully balanced cup of coffee as he strolled from table to table in the mess hall. "I got this from Personnel," he would say in preface to some improbable hearsay about the distant brass (the colonel had syphilis; the stockade commander had weaseled out of a combat assignment; the training program had been cut short and we'd all be overseas in a month). But one Saturday noon he had something less remote; he had gotten it from his own company orderly room, and it sounded plausible. For weeks, he told us, the plump lieutenant had been trying to get Reece transferred; now it appeared to be in the works, and next week might well be Reece's last as a platoon sergeant. "His days are numbered," the clerk said darkly.

"Whaddya mean, transferred?" D'Allessandro asked. "Transferred where?"

"Keep your voice down," the clerk said, with an uneasy glance toward the noncoms' table, where Reece bent stolidly over his food. "I dunno. That part I dunno. Anyway, it's a lousy deal. You kids got the best damn platoon sergeant on the post, if you wanna know something. He's too *damn* good, in fact; that's his trouble. Too good for a half-assed second lieutenant to handle. In the Army it never pays to be that good."

"You're right," D'Allessandro said solemnly. "It never pays."

"Yeah?" Schacht inquired, grinning. "Is that right, Squad Leader? Tell us about it, Squad Leader." And the talk at our table degenerated into wisecracks. The clerk drifted away.

Reece must have heard the story about the same time we did; at any rate that weekend marked a sudden change in his behavior. He left for town with the tense look of a man methodically planning to get drunk, and on Monday morning he almost missed Reveille. He nearly always had a hangover on Monday mornings, but it had never before interfered with his day's work; he had always been there to get us up and out with his angry tongue. This time, though, there was an odd silence in the barracks as we dressed. "Hey, he isn't *here*," somebody called from the door of Reece's room near the stairs. "Reece isn't *here*." The squad leaders were admirably quick to take the initiative. They coaxed and prodded until we had all tumbled outside and into formation in the dark, very nearly as fast as we'd have done it under Reece's supervision. But the night's

CQ, in making his rounds, had already discovered Reece's absence and run off to rouse the lieutenant.

The company officers rarely stood Reveille, particularly on Mondays, but now as we stood leaderless in the company street our lieutenant came jogging around the side of the barracks. By the lights of the building we could see that his shirt was half buttoned and his hair wild; he looked puffy with sleep and badly confused. Still running, he called, "All right, you men, uh —"

All the squad leaders drew their breath to call us to attention, but they got no further than a ragged "Tetch—" when Reece emerged out of the gloaming, stepped up in front of the lieutenant, and said, "P'toon! Tetch—*hut!*" There he was, a little winded from running, still wearing the wrinkled suntans of the night before, but plainly in charge. He called the roll by squads; then he kicked out one stiff leg in the ornate, Regular Army way of doing an about-face, neatly executed the turn and ended up facing the lieutenant in a perfect salute. "All presen'accounted for, sir," he said.

The lieutenant was too startled to do anything but salute back, sloppily, and mumble "All right, Sergeant." I guess he felt he couldn't even say, "See that this doesn't happen again," since, after all, nothing very much had happened, except that he'd been gotten out of bed for Reveille. And I guess he spent the rest of the day wondering whether he should have reprimanded Reece for being out of uniform; he looked as if the question was already bothering him as he turned to go back to his quarters. Dismissed, our formation broke up in a thunderclap of laughter that he pretended not to hear.

But Sergeant Reece soon spoiled the joke. He didn't even thank the squad leaders for helping him out of a tight spot, and for the rest of the day he treated us to the kind of petty nagging we thought we had outgrown. On the drill field he braced little Fogarty and said, "When'd yew shave last?"

Like many of our faces, Fogarty's bore only a pale fuzz that hardly needed shaving at all. "About a week ago," he said.

" 'Bout a week ago, *Sah*jint," Reece corrected.

"About a week ago, Sergeant," Fogarty said.

Reece curled back his thin lips. "Yew look lak a mangy ole mungrel bitch," he said. "Doan yew know you're s'posed to shave ever' day?"

"I wouldn't have nothing to *shave* every day."

"Wouldn't have nothin' to shave, *Sah*jint."

Fogarty swallowed, blinking. "Nothing to shave, Sergeant," he said.

We all felt badly let down. "What the hell's he think we are," Schacht demanded that noon, "a bunch of rookies?" And D'Allessandro grumbled in mutinous agreement.

A bad hangover might have excused Reece that day, but it could hardly have accounted for the next day and the day after that. He was bullying us without reason and without relief, and he was destroying everything he had built up so carefully in the many weeks before; the whole delicate structure of our respect for him crumbled and fell.

"It's final," the company clerk said grimly at supper Wednesday night. "The orders are cut. Tomorrow's his last day."

"So?" Schacht inquired. "Where's he going?"

"Keep your voice down," the clerk said. "Gonna work with the instuctors. Spend part of his time out on the bivouac area and part on the bayonet course."

Schacht laughed, nudging D'Allessandro. "Hod damn," he said, "he'll eat that up, won't he? Specially the bayonet part. Bastard'll get to show off every day. He'll like that."

"Whaddya, *kidding*?" the clerk asked, offended. "Like it my ass. That guy loved his job. You think I'm kidding? He *loved* his job, and it's a lousy break. You kids don't know when you're well off."

D'Allessandro took up the argument, narrowing his eyes. "Yeah?" he said. "You think so? You oughta see him out there every day this week. Every day."

The clerk leaned forward so earnestly that some of his coffee

spilled. "Listen," he said. "He's known about this all week —
how the hellya *want* him to act? How the hell would *you* act
if you knew somebody was screwing you out of the thing you
liked best? Can'tcha see he's under a strain?"

But that, we all told him with our surly stares, was no excuse
for being a dumb Rebel bastard.

"Some of you kids act too big for your pants," the clerk
said, and went away in a·sulk.

"Ah, don't believe everything you hear," Schacht said. "I'll
believe he's transferred when I see it."

But it was true. That night Reece sat up late in his room,
drinking morosely with one of his cronies. We could hear their
low, blurred voices in the darkness, and the occasional clink
of their whiskey bottle. The following day he was neither easy
nor hard on us in the field, but brooding and aloof as if he had
other things on his mind. And when he marched us back that
evening he kept us standing in formation in front of the barracks for a few moments, at ease, before dismissing us. His
restless glance seemed to survey all our faces in turn. Then he
began to speak in a voice more gentle than any we had ever
heard him use. "I won't be seein' yew men any more after today," he said. "I'm bein' transferred. One thing yew can always
count on in th' Army, and that is, if yew find somethin' good,
some job yew like, they always transfer your ass somewheres
else."

I think we were all touched — I know I was; it was the closest
he had ever come to saying he liked us. But it was too late. Anything he said or did now would have been too late, and our pre-
dominant feeling was relief. Reece seemed to sense this, and
seemed to cut short the things he had planned to say.

"I know there ain't no call for me to make a speech," he said,
"and I ain't gonna make one. Onliest thing I want to say is —"
He lowered his eyes and stared at his dusty service shoes. "I
want to wish all yew men a lot of luck. Y'all keep your nose
clean, hear? And stay outa trouble?" The next words could

scarcely be heard. "And doan let nobody push y'around."

A short, painful silence followed, as painful as the parting of disenchanted lovers. Then he drew himself straight. "P'toon! Tetch—*hut!*" He looked us over once more with hard and glittering eyes. "*Dis*-missed."

And when we came back from chow that night we found he had already packed his barracks bags and cleared out. We didn't even get to shake his hand.

Our new platoon sergeant was there in the morning, a squat, jolly cab driver from Queens who insisted that we call him only by his first name, which was Ruby. He was every inch a Good Joe. He turned us loose at the Lister bags every chance he got, and confided with a giggle that, through a buddy of his in the PX, he often got his own canteen filled with Coca-Cola and crushed ice. He was a slack drillmaster, and on the road he never made us count cadence except when we passed an officer, never made us chant or sing anything except a ragged version of "Give My Regards to Broadway," which he led with fervor although he didn't know all the words.

It took us a little while to adjust to him, after Reece. Once when the lieutenant came to the barracks to give one of his little talks about playing ball, ending up with his usual "All right, Sergeant," Ruby hooked his thumbs in his cartridge belt, slouched comfortably, and said, "Fellas, I hope yez all listened and gave ya attention to what the lieutenant said. I think I can speak fa yez all as well as myself when I say, Lieutenant, we're *gonna* play ball wit' you, like you said, because this here is one platoon that knows a Good Joe when we see one."

As flustered by this as he had ever been by Reece's silent scorn, the lieutenant could only blush and stammer, "Well, uh — thank you, Sergeant. Uh — I guess that's all, then. Carry on." And as soon as the lieutenant was out of sight we all began to make loud retching noises, to hold our noses or go through the motions of shoveling, as if we stood knee-deep in manure. "Christ, Ruby," Schacht cried, "what the hella *you* buckin' for?"

Ruby hunched his shoulders and spread his hands, bubbling with good-natured laughter. "To stay alive," he said. "To stay alive, whaddya think?" And he defended the point vigorously over the mounting din of our ridicule. "Whatsa matta?" he demanded. "Whatsa matta? Don'tcha think he does it to the captain? Don'tcha think the captain does it up at Battalion? Listen, wise up, will yez? *Evvybody* does it! *Evvybody* does it! What the hellya think makes the Army *go*?" Finally he dismissed the whole subject with cab-driverly nonchalance. "Arright, arright, just stick around. *Yull* find out. Wait'll you kids got *my* time in the Army, *then* yez can talk." But by that time we were all laughing with him; he had won our hearts.

In the evenings, at the PX, we would cluster around him while he sat behind a battery of beer bottles, waving his expressive hands and talking the kind of relaxed, civilian language we all could understand. "Ah, I got this brother-in-law, a real smott bastid. Know how *he* got outa the Army? Know how *he* got out?" There would follow an involved, unlikely tale of treachery to which the only expected response was a laugh. "Sure!" Ruby would insist, laughing. "Don'tcha believe me? Don'tcha believe me? And this other guy I know, boy, talk about bein' *smott* — I'm tellin' ya, this bastid's *really* smott. Know how *he* got out?"

Sometimes our allegiance wavered, but not for long. One evening a group of us sat around the front steps, dawdling over cigarettes before we pushed off to the PX, and discussing at length — as if to convince ourselves — the many things that made life with Ruby so enjoyable. "Well yeah," little Fogarty said, "but I dunno. With Ruby it don't seem much like soldiering any more."

This was the second time Fogarty had thrown us into a momentary confusion, and for the second time D'Allessandro cleared the air. "So?" he said with a shrug. "Who the hell wants to soldier?"

That said it perfectly. We could spit in the dust and amble off toward the PX now, round-shouldered, relieved, confident that Sergeant Reece would not haunt us again. Who the hell wanted to soldier? "Not *me*," we could all say in our hearts, "not *this* chicken," and our very defiance would dignify the attitude. An attitude was all we needed anyway, all we had ever needed, and this one would always sit more comfortably than Reece's stern, demanding creed. It meant, I guess, that at the end of our training cycle the camp delivered up a bunch of shameless little wise guys to be scattered and absorbed into the vast disorder of the Army, but at least Reece never saw it happen, and he was the only one who might have cared.

— *1952*

No Pain Whatsoever

MYRA straightened herself in the back seat and smoothed her skirt, pushing Jack's hand away.

"All right, baby," he whispered, smiling, "take it easy."

"You take it easy, Jack," she told him. "I mean it, now."

His hand yielded, limp, but his arm stayed indolently around her shoulders. Myra ignored him and stared out the window. It was early Sunday evening, late in December, and the Long Island streets looked stale; dirty crusts of snow lay shriveled on the sidewalk, and cardboard images of Santa Claus leered out of closed liquor stores.

"I still don't feel right about you driving me all the way out here," Myra called to Marty, who was driving, to be polite.

" 'S all right," Marty grumbled. Then he sounded his horn and added, to the back of a slow truck, "Get that son of a bitch outa the way."

Myra was annoyed — why did Marty always have to be such a grouch? — but Irene, Marty's wife, squirmed around in the front seat with her friendly grin. "Marty don't mind," she said. "It's good for 'm, getting out on a Sunday insteada laying around the house."

"Well," Myra said, "I certainly do appreciate it." The truth was that she would much rather have taken the bus, alone, as usual. In the four years she had been coming out here to visit her husband every Sunday she had grown used to the long ride, and she liked stopping at a little cafeteria in Hempstead, where you had to change buses, for coffee and cake on the way home. But today she and Jack had gone over to Irene and Marty's for dinner, and the dinner was so late that Marty had to offer to drive her out to the hospital, and she had to accept. And then of course Irene had to come along, and Jack too, and they all acted as if they were doing her a favor. But you had to be polite. "It certainly is nice," Myra called, "to be riding out here in a car, instead of a — *don't* Jack!"

Jack said, "*Sh-h-h*, take it easy, baby," but she threw off his hand and twisted away. Watching them, Irene put her tongue between her teeth and giggled, and Myra felt herself blushing. It wasn't that there was anything to be ashamed of — Irene and Marty knew all about Jack and everything; most of her friends did, and nobody blamed her (after all, wasn't it almost like being a widow?) — it was just that Jack ought to know better. Couldn't he at least have the decency to keep his hands to himself now, of all times?

"There," Marty said. "Now we'll make some time." The truck had turned off and they were picking up speed, leaving the streetcar tracks and stores behind as the street became a road and then a highway.

"Care to hear the radio, kids?" Irene called. She clicked one of the dial tabs and a voice urged everyone to enjoy television in their own homes, now, tonight. She clicked another and a voice said, "Yes, your money buys more in a Crawford store!"

"Turn that son of a bitch off," Marty said, and sounding the horn again, he pulled out into the fast lane.

When the car entered the hospital grounds, Irene turned around in the front seat and said, "Say, this is a beautiful place. I mean it, isn't this a beautiful place? Oh, look, they got a Christmas tree up, with lights and all."

"Well," Marty said, "where to?"

"Straight ahead," Myra told him, "down to that big circle, where the Christmas tree is. Then you turn right, out around the Administration Building, and on out to the end of that street." He made the turn correctly, and as they approached the long, low TB building, she said, "Here it is, Marty, this one right here." He drew up to the curb and stopped, and she gathered together the magazines she had brought for her husband and stepped out on the thin gray snow.

Irene hunched her shoulders and turned around, hugging herself. "Oo-oo, it's *cold* out there, isn't it? Listen, honey, what time is it you'll be through, now? Eight o'clock, is it?"

"That's right," Myra said, "but listen, why don't you people go on home? I can just as soon take the bus back, like I always do."

"Whaddya think I am, crazy?" Irene said. "You think I want to drive all the way home with Jack moping there in the back seat?" She giggled and winked. "Be hard enough just trying to keep him happy while you're inside, let alone driving all the way home. No, listen, we'll cruise around a little, honey, maybe have a little drink or something, and then we'll come back here for you at eight o'clock sharp."

"Well okay, but I'd really just as soon —"

"Right here," Irene said. "We'll see you right here in front of the building at eight o'clock sharp. Now hurry up and shut the door before we all freeze to death."

Myra smiled as she slammed the door, but Jack, sulking, did not look up to smile back, or wave. Then the car rolled away and she walked up the path and the steps to the TB building.

The small waiting room smelled of steam heat and wet overshoes, and she hurried through it, past the door marked NURSES' OFFICE — CLEAN AREA and into the big, noisy center ward. There were thirty-six beds in the center ward, divided in half by a wide aisle and subdivided by shoulder-high partitions into open cubicles of six beds each. All the sheets and the hospital pajamas were dyed yellow, to distinguish them from uncontaminated linen in the hospital laundry, and this combined with the pale green of the walls made a sickly color scheme that

Myra could never get used to. The noise was terrible too; each patient had a radio, and they all seemed to be playing different stations at once. There were clumps of visitors at some of the beds — one of the newer men lay with his arms around his wife in a kiss — but at other beds the men looked lonely, reading or listening to their radios.

Myra's husband didn't see her until she was right beside his bed. He was sitting up, cross-legged, frowning over something in his lap. "Hello, Harry," she said.

He looked up. "Oh, hi there, honey, didn't see you coming."

She leaned over and kissed him quickly on the cheek. Sometimes they kissed on the lips, but you weren't supposed to.

Harry glanced at his watch. "You're late. Was the bus late?"

"I didn't come on the bus," she said, taking off her coat. "I got a ride out. Irene, the girl that works in my office? She and her husband drove me out in their car."

"Oh, that's nice. Whyn't you bring 'em on in?"

"Oh, they couldn't stay — they had someplace else to go. But they both said to give you their regards. Here, I brought you these."

"Oh, thanks, that's swell." He took the magazines and spread them out on the bed: *Life, Collier's* and *Popular Science.* "That's swell, honey. Sit down and stay awhile."

Myra laid her coat over the back of the bedside chair and sat down. "Hello there, Mr. Chance," she said to a very long Negro in the next bed who was nodding and grinning at her.

"How're you, Mrs. Wilson?"

"Fine, thanks, and you?"

"Oh, no use complaining," Mr. Chance said.

She peered across Harry's bed at Red O'Meara, who lay listening to his radio on the other side. "Hi there, Red."

"Oh, hi, Mrs. Wilson. Didn't see you come in."

"Your wife coming in tonight, Red?"

"She comes Saturdays now. She was here last night."

"Oh," Myra said, "well, tell her I said hello."

"I sure will, Mrs. Wilson."

Then she smiled at the elderly man across the cubicle whose name she could never remember, who never had any visitors, and he smiled back, looking rather shy. She settled herself on the little steel chair, opening her handbag for cigarettes. "What's that thing on your lap, Harry?" It was a ring of blond wood a foot wide, with a great deal of blue knitting wool attached to little pegs around its edge.

"Oh, this?" Harry said, holding it up. "It's what they call rake-knitting. Something I got from occupational therapy."

"*What*-knitting?"

"Rake-knitting. See, what you do, you take this little hook and kind of pry the wool up and over each peg, like that, and you keep on doing that around and around the ring until you got yourself a muffler or a stocking cap — something like that."

"Oh, *I* see," Myra said. "It's like what we used to do when I was a kid, only we did it with a regular little spool, with nails stuck in it? You wind string around the nails and pull it through the spool and it makes sort of a knitted rope, like."

"Oh, yeah?" Harry said. "With a spool, huh? Yeah, I think my sister used to do that too, now that I think of it. With a spool. You're right, this is the same principle, only bigger."

"What're you going to make?"

"Oh, I don't know, I'm just fooling around with it. Thought I might make a stocking cap or something. I don't know." He inspected his work, turning the knitting-rake around in his hands, then leaned over and put it away in his bed stand. "It's just something to do."

She offered him the pack and he took a cigarette. When he bent forward to take the match the yellow pajamas gaped open and she saw his chest, unbelievably thin, partly caved-in on one side where the ribs were gone. She could just see the end of the ugly, newly healed scar from the last operation.

"Thanks, honey," he said, the cigarette wagging in his lips, and he leaned back against the pillows, stretching out his socked feet on the spread.

"How're you feeling, Harry?" she said.

"Feeling fine."

"You're looking better," she lied. "If you can gain a little weight now, you'll look fine."

"Pay up," said a voice over the din of the radios, and Myra looked around to see a little man coming down the center aisle in a wheelchair, walking the chair slowly with his feet, as all TB patients did to avoid the chest strain of turning the wheels with their hands. He was headed for Harry's bed, grinning with yellow teeth. "Pay up," he said again as the wheelchair came to a stop beside the bed. A piece of rubber tubing protruded from some kind of bandage on his chest. It coiled across his pajama top, held in place by a safety pin, and ended in a small rubber-capped bottle which rode heavily in his breast pocket. "Come on, come on," he said. "Pay up."

"Oh, yeah!" Harry said, laughing. "I forgot all about it, Walter." From the drawer of his bed stand he got out a dollar bill and handed it to the man, who folded it with thin fingers and put it in his pocket, along with the bottle.

"Okay, Harry," he said. "All squared away now, right?"

"Right, Walter."

He backed the wheelchair up and turned it around, and Myra saw that his chest, back and shoulders were crumpled and misshapen. "Sorry to butt in," he said, turning the sickly grin on Myra.

She smiled. "That's all right." When he had gone up the aisle again, she said, "What was that all about?"

"Oh, we had a bet on the fight Friday night. I'd forgotten all about it."

"Oh. Have I met him before?"

"Who, Walter? Sure, I think so, honey. You must've met him when I was over in surgery. Old Walter was in surgery more'n two years; they just brought him back here last week. Kid's had a rough time of it. He's got plenty of guts."

"What's that thing on his pajamas? That bottle?"

"He's draining," Harry said, settling back against the yellow pillows. "Old Walter's a good guy; I'm glad he's back." Then he lowered his voice, confidentially. "Matter of fact, he's one of the few really good guys left in this ward, with so many of the old crowd gone now, or over in surgery."

"Don't you like the new boys?" Myra asked, keeping her own voice low so that Red O'Meara, who was relatively new, wouldn't hear. "They seem perfectly nice to me."

"Oh, they're all right, I guess," Harry said. "I just mean, well, I get along better with guys like Walter, that's all. We been through a lot together, or something. I don't know. These new guys get on your nerves sometimes, the way they talk. For instance, there's not one of them knows anything about TB, and they all of them think they know it all; you can't tell them anything. I mean, a thing like that can get on your nerves."

Myra said she guessed she saw what he meant, and then it seemed that the best thing to do was change the subject. "Irene thought the hospital looked real pretty, with the Christmas tree and all."

"Oh, yeah?" Very carefully, Harry reached over and flicked his cigarette into the spotless ashtray on his bed stand. All his habits were precise and neat from living so long in bed. "How're things going at the office, honey?"

"Oh, all right, I guess. Remember I told you about that girl Janet that got fired for staying out too long at lunch, and we were all scared they'd start cracking down on that half-hour lunch period?"

"Oh, yeah," Harry said, but she could tell he didn't remember and wasn't really listening.

"Well, it seems to be all blown over now, because last week Irene and three other girls stayed out almost two hours and nobody said a word. And one of them, a girl named Rose, has been kind of expecting to get fired for a couple of months now, and they didn't even say anything to her."

"Oh, yeah?" Harry said. "Well, that's good."

There was a pause. "Harry?" she said.

"What, honey?"

"Have they told you anything new?"

"Anything new?"

"I mean, about whether or not you're going to need the operation on the other side."

"Oh, *no*, honey. I told you, we can't expect to hear anything on that for quite some time yet — I thought I explained all that." His mouth was smiling and his eyes frowning to show it had been a foolish question. It was the same look he always used to give her at first, long ago, when she would say, "But when do you *think* they'll let you come home?" Now he said, "Thing is, I've still got to get over this *last* one. You got to do one thing at a time in this business; you need a long postoperative period before you're really in the clear, especially with a record of breakdowns like I've had in the last — what is it, now — four years? No, what they'll do is wait awhile, I don't know, maybe six months, maybe longer, and see how this side's coming along. Then they'll decide about the other side. Might give me more surgery and they might not. You can't count on anything in this business, honey, you know that."

"No, of course, Harry, I'm sorry. I don't mean to ask stupid questions. I just meant, well, how're you feeling and everything. You still have any pain?"

"None at all, any more," Harry said. "I mean, as long as I don't go raising my arm too high or anything. When I do that it hurts, and sometimes I start to roll over on that side in my sleep, and that hurts too, but as long as I stay — you know — more or less in a normal position, why, there's no pain whatsoever."

"That's good," she said, "I'm awfully glad to hear that, anyway."

Neither of them spoke for what seemed a long time, and in the noise of radios and the noise of laughing and coughing from other beds, their silence seemed strange. Harry began to riffle *Popular Science* absently with his thumb. Myra's eyes strayed to the framed picture on his bed stand, an enlarged snapshot of the two of them just before their marriage, taken in her mother's back yard in Michigan. She looked very young in the picture, leggy in her 1945 skirt, not knowing how to dress or even how to stand, knowing nothing and ready for anything with a child's smile. And Harry — but the surprising thing was that Harry looked older in the picture, somehow, than he did now. Probably it was the thicker face and build, and of course the clothes helped — the dark, decorated Eisenhower jacket and the gleaming boots. Oh, he'd been good-looking, all right, with his set jaw and hard gray eyes — much better looking, for instance, than a too stocky, too solid man like Jack. But now with the loss of weight there had been a softening about the lips and eyes that gave him the look of a thin little boy. His face had changed to suit the pajamas.

"Sure am glad you brought me this," Harry said of his *Popular Science*. "They got an article in here I want to read."

"Good," she said, and she wanted to say: Can't it wait until I've gone?

Harry flipped the magazine on its face, fighting the urge to read, and said, "How's everything else, honey? Outside of the office, I mean."

"All right," she said. "I had a letter from Mother the other day, kind of a Christmas letter. She sent you her best regards."

"Good," Harry said, but the magazine was winning. He flipped it over again, opened it to his article and read a few lines very casually — as if only to make sure it was the right article — and then he lost himself in it.

Myra lighted a fresh cigarette from the butt of her last one, picked up the *Life* and began to turn the pages. From time to time she looked up to watch him; he lay biting a knuckle as he read, scratching the sole of one socked foot with the curled toe of the other.

They spent the rest of the visiting hour that way. Shortly before eight o'clock a group of people came down the aisle, smiling and trundling a studio piano on rubber-tired casters — the Sunday night Red Cross entertainers. Mrs. Balacheck led the procession; a kindly, heavy-set woman in uniform, who played. Then came the piano, pushed by a pale young tenor whose lips were always wet, and then the female singers: a swollen soprano in a taffeta dress that looked tight under the arms and a stern-faced, lean contralto with a briefcase. They wheeled the piano close to Harry's bed, in the approximate middle of the ward, and began to unpack their sheet music.

Harry looked up from his reading. "Evening, Mrs. Balacheck."

Her glasses gleamed at him. "How're you tonight, Harry? Like to hear a few Christmas carols tonight?"

"Yes, ma'am."

One by one the radios were turned off and the chattering died. But just before Mrs. Balacheck hit the keys a stocky nurse intervened, thumping rubber-heeled down the aisle with a hand outstretched to ward off the music until she could make an announcement. Mrs. Balacheck sat back, and the nurse, craning her neck, called, "Visiting hour's over!" to one end of the ward and, "Visiting hour's over!" to the other. Then she nodded to Mrs. Balacheck, smiling behind her sterilized linen mask, and thumped away again. After a moment's whispered counsel, Mrs. Balacheck began to play an introductory "Jingle Bells," her cheeks wobbling, to cover the disturbance of departing visitors, while the singers retired to cough quietly among themselves; they would wait until their audience settled down.

"Gee," Harry said, "I didn't realize it was that late. Here, I'll walk you out to the door." He sat up slowly and swung his feet to the floor.

"No, don't bother, Harry," Myra said. "You lie still."

"No, that's all right," he said, wriggling into his slippers. "Will you hand me the robe, honey?" He stood up, and she helped him on with a corduroy VA bathrobe that was too short for him.

"Good night, Mr. Chance," Myra said, and Mr. Chance grinned and nodded. Then she said good night to Red O'Meara and the elderly man, and as they passed his wheelchair in the aisle, she said goodnight to Walter. She took Harry's arm, startled at its thinness, and matched his slow steps very carefully. They stood facing each other in the small awkward crowd of visitors that lingered in the waiting room.

"Well," Harry said, "take care of yourself now, honey. See you next week."

"Oo-oo," somebody's mother said, plodding hump-shouldered out the door, "it *is* cold tonight." She turned back to wave to her son, then grasped her husband's arm and went down the steps to the snow-blown path. Someone else caught the door and held it open for other visitors to pass through, filling the room with a cold draft, and then it closed again, and Myra and Harry were alone.

"All right, Harry," Myra said, "you go back to bed and listen to the music, now." He looked very frail standing there with his robe hanging open. She reached up and closed it neatly over his chest, took the dangling belt and knotted it firmly, while he smiled down at her. "Now you go on back in there before you catch cold."

"Okay. Goodnight, honey."

"Goodnight," she said, and standing on tiptoe, she kissed his cheek. "Goodnight, Harry."

At the door she turned to watch him walk back to the ward in the tight, high-waisted robe. Then she went outside and down the steps, turning up her coat collar in the sudden cold. Marty's car was not there; the road was bare except for the dwindling backs of the other visitors, passing under a street lamp now as they made their way down to the bus stop near the Administration Building. She drew the coat more closely around her and stood close to the building for shelter from the wind.

"Jingle Bells" ended inside, to muffled applause, and after a moment the program began in earnest. A few solemn chords sounded on the piano, and then the voices came through:

> *"Hark, the herald angels sing,*
> *Glory to the new-born King . . ."*

All at once Myra's throat closed up and the street lights swam in her eyes. Then half her fist was in her mouth and she was sobbing wretchedly, making little puffs of mist that floated away in the dark. It took her a long time to stop, and each sniffling intake of breath made a high sharp noise that sounded as if it could be heard for miles. Finally it was over, or nearly over; she managed to control her shoulders, to blow her nose and put her handkerchief away, closing her bag with a reassuring, businesslike snap.

Then the lights of the car came probing up the road. She ran down the path and stood waiting in the wind.

Inside the car a warm smell of whiskey hung among the cherry-red points of cigarettes, and Irene's voice squealed, "Oo-oo! Hurry up and shut the *door!*"

Jack's arms gathered her close as the door slammed, and in a thick whisper he said, "Hello, baby."

They were all a little drunk; even Marty was in high spirits. "Hold tight, everybody!" he called, as they swung around the Administration Building, past the Christmas tree, and leveled off for the straightaway to the gate, gaining speed. "Everybody hold tight!"

Irene's face floated chattering over the back of the front seat. "Myra, honey, listen, we found the most adorable little place down the road, kind of a roadhouse, like, only real inexpensive and everything? So listen, we wanna take you back there for a little drink, okay?"

"Sure," Myra said, "fine."

"'Cause I mean, we're way ahead of you now anyway, and anyway I want you to see this place . . . Marty, will you take it *easy!*" She laughed. "Honestly, anybody else driving this car with what he's had to drink in him, I'd be scared to death, you know it? But you never got to worry about old Marty. He's the best old driver in the world, drunk, sober, I don't care *what* he is."

But they weren't listening. Deep in a kiss, Jack slipped his hand inside her coat, expertly around and inside all the other layers until it held the flesh of her breast. "All over being mad at me, baby?" he mumbled against her lips. "Wanna go have a little drink?"

Her hands gripped the bulk of his back and clung there. Then she let herself be turned so that his other hand could creep secretly up her thigh. "All right," she whispered, "but let's only have one and then afterwards —"

"Okay, baby, okay."

"— and then afterwards, darling, let's go right home."

— 1951

A Glutton for Punishment

For a little while when Walter Henderson was nine years old he thought falling dead was the very zenith of romance, and so did a number of his friends. Having found that the only truly rewarding part of any cops-and-robbers game was the moment when you pretended to be shot, clutched your heart, dropped your pistol and crumpled to the earth, they soon dispensed with the rest of it — the tiresome business of choosing up sides and sneaking around — and refined the game to its essence. It became a matter of individual performance, almost an art. One of them at a time would run dramatically along the crest of a hill, and at a given point the ambush would occur: a simultaneous jerking of aimed toy pistols and a chorus of those staccato throaty sounds — a kind of hoarse-whispered *"Pk-k-ew! Pk-k-ew!"* — with which little boys simulate the noise of gunfire. Then the performer would stop, turn, stand poised for a moment in graceful agony, pitch over and fall down the hill in a whirl of arms and legs and a splendid cloud of dust, and finally sprawl flat at the bottom, a rumpled corpse. When he got up and brushed off his clothes, the others would criticize his form ("Pretty good," or "Too stiff," or "Didn't look natural"), and then it would be the next player's turn. That was all there was to the game, but Walter Henderson loved it. He was a slight, poorly coordinated boy, and this was the only thing even faintly like a sport at which he excelled. No-

body could match the abandon with which he flung his limp
body down the hill, and he reveled in the small acclaim it won
him. Eventually the others grew bored with the game, after
some older boys had laughed at them; Walter turned reluctantly to more wholesome forms of play, and soon he had
forgotten about it.

But he had occasion to remember it, vividly, one May afternoon nearly twenty-five years later in a Lexington Avenue office
building, while he sat at his desk pretending to work and waiting to be fired. He had become a sober, keen-looking young
man now, with clothes that showed the influence of an Eastern
university and neat brown hair that was just beginning to thin
out on top. Years of good health had made him less slight, and
though he still had trouble with his coordination it showed up
mainly in minor things nowadays, like an inability to coordinate
his hat, his wallet, his theater tickets and his change without
making his wife stop and wait for him, or a tendency to push
heavily against doors marked "Pull." He looked, at any rate,
the picture of sanity and competence as he sat there in the
office. No one could have told that the cool sweat of anxiety
was sliding under his shirt, or that the fingers of his left hand,
concealed in his pocket, were slowly grinding and tearing a book
of matches into a moist cardboard pulp. He had seen it coming
for weeks, and this morning, from the minute he got off the
elevator, he had sensed that this was the day it would happen.
When several of his superiors said, "Morning, Walt," he had
seen the faintest suggestion of concern behind their smiles; then
once this afternoon, glancing out over the gate of the cubicle
where he worked, he'd happened to catch the eye of George
Crowell, the department manager, who was hesitating in the
door of his private office with some papers in his hand. Crowell
turned away quickly, but Walter knew he had been watching
him, troubled but determined. In a matter of minutes, he felt
sure, Crowell would call him in and break the news — with
difficulty, of course, since Crowell was the kind of boss who

took pride in being a regular guy. There was nothing to do now but let the thing happen and try to take it as gracefully as possible.

That was when the childhood memory began to prey on his mind, for it suddenly struck him — and the force of it sent his thumbnail biting deep into the secret matchbook — that letting things happen and taking them gracefully had been, in a way, the pattern of his life. There was certainly no denying that the role of good loser had always held an inordinate appeal for him. All through adolescence he had specialized in it, gamely losing fights with stronger boys, playing football badly in the secret hope of being injured and carried dramatically off the field ("You got to hand it to old Henderson for *one* thing, anyway," the high-school coach had said with a chuckle, "he's a real little glutton for punishment"). College had offered a wider scope to his talent — there were exams to be flunked and elections to be lost — and later the Air Force had made it possible for him to wash out, honorably, as a flight cadet. And now, inevitably, it seemed, he was running true to form once more. The several jobs he'd held before this had been the beginner's kind at which it isn't easy to fail; when the opportunity for this one first arose it had been, in Crowell's phrase, "a real challenge."

"Good," Walter had said. "That's what I'm looking for." When he related that part of the conversation to his wife she had said, "Oh, wonderful!" and they'd moved to an expensive apartment in the East Sixties on the strength of it. And lately, when he started coming home with a beaten look and announcing darkly that he doubted if he could hold on much longer, she would enjoin the children not to bother him ("Daddy's very tired tonight"), bring him a drink and soothe him with careful, wifely reassurance, doing her best to conceal her fear, never guessing, or at least never showing, that she was dealing with a chronic, compulsive failure, a strange little boy in love with the attitudes of collapse. And the amazing thing, he thought — the really amazing thing — was that he himself had never looked at it that way before.

"Walt?"

The cubicle gate had swung open and George Crowell was standing there, looking uncomfortable. "Will you step into my office a minute?"

"Right, George." And Walter followed him out of the cubicle, out across the office floor, feeling many eyes on his back. Keep it dignified, he told himself. The important thing is to keep it dignified. Then the door closed behind them and the two of them were alone in the carpeted silence of Crowell's private office. Automobile horns blared in the distance, twenty-one stories below; the only other sounds were their breathing, the squeak of Crowell's shoes as he went to his desk and the creak of his swivel chair as he sat down. "Pull up a chair, Walt," he said. "Smoke?"

"No thanks." Walter sat down and laced his fingers tight between his knees.

Crowell shut the cigarette box without taking one for himself, pushed it aside and leaned forward, both hands spread flat on the plate-glass top of the desk. "Walt, I might as well give you this straight from the shoulder," he said, and the last shred of hope slipped away. The funny part was that it came as a shock, even so. "Mr. Harvey and I have felt for some time that you haven't quite caught on to the work here, and we've both very reluctantly come to the conclusion that the best thing to do, in your own best interests as well as ours, is to let you go. Now," he added quickly, "this is no reflection on you personally, Walt. We do a highly specialized kind of work here and we can't expect everybody to stay on top of the job. In your case particularly, we really feel you'd be happier in some organization better suited to your — abilities."

Crowell leaned back, and when he raised his hands their moisture left two gray, perfect prints on the glass, like the hands of a skeleton. Walter stared at them, fascinated, while they shriveled and disappeared.

"Well," he said, and looked up. "You put that very nicely, George. Thanks."

Crowell's lips worked into an apologetic, regular guy's smile. "Awfully sorry," he said. "These things just happen." And he began to fumble with the knobs of his desk drawers, visibly relieved that the worst was over. "Now," he said, "we've made out a check here covering your salary through the end of next month. That'll give you something in the way of — severance pay, so to speak — to tide you over until you find something." He held out a long envelope.

"That's very generous," Walter said. Then there was a silence, and Walter realized it was up to him to break it. He got to his feet. "All right, George. I won't keep you."

Crowell got up quickly and came around the desk with both hands held out — one to shake Walter's hand, the other to put on his shoulder as they walked to the door. The gesture, at once friendly and humiliating, brought a quick rush of blood to Walter's throat, and for a terrible second he thought he might be going to cry. "Well, boy," Crowell said, "good luck to you."

"Thanks," he said, and he was so relieved to find his voice steady that he said it again, smiling. "Thanks. So long, George."

There was a distance of some fifty feet to be crossed on the way back to his cubicle, and Walter Henderson accomplished it with style. He was aware of how trim and straight his departing shoulders looked to Crowell; he was aware too, as he threaded his way among desks whose occupants either glanced up shyly at him or looked as if they'd like to, of every subtle play of well-controlled emotion in his face. It was as if the whole thing were a scene in a movie. The camera had opened the action from Crowell's viewpoint and dollied back to take in the entire office as a frame for Walter's figure in lonely, stately passage; now it came in for a long-held close-up of

Walter's face, switched to other brief views of his colleagues' turning heads (Joe Collins looking worried, Fred Holmes trying to keep from looking pleased), and switched again to Walter's viewpoint as it discovered the plain, unsuspecting face of Mary, his secretary, who was waiting for him at his desk with a report he had given her to type.

"I hope this is all right, Mr. Henderson."

Walter took it and dropped it on the desk. "Forget it, Mary," he said. "Look, you might as well take the rest of the day off, and go see the personnel manager in the morning. You'll be getting a new job. I've just been fired."

Her first expression was a faint, suspicious smile — she thought he was kidding — but then she began to look pale and shaken. She was very young and not too bright; they had probably never told her in secretarial school that it was possible for your boss to get fired. "Why, that's *terrible*, Mr. Henderson. I — well, but why would they *do* such a thing?"

"Oh, I don't know," he said. "Lot of little reasons, I guess." He was opening and slamming the drawers of his desk, cleaning out his belongings. There wasn't much: a handful of old personal letters, a dry fountain pen, a cigarette lighter with no flint, and half of a wrapped chocolate bar. He was aware of how poignant each of these objects looked to her, as she watched him sort them out and fill his pockets, and he was aware of the dignity with which he straightened up, turned, took his hat from the stand and put it on.

"Doesn't affect you, of course, Mary," he said. "They'll have a new job for you in the morning. Well." He held out his hand. "Good luck."

"Thank you; the same to you. Well, then, g'night" — and here she brought her chewed fingernails up to her lips for an uncertain little giggle — "I mean, g'bye, then, Mr. Henderson."

The next part of the scene was at the water cooler, where Joe Collins's sober eyes became enriched with sympathy as Walter approached him.

"Joe," Walter said. "I'm leaving. Got the ax."

"No!" But Collins's look of shock was plainly an act of kindness; it couldn't have been much of a surprise. "Jesus, Walt, what the hell's the matter with these people?"

Then Fred Holmes chimed in, very grave and sorry, clearly pleased with the news: "Gee, boy, that's a damn shame."

Walter led the two of them away to the elevators, where he pressed the "down" button; and suddenly other men were bearing down on him from all corners of the office, their faces stiff with sorrow, their hands held out.

"Awful sorry, Walt . . ."

"Good luck, boy . . ."

"Keep in touch, okay, Walt? . . ."

Nodding and smiling, shaking hands, Walter said, "Thanks," and "So long," and "I certainly will"; then the red light came on over one of the elevators with its little mechanical "ding!" and in another few seconds the doors slid open and the operator's voice said, "Down!" He backed into the car, still wearing his fixed smile and waving a jaunty salute to their earnest, talking faces, and the scene found its perfect conclusion as the doors slid shut, clamped, and the car dropped in silence through space.

All the way down he stood with the ruddy, bright-eyed look of a man fulfilled by pleasure; it wasn't until he was out on the street, walking rapidly, that he realized how completely he had enjoyed himself.

The heavy shock of this knowledge slowed him down, until he came to a stop and stood against a building front for the better part of a minute. His scalp prickled under his hat, and his fingers began to fumble with the knot of his tie and the button of his coat. He felt as if he had surprised himself in some obscene and shameful act, and he had never felt more helpless, or more frightened.

Then in a burst of action he set off again, squaring his hat and setting his jaw, bringing his heels down hard on the pavement, trying to look hurried and impatient and impelled by

business. A man could drive himself crazy trying to psycho-
analyze himself in the middle of Lexington Avenue, in the
middle of the afternoon. The thing to do was get busy, now, and
start looking for a job.

The only trouble, he realized, coming to a stop again and
looking around, was that he didn't know where he was going.
He was somewhere in the upper Forties, on a corner that was
bright with florist shops and taxicabs, alive with well-dressed
men and women walking in the clear spring air. A telephone
was what he needed first. He hurried across the street to a drugstore and made his way through smells of toilet soap and perfume and ketchup and bacon to the rank of phone booths
along the rear wall; he got out his address book and found the
page showing the several employment agencies where his ap-
plications were filed; then he got his dimes ready and shut himself into one of the booths.

But all the agencies told him the same thing: no openings
in his field at the moment; no point in his coming in until they
called him. When he was finished he dug for the address book
again, to check the number of an acquaintance who had told
him, a month before, that there might soon be an opening in
his office. The book wasn't in his inside pocket; he plunged his
hands into the other pockets of his coat and then his pants,
cracking an elbow painfully against the wall of the booth, but
all he could find were the old letters and the piece of chocolate from his desk. Cursing, he dropped the chocolate on the
floor and, as if it were a lighted cigarette, stepped on it. These
exertions in the heat of the booth made his breathing rapid
and shallow. He was feeling faint by the time he saw the address book right in front of him, on top of the coin box, where
he'd left it. His finger trembled in the dial, and when he started
to speak, clawing the collar away from his sweating neck with
his free hand, his voice was as weak and urgent as a beggar's.

"Jack," he said. "I was just wondering — just wondering if

you'd heard anything new on the opening you mentioned a while back."

"On the which?"

"The opening. You know. You said there might be a job in your —"

"Oh, that. No, haven't heard a thing, Walt. I'll be in touch with you if anything breaks."

"Okay, Jack." He pulled open the folding door of the booth and leaned back against the stamped-tin wall, breathing deeply to welcome the rush of cool air. "I just thought it might've slipped your mind or something," he said. His voice was almost normal again. "Sorry to bother you."

"Hell, that's okay," said the hearty voice in the receiver. "What's the matter, boy? Things getting a little sticky where you are?"

"*Oh* no," Walter found himself saying, and he was immediately glad of the lie. He almost never lied, and it always surprised him to discover how easy it could be. His voice gained confidence. "No, I'm all *right* here, Jack, it's just that I didn't want to — *you* know, I thought it might have slipped your mind, is all. How's the family?"

When the conversation was over, he guessed there was nothing more to do but go home. But he continued to sit in the open booth for a long time, with his feet stretched out on the drugstore floor, until a small, canny smile began to play on his face, slowly dissolving and changing into a look of normal strength. The ease of the lie had given him an idea that grew, the more he thought it over, into a profound and revolutionary decision.

He would not tell his wife. With luck he was sure to find some kind of work before the month was out, and in the meantime, for once in his life, he would keep his troubles to himself. Tonight, when she asked how the day had gone, he would say, "Oh, all right," or even "Fine." In the morning he would leave the house at the usual time and stay away all day, and he would go on doing the same thing every day until he had a job.

The phrase "Pull yourself together" occurred to him, and there was more than determination in the way he pulled himself together there in the phone booth, the way he gathered up his coins and straightened his tie and walked out to the street: there was a kind of nobility.

Several hours had to be killed before the normal time of his homecoming, and when he found himself walking west on Forty-second Street he decided to kill them in the Public Library. He mounted the wide stone steps importantly, and soon he was installed in the reading room, examining a bound copy of last year's *Life* magazines and going over and over his plan, enlarging and perfecting it.

He knew, sensibly, that there would be nothing easy about the day-to-day deception. It would call for the constant vigilance and cunning of an outlaw. But wasn't it the very difficulty of the plan that made it worthwhile? And in the end, when it was all over and he could tell her at last, it would be a reward worth every minute of the ordeal. He knew just how she would look at him when he told her — in blank disbelief at first and then, gradually, with the dawning of a kind of respect he hadn't seen in her eyes for years.

"You mean you kept it to yourself all this *time?* But *why,* Walt?"

"Oh well," he would say casually, even shrugging, "I didn't see any point in upsetting you."

When it was time to leave the library he lingered in the main entrance for a minute, taking deep pulls from a cigarette and looking down over the five o'clock traffic and crowds. The scene held a special nostalgia for him, because it was here, on a spring evening five years before, that he had come to meet her for the first time. "Can you meet me at the top of the library steps?" she had asked over the phone that morning, and it wasn't until many months later, after they were married, that this struck him as a peculiar meeting place. When he asked her about it then, she laughed at him. "Of *course* it was inconvenient — that was the whole point. I wanted to pose up there, like a princess in a castle or something, and make you climb up all those lovely steps to claim me."

And that was exactly how it had seemed. He'd escaped from the office ten minutes early that day and hurried to Grand Central to wash and shave in a gleaming subterranean dressing room; he had waited in a fit of impatience while a very old, stout, slow attendant took his suit away to be pressed. Then, after tipping the attendant more than he could afford, he had raced outside and up Forty-second Street, tense and breathless as he strode past shoe stores and milk bars, as he winnowed his way through swarms of intolerably slow-moving pedestrians who had no idea of how urgent his mission was. He was afraid of being late, even half afraid that it was all some kind of a joke and she wouldn't be there at all. But as soon as he hit Fifth Avenue he saw her up there in the distance, alone, standing at the top of the library steps — a slender, radiant brunette in a fashionable black coat.

He slowed down, then. He crossed the avenue at a stroll, one hand in his pocket, and took the steps with such an easy, athletic nonchalance that nobody could have guessed at the hours of anxiety, the days of strategic and tactical planning this particular moment had cost him.

When he was fairly certain she could see him coming he looked up at her again, and she smiled. It wasn't the first time he had seen her smile that way, but it was the first time he could be sure it was intended wholly for him, and it caused warm tremors of pleasure in his chest. He couldn't remember the words of their greeting, but he remembered being quite sure that they were all right, that it was starting off well — that her wide shining eyes were seeing him exactly as he most wanted to be seen. The things he said, whatever they were, struck her as witty, and the things she said, or the sound of her voice when she said them, made him feel taller and stronger and broader of shoulder than ever before in his life. When they turned and started down the steps together he took hold of her upper arm, claiming her, and felt the light jounce of her breast on the backs of his fingers with each step. And the evening before them, spread out and waiting at their feet, seemed miraculously long and miraculously rich with promise.

Starting down alone, now, he found it strengthening to have one clear triumph to look back on — one time in his life, at least, when he had denied the possibility of failure, and won. Other memories came into focus when he crossed the avenue and started back down the gentle slope of Forty-second Street: they had come this way that evening too, and walked to the Biltmore for a drink, and he remembered how she had looked sitting beside him in the semidarkness of the cocktail lounge, squirming forward from the hips while he helped her out of the sleeves of her coat and then settling back, giving her long hair a toss and looking at him in a provocative sidelong way as she raised the glass to her lips. A little later she had said, "Oh, let's go down to the river — I love the river at this time of day," and they had left the hotel and walked there. He walked there now, down through the clangor of Third Avenue and up toward Tudor City — it seemed a much longer walk alone — until he was standing at the little balustrade, looking down over the swarm of sleek cars on the East River Drive and at the slow, gray water moving beyond it. It was on this very spot, while a tugboat moaned somewhere under the darkening skyline of Queens, that he had drawn her close and kissed her for the first time. Now he turned away, a new man, and set out to walk all the way home.

The first thing that hit him, when he let himself in the apartment door, was the smell of Brussels sprouts. The children were still at their supper in the kitchen: he could hear their high mumbled voices over the clink of dishes, and then his wife's voice, tired and coaxing. When the door slammed he

heard her say, "There's Daddy now," and the children began
to call, "Daddy! Daddy!"

He put his hat carefully in the hall closet and turned around
just as she appeared in the kitchen doorway, drying her hands
on her apron and smiling through her tiredness. "Home on
time for once," she said. "How lovely. I was afraid you'd be
working late again."

"No," he said. "No, I didn't have to work late." His voice
had an oddly foreign, amplified sound in his own ears, as if
he were speaking in an echo chamber.

"You do look tired, though, Walt. You look worn out."

"Walked home, that's all. Guess I'm not used to it. How's
everything?"

"Oh, fine." But she looked worn out herself.

When they went together into the kitchen he felt encircled
and entrapped by its humid brightness. His eyes roamed dole-
fully over the milk cartons, the mayonnaise jars and soup cans
and cereal boxes, the peaches lined up to ripen on the window-
sill, the remarkable frailty and tenderness of his two children,
whose chattering faces were lightly streaked with mashed
potato.

Things looked better in the bathroom, where he took longer
than necessary over the job of washing up for dinner. At least
he could be alone here, braced by splashings of cold water; the
only intrusion was the sound of his wife's voice rising in impatience with the older child: "All right, Andrew Henderson.
No story for *you* tonight unless you finish up all that custard
now." A little later came the scraping of chairs and stacking of
dishes that meant their supper was over, and the light scuffle of
shoes and the slamming door that meant they had been turned
loose in their room for an hour to play before bath time.

Walter carefully dried his hands; then he went out to the living-room sofa and settled himself there with a magazine, taking
very slow, deep breaths to show how self-controlled he was. In
a minute she came in to join him, her apron removed and her

lipstick replenished, bringing the cocktail pitcher full of ice. "Oh," she said with a sigh. "Thank God that's over. Now for a little peace and quiet."

"I'll get the drinks, honey," he said, bolting to his feet. He had hoped his voice might sound normal now, but it still came out with echo-chamber resonance.

"You will not," she commanded. "You sit down. You deserve to sit still and be waited on, when you come home looking so tired. How did the day go, Walt?"

"Oh, all right," he said, sitting down again. "Fine." He watched her measuring out the gin and vermouth, stirring the pitcher in her neat, quick way, arranging the tray and bringing it across the room.

"There," she said, settling herself close beside him. "Will you do the honors, darling?" And when he had filled the chilled glasses she raised hers and said, "Oh, lovely. Cheers." This bright cocktail mood was a carefully studied effect, he knew. So was her motherly sternness over the children's supper; so was the brisk, no-nonsense efficiency with which, earlier today, she had attacked the supermarket; and so, later tonight, would be the tenderness of her surrender in his arms. The orderly rotation of many careful moods was her life, or rather, was what her life had become. She managed it well, and it was only rarely, looking very closely at her face, that he could see how much the effort was costing her.

But the drink was a great help. The first bitter, ice-cold sip of it seemed to restore his calm, and the glass in his hand looked reassuringly deep. He took another sip or two before daring to look at her again, and when he did it was a heartening sight. Her smile was almost completely free of tension, and soon they were chatting together as comfortably as happy lovers.

"Oh, isn't it nice just to sit down and unwind?" she said, allowing her head to sink back into the upholstery. "And isn't it lovely to think it's Friday night?"

"Sure is," he said, and instantly put his mouth in his drink to hide his shock. Friday night! That meant there would be two days before he could even begin to look for a job—two days of mild imprisonment in the house, or of dealing with tricycles and popsicles in the park, without a hope of escaping the burden of his secret. "Funny," he said. "I'd almost forgotten it was Friday."

"Oh, how *can* you forget?" She squirmed luxuriously deeper into the sofa. "I look forward to it all week. Pour me just a tiny bit more, darling, and then I must get back to the chores."

He poured a tiny bit more for her and a full glass for himself. His hand was shaking and he spilled a little of it, but she didn't seem to notice. Nor did she seem to notice that his replies grow more and more strained as she kept the conversation going. When she got back to the chores — basting the roast, drawing the children's baths, tidying up their room for the night — Walter sat alone and allowed his mind to slide into a heavy, gin-fuddled confusion. Only one persistent thought came through, a piece of self-advice that was as clear and cold as the drink that rose again and again to his lips: Hold on. No matter what she says, no matter what happens tonight or tomorrow or the next day, just hold on. Hold on.

But holding on grew less and less easy as the children's splashing bath-noises floated into the room; it was more difficult still by the time they were brought in to say goodnight, carrying their teddy bears and dressed in clean pajamas, their faces shining and smelling of soap. After that, it became impossible to stay seated on the sofa. He sprang up and began stalking around the floor, lighting one cigarette after another, listening to his wife's clear, modulated reading of the bedtime story in the next room ("You may go into the fields, or down the lane, but *don't* go into Mr. McGregor's garden . . .").

When she came out again, closing the children's door behind her, she found him standing like a tragic statue at the window, looking down into the darkening courtyard. "What's the matter, Walt?"

He turned on her with a false grin. "Nothing's the matter," he said in the echo-chamber voice, and the movie camera started rolling again. It came in for a close-up of his own tense face, then switched over to observe her movements as she hovered uncertainly at the coffee table.

"Well," she said. "I'm going to have one more cigarette and then I must get the dinner on the table." She sat down again — not leaning back this time, or smiling, for this was her busy, getting-the-dinner-on-the-table mood. "Have you got a match, Walt?"

"Sure." And he came toward her, probing in his pocket as if to bring forth something he had been saving to give her all day.

"God," she said. "Look at those matches. What *happened* to them?"

"These?" He stared down at the raddled, twisted matchbook as if it were a piece of incriminating evidence. "Must've been kind of tearing them up or something," he said. "Nervous habit."

"Thanks," she said, accepting the light from his trembling fingers, and then she began to look at him with wide, dead-serious eyes. "Walt, there *is* something wrong, isn't there?"

"Of course not. Why should there be anything wi—"

"Tell me the truth. Is it the job? Is it about — what you were afraid of last week? I mean, did anything happen today to make you think they might — Did Crowell say anything? Tell me." The faint lines on her face seemed to have deepened. She looked severe and competent and suddenly much older, not even very pretty any more — a woman used to dealing with emergencies, ready to take charge.

He began to walk slowly away toward an easy chair across the room, and the shape of his back was an eloquent statement of impending defeat. At the edge of the carpet he stopped and seemed to stiffen, a wounded man holding himself together; then he turned around and faced her with the suggestion of a melancholy smile.

"Well, darling —" he began. His right hand came up and touched the middle button of his shirt, as if to unfasten it, and then with a great deflating sigh he collapsed backward into the chair, one foot sliding out on the carpet and the other curled beneath him. It was the most graceful thing he had done all day. "They got me," he said.

— 1953

A Wrestler with Sharks

Nobody had much respect for *The Labor Leader*. Even Finkel and Kramm, its owners, the two sour brothers-in-law who'd dreamed it up in the first place and who somehow managed to make a profit on it year after year — even they could take little pride in the thing. At least, that's what I used to suspect from the way they'd hump grudgingly around the office, shivering the bile-green partitions with their thumps and shouts, grabbing and tearing at galley proofs, breaking pencil points, dropping wet cigar butts on the floor and slamming telephones contemptuously into their cradles. *The Labor Leader* was all either of them would ever have for a life's work, and they seemed to hate it.

You couldn't blame them: the thing was a monster. In format it was a fat biweekly tabloid, badly printed, that spilled easily out of your hands and was very hard to put together again in the right order; in policy it called itself "An Independent Newspaper Pledged to the Spirit of the Trade Union Movement," but its real pitch was to be a kind of trade journal for union officials, who subscribed to it out of union funds and who must surely have been inclined to tolerate, rather than to want or need, whatever thin sustenance it gave to them. The *Leader*'s coverage of national events "from the labor angle" was certain to be stale, likely to be muddled, and often opaque with typographical errors; most of its dense columns were filled with flattering reports on the doings of the unions whose leaders were on the subscription list, often to the exclusion of much bigger news about those whose leaders weren't. And every issue carried scores of simple-minded ads urging "Harmony" in the names of various small industrial firms that Finkel and Kramm had been able to beg or browbeat into buying space — a compromise that would almost certainly have hobbled a real labor paper but that didn't, typically enough, seem to cramp the *Leader*'s style at all.

There was a fast turnover on the editorial staff. Whenever somebody quit, the *Leader* would advertise in the help-wanted section of the *Times*, offering a "moderate salary commensurate with experience." This always brought a good crowd to the sidewalk outside the *Leader* office, a gritty storefront on the lower fringe of the garment district, and Kramm, who was the editor (Finkel was the publisher), would keep them all waiting for half an hour before he picked up a sheaf of application forms, shot his cuffs, and gravely opened the door — I think he enjoyed this occasional chance to play the man of affairs.

"All right, take your time," he'd say, as they jostled inside and pressed against the wooden rail that shielded the inner offices. "Take your time, gentlemen." Then he would raise a hand and say, "May I have your attention, please?" And he'd begin to explain the job. Half the applicants would go away when he got to the part about the salary structure, and most of those who remained offered little competition to anyone who was sober, clean and able to construct an English sentence.

That's the way we'd all been hired, the six or eight of us who frowned under the *Leader*'s sickly fluorescent lights that winter, and most of us made no secret of our desire for better things. I went to work there a couple of weeks after losing my job on one of the metropolitan dailies, and stayed only until I was rescued the next spring by the big picture magazine that still employs me. The others had other explanations, which, like me, they spent a great deal of time discussing: it was a great place for shrill and redundant hard-luck stories.

But Leon Sobel joined the staff about a month after I did, and from the moment Kramm led him into the editorial room we all knew he was going to be different. He stood among the messy desks with the look of a man surveying new fields to conquer, and when Kramm introduced him around (forgetting half our names) he made a theatrically solemn business out of shaking hands. He was about thirty-five, older than most of us, a very small, tense man with black hair that seemed to explode from his skull and a humorless thin-lipped face that was blotched with the scars of acne. His eyebrows were always in motion when he talked, and his eyes, not so much piercing as anxious to pierce, never left the eyes of his listener.

The first thing I learned about him was that he'd never held an office job before: he had been a sheet-metal worker all his adult life. What's more, he hadn't come to the *Leader* out of need, like the rest of us, but, as he put it, out of principle. To do so, in fact, he had given up a factory job paying nearly twice the money.

"What'sa matter, don'tcha believe me?" he asked, after telling me this.

"Well, it's not that," I said. "It's just that I —"

"Maybe you think I'm crazy," he said, and screwed up his face into a canny smile.

I tried to protest, but he wouldn't have it. "Listen, don't worry, McCabe. I'm called crazy a lotta times already. It don't bother me. My wife says, 'Leon, you gotta expect it.' She says, 'People never understand a man who wants something more outa life than just money.' And she's right! She's right!"

"No," I said. "Wait a second. I —"

"People think you gotta be one of two things: either you're a shark, or you gotta lay back and let the sharks eatcha alive — this is the world. Me, I'm the kinda guy's gotta go out and wrestle with the sharks. Why? I dunno why. This is crazy? Okay."

"Wait a second," I said. And I tried to explain that I had nothing whatever against his striking a blow for social justice, if that was what he had in mind; it was just that I thought *The Labor Leader* was about the least likely place in the world for him to do it.

But his shrug told me I was quibbling. "So?" he said. "It's a paper, isn't it? Well, I'm a writer. And what good's a writer if he don't get printed? Listen." He lifted one haunch and placed it on the edge of my desk — he was too short a man to do this gracefully, but the force of his argument helped him to bring it off. "Listen, McCabe. You're a young kid yet. I wanna tellya something. Know how many books I wrote already?" And now his hands came into play, as they always did sooner or later. Both stubby fists were thrust under my nose and allowed to shake there for a moment before they burst into a thicket of stiff, quivering fingers — only the thumb of one hand remained folded down. "Nine," he said, and the hands fell limp on his thigh, to rest until he needed them again. "Nine. Novels, philosophy, political theory — the entire gamut. And not one of 'em published. Believe me, I been around awhile."

"I believe you," I said.

"So finally I sat down and figured: What's the answer? And I figured this: The trouble with my books is, they tell the truth. And the truth is a funny thing, McCabe. People wanna read it, but they only wanna read it when it comes from somebody they already know their name. Am I right? So all right. I figure, I wanna write these books, first I gotta build up a name for myself. This is worth any sacrifice. This is the only way. You know something, McCabe? The last one I wrote took me two years?" Two fingers sprang up to illustrate the point, and dropped again. "Two years, working four, five hours every night and all day long on the weekends. And then you oughta seen the crap I got from the publishers. Every damn publisher in town. My

wife cried. She says, 'But why, Leon? Why?' " Here his lips
curled tight against his small, stained teeth, and the fist of one
hand smacked the palm of the other on his thigh, but then he
relaxed. "I told her, 'Listen, honey. You know why.' " And now
he was smiling at me in quiet triumph. "I says, 'This book told
the truth. That's why.' " Then he winked, slid off my desk and
walked away, erect and jaunty in his soiled sport shirt and his
dark serge pants that hung loose and shiny in the seat. That
was Sobel.

It took him a little while to loosen up in the job: for the
first week or so, when he wasn't talking, he went at everything
with a zeal and a fear of failure that disconcerted everyone but
Finney, the managing editor. Like the rest of us, Sobel had a
list of twelve or fifteen union offices around town, and the main
part of his job was to keep in touch with them and write up
whatever bits of news they gave out. As a rule there was nothing
very exciting to write about: the average story ran two or three
paragraphs with a single-column head:

PLUMBERS WIN
3¢ PAY HIKE

or something like that. But Sobel composed them all as carefully as sonnets, and after he'd turned one in he would sit
chewing his lips in anxiety until Finney raised a forefinger
and said, "C'mere a second, Sobel."

Then he'd go over and stand, nodding apologetically, while
Finney pointed out some niggling grammatical flaw. "Never
end a sentence with a preposition, Sobel. You don't wanna
say, 'gave the plumbers new grounds to bargain on.' You wanna
say, 'gave the plumbers new grounds on which to bargain.' "

Finney enjoyed these lectures. The annoying thing, from a
spectator's point of view, was that Sobel took so long to
learn what everyone else seemed to know instinctively: that
Finney was scared of his own shadow and would back down
on anything at all if you raised your voice. He was a frail,

nervous man who dribbled on his chin when he got excited and raked trembling fingers through his thickly oiled hair, with the result that his fingers spread hair oil, like a spoor of his personality, to everything he touched: his clothes, his pencils, his telephone and his typewriter keys. I guess the main reason he was managing editor was that nobody else would submit to the bullying he took from Kramm: their editorial conferences always began with Kramm shouting "Finney! Finney!" from behind his partition, and Finney jumping like a squirrel to hurry inside. Then you'd hear the relentless drone of Kramm's demands and the quavering sputter of Finney's explanations, and it would end with a thump as Kramm socked his desk. "No, Finney. No, no, *no!* What's the matter with you? I gotta draw you a picture? All right, all right, get outa here, I'll do it myself." At first you might wonder why Finney took it — nobody could need a job that badly — but the answer lay in the fact that there were only three by-lined pieces in *The Labor Leader:* a boiler-plated sports feature that we got from a syndicate, a ponderous column called "LABOR TODAY, by Julius Kramm," that ran facing the editorial page, and a double-column box in the back of the book with the heading:

BROADWAY BEAT
by WES FINNEY

There was even a thumbnail picture of him in the upper left-hand corner, hair slicked down and teeth bared in a confident smile. The text managed to work in a labor angle here and there — a paragraph on Actors' Equity, say, or the stagehands' union — but mostly he played it straight, in the manner of two or three real Broadway-and-nightclub columnists. "Heard about the new thrush at the Copa?" he would ask the labor leaders; then he'd give them her name, with a sly note about her bust and hip measurements and a folksy note about the state from which she "hailed," and he'd wind it up like this: "She's got the whole town talking, and turning up in droves. Their verdict, in which this department wholly concurs: the lady has class." No reader could have guessed that Wes Finney's shoes needed repair, that he got no complimentary tickets to anything and never went out except to take in a movie or to crouch over a liverwurst sandwich at the Automat. He wrote the column on his own time and got extra money for it — the figure I heard was fifty dollars a month. So it was a mutually satisfactory deal: for that small sum Kramm held his whipping boy in absolute bondage; for that small torture Finney could paste clippings in a scrapbook, with all the contamination of *The Labor Leader* sheared away into the wastebasket of his furnished room, and whisper himself to sleep with dreams of ultimate freedom.

Anyway, this was the man who could make Sobel apologize for the grammar of his news stories, and it was a sad thing to watch. Of course, it couldn't go on forever, and one day it stopped.

Finney had called Sobel over to explain about split infinitives, and Sobel was wrinkling his brow in an effort to understand. Neither of them noticed that Kramm was standing in the doorway of his office a few feet away, listening, and looking at the wet end of his cigar as if it tasted terrible.

"Finney," he said. "You wanna be an English teacher, get a job in the high school."

Startled, Finney stuck a pencil behind his ear without noticing that another pencil was already there, and both pencils clattered to the floor. "Well, I —" he said. "Just thought I'd —"

"Finney, this does not interest me. Pick up your pencils and listen to me, please. For your information, Mr. Sobel is not supposed to be a literary Englishman. He is supposed to be a literate American, and this I believe he is. Do I make myself clear?"

And the look on Sobel's face as he walked back to his own desk was that of a man released from prison.

From that moment on he began to relax; or almost from that

moment — what seemed to clinch the transformation was O'-Leary's hat.

O'Leary was a recent City College graduate and one of the best men on the staff (he has since done very well; you'll often see his by-line in one of the evening papers), and the hat he wore that winter was of the waterproof cloth kind that is sold in raincoat shops. There was nothing very dashing about it — in fact its floppiness made O'Leary's face look too thin — but Sobel must secretly have admired it as a symbol of journalism, or of nonconformity, for one morning he showed up in an identical one, brand new. It looked even worse on him than on O'Leary, particularly when worn with his lumpy brown overcoat, but he seemed to cherish it. He developed a whole new set of mannerisms to go with the hat: cocking it back with a flip of the index finger as he settled down to make his morning phone calls ("This is Leon Sobel, of *The Labor Leader* . . ."), tugging it smartly forward as he left the office on a reporting assignment, twirling it onto a peg when he came back to write his story. At the end of the day, when he'd dropped the last of his copy into Finney's wire basket, he would shape the hat into a careless slant over one eyebrow, swing the overcoat around his shoulders and stride out with a loose salute of farewell, and I used to picture him studying his reflection in the black subway windows all the way home to the Bronx.

He seemed determined to love his work. He even brought in a snapshot of his family — a tired, abjectly smiling woman and two small sons — and fastened it to his desk top with cellophane tape. Nobody else ever left anything more personal than a book of matches in the office overnight.

One afternoon toward the end of February, Finney summoned me to his oily desk. "McCabe," he said. "Wanna do a column for us?"

"What kind of a column?"

"Labor gossip," he said. "Straight union items with a gossip or a chatter angle — little humor, personalities, stuff like that.

Mr. Kramm thinks we need it, and I told him you'd be the best man for the job."

I can't deny that I was flattered (we are all conditioned by our surroundings, after all), but I was also suspicious. "Do I get a by-line?"

He began to blink nervously. "Oh, no, no by-line," he said. "Mr. Kramm wants this to be anonymous. See, the guys'll give you any items they turn up, and you'll just collect 'em and put 'em in shape. It's just something you can do on office time, part of your regular job. See what I mean?"

I saw what he meant. "Part of my regular salary too," I said. "Right?"

"That's right."

"No thanks," I told him, and then, feeling generous, I suggested that he try O'Leary.

"Nah, I already asked him," Finney said. "He don't wanna do it either. Nobody does."

I should have guessed, of course, that he'd been working down the list of everyone in the office. And to judge from the lateness of the day, I must have been close to the tail end.

Sobel fell in step with me as we left the building after work that night. He was wearing his overcoat cloak-style, the sleeves dangling, and holding his cloth hat in place as he hopped nimbly to avoid the furrows of dirty slush on the sidewalk. "Letcha in on a little secret, McCabe," he said. "I'm doin' a column for the paper. It's all arranged."

"Yeah?" I said. "Any money in it?"

"Money?" He winked. "I'll tell y' about that part. Let's get a cuppa coffee." He led me into the tiled and steaming brilliance of the Automat, and when we were settled at a damp corner table he explained everything. "Finney says no money, see? So I said okay. He says no by-line either. I said okay." He winked again. "Playin' it smart."

"How do you mean?"

"How do I mean?" He always repeated your question like

that, savoring it, holding his black eyebrows high while he made you wait for the answer. "Listen, I got this Finney figured out. *He* don't decide these things. You think he decides anything around that place? You better wise up, McCabe. Mr. *Kramm* makes the decisions. And Mr. Kramm is an intelligent man, don't kid yourself." Nodding, he raised his coffee cup, but his lips recoiled from the heat of it, puckered, and blew into the steam before they began to sip with gingerly impatience.

"Well," I said, "okay, but I'd check with Kramm before you start counting on anything."

"Check?" He put his cup down with a clatter. "What's to check? Listen, Mr. Kramm wants a column, right? You think he cares if I get a by-line or not? Or the money, either — you think if I write a good column he's gonna quibble over payin' me for it? Ya crazy. *Finney's* the one, don'tcha see? *He* don't wanna gimme a break because he's worried about losing his *own* column. Get it? So all right. I check with nobody until I got that column written." He prodded his chest with a stiff thumb. "On my own time. Then I take it to Mr. Kramm and we talk business. You leave it to me." He settled down comfortably, elbows on the table, both hands cradling the cup just short of drinking position while he blew into the steam.

"Well," I said. "I hope you're right. Be nice if it does work out that way."

"Ah, it may not," he conceded, pulling his mouth into a grimace of speculation and tilting his head to one side. "*You* know. It's a gamble." But he was only saying that out of politeness, to minimize my envy. He could afford to express doubt because he felt none, and I could tell he was already planning the way he'd tell his wife about it.

The next morning Finney came around to each of our desks with instructions that we were to give Sobel any gossip or chatter items we might turn up; the column was scheduled to begin in the next issue. Later I saw him in conference with Sobel, briefing him on how the column was to be written, and I noticed that

Finney did all the talking: Sobel just sat there making thin, contemptuous jets of cigarette smoke.

We had just put an issue to press, so the deadline for the column was two weeks away. Not many items turned up at first — it was hard enough getting news out of the unions we covered, let alone "chatter." Whenever someone did hand him a note, Sobel would frown over it, add a scribble of his own and drop it in a desk drawer; once or twice I saw him drop one in the wastebasket. I only remember one of the several pieces I gave him: the business agent of a steamfitters' local I covered had yelled at me through a closed door that he couldn't be bothered that day because his wife had just had twins. But Sobel didn't want it. "So, the guy's got twins," he said. "So what?"

"Suit yourself," I said. "You getting much other stuff?"

He shrugged. "Some. I'm not worried. I'll tellya one thing, though — I'm not using a lotta this crap. This chatter. Who the hell's gonna read it? You can't have a whole column fulla crap like that. Gotta be something to hold it together. Am I right?"

Another time (the column was all he talked about now) he chuckled affectionately and said, "My wife says I'm just as bad now as when I was working on my books. Write, write, write. She don't care, though," he added. "She's really getting excited about this thing. She's telling everybody — the neighbors, everybody. Her brother come over Sunday, starts asking me how the job's going — you know, in a wise-guy kinda way? I just kept quiet, but my wife pipes up: 'Leon's doing a column for the paper now' — and she tells him all about it. Boy, you oughta seen his face."

Every morning he brought in the work he had done the night before, a wad of handwritten papers, and used his lunch hour to type it out and revise it while he chewed a sandwich at his desk. And he was the last one to go home every night; we'd leave him there hammering his typewriter in a trance of concentration. Finney kept bothering him — "How you coming on that feature, Sobel?" — but he always parried the question with squinted eyes and a truculent lift of the chin. "Whaddya worried about? You'll get it." And he would wink at me.

On the morning of the deadline he came to work with a little patch of toilet paper on his cheek; he had cut himself shaving in his nervousness, but otherwise he looked as confident as ever. There were no calls to make that morning — on deadline days we all stayed in to work on copy and proofs — so the first thing he did was to spread out the finished manuscript for a final reading. His absorption was so complete that he didn't look up until Finney was standing at his elbow. "You wanna gimme that feature, Sobel?"

Sobel grabbed up the papers and shielded them with an arrogant forearm. He looked steadily at Finney and said, with a firmness that he must have been rehearsing for two weeks: "I'm showing this to Mr. Kramm. Not you."

Finney's whole face began to twitch in a fit of nerves. "Nah, nah, Mr. Kramm don't need to see it," he said. "Anyway, he's not in yet. C'mon, lemme have it."

"You're wasting your time, Finney," Sobel said. "I'm waiting for Mr. Kramm."

Muttering, avoiding Sobel's triumphant eyes, Finney went back to his own desk, where he was reading proof on BROAD-WAY BEAT.

My own job that morning was at the layout table, pasting up the dummy for the first section. I was standing there, working with the unwieldly page forms and the paste-clogged scissors, when Sobel sidled up behind me, looking anxious. "You wanna read it, McCabe?" he asked. "Before I turn it in?" And he handed me the manuscript.

The first thing that hit me was that he had clipped a photograph to the top of page 1, a small portrait of himself in his cloth hat. The next thing was his title:

SOBEL SPEAKING
by Leon Sobel

I can't remember the exact words of the opening paragraph, but it went something like this:

This is the "debut" of a new department in *The Labor Leader* and, moreover, it is also "something new" for your correspondent, who has never handled a column before. However, he is far from being a novice with the written word, on the contrary he is an "ink-stained veteran" of many battles on the field of ideas, to be exact nine books have emanated from his pen.

Naturally in those tomes his task was somewhat different than that which it will be in this column, and yet he hopes that this column will also strive as they did to penetrate the basic human mystery, in other words, to tell the truth.

When I looked up I saw he had picked open the razor cut cut on his cheek and it was bleeding freely. "Well," I said, "for one thing, I wouldn't give it to him with your picture that way — I mean, don't you think it might be better to let him read it first, and then —"

"Okay," he said, blotting at his face with a wadded gray handkerchief. "Okay, I'll take the picture off. G'ahead, read the rest."

But there wasn't time to read the rest. Kramm had come in, Finney had spoken to him, and now he was standing in the door of his office, champing crossly on a dead cigar. "You wanted to see me, Sobel?" he called.

"Just a second," Sobel said. He straightened the pages of SOBEL SPEAKING and detached the photograph, which he jammed into his hip pocket as he started for the door. Halfway there he remembered to take off his hat, and threw it unsuccessfully at the hat stand. Then he disappeared behind the partition, and we all settled down to listen.

It wasn't long before Kramm's reaction came through. "No

Sobel. No, no, *no!* What *is* this? What are you tryna put *over* on me here?"

Outside, Finney winced comically and clapped the side of his head, giggling, and O'Leary had to glare at him until he stopped.

We heard Sobel's voice, a blurred sentence or two of protest, and then Kramm came through again: " 'Basic human mystery' — this is gossip? This is chatter? You can't follow instructions? Wait a minute — Finney! Finney!"

Finney loped to the door, delighted to be of service, and we heard him making clear, righteous replies to Kramm's interrogation: Yes, he had told Sobel what kind of a column was wanted; yes, he had specified that there was to be no by-line; yes, Sobel had been provided with ample gossip material. All we heard from Sobel was something indistinct, said in a very tight, flat voice. Kramm made a guttural reply, and even though we couldn't make out the words we knew it was all over. Then they came out, Finney wearing the foolish smile you sometimes see in the crowds that gape at street accidents, Sobel as expressionless as death.

He picked his hat off the floor and his coat off the stand, put them on, and came over to me. "So long, McCabe," he said. "Take it easy."

Shaking hands with him, I felt my face jump into Finney's idiot smile, and I asked a stupid question. "You leaving?"

He nodded. Then he shook hands with O'Leary — "So long, kid" — and hesitated, uncertain whether to shake hands with the rest of the staff. He settled for a little wave of the forefinger, and walked out to the street.

Finney lost no time in giving us all the inside story in an eager whisper: "The guy's *crazy!* He says to Kramm, 'You take this column or I quit' — just like that. Kramm just looks at him and says, 'Quit? Get outa here, you're fired.' I mean, what *else* could he say?"

Turning away, I saw that the snapshot of Sobel's wife and

sons still lay taped to his desk. I stripped it off and took it out to the sidewalk. "Hey, Sobel!" I yelled. He was a block away, very small, walking toward the subway. I started to run after him, nearly breaking my neck on the frozen slush. "Hey *Sobel!*" But he didn't hear me.

Back at the office I found his address in the Bronx telephone directory, put the picture in an envelope and dropped it in the mail, and I wish that were the end of the story.

But that afternoon I called up the editor of a hardware trade journal I had worked on before the war, who said he had no vacancies on his staff but might soon, and would be willing to interview Sobel if he wanted to drop in. It was a foolish idea: the wages there were even lower than on the *Leader*, and besides, it was a place for very young men whose fathers wanted them to learn the hardware business — Sobel would probably have been ruled out the minute he opened his mouth. But it seemed better than nothing, and as soon as I was out of the office that night I went to a phone booth and looked up Sobel's name again.

A woman's voice answered, but it wasn't the high, faint voice I'd expected. It was low and melodious — that was the first of my several surprises.

"Mrs. Sobel?" I asked, absurdly smiling into the mouthpiece. "Is Leon there?"

She started to say, "Just a minute," but changed it to "Who's calling, please? I'd rather not disturb him right now."

I told her my name and tried to explain about the hardware deal.

"I don't understand," she said. "What kind of a paper is it, exactly?"

"Well, it's a trade journal," I said. "It doesn't amount to much, I guess, but it's — *you* know, a pretty good little thing, of its kind."

"I see," she said. "And you want him to go in and apply for a job? Is that it?"

"Well I mean, if he *wants* to, is all," I said. I was beginning to sweat. It was impossible to reconcile the wan face in Sobel's snapshot with this serene, almost beautiful voice. "I just thought he might like to give it a try, is all."

"Well," she said, "just a minute, I'll ask him." She put down the phone, and I heard them talking in the background. Their words were muffled at first, but then I heard Sobel say, "Ah, I'll talk to him — I'll just say thanks for calling." And I heard her answer, with infinite tenderness, "No, honey, why should you? He doesn't deserve it."

"McCabe's all right," he said.

"No he's not," she told him, "or he'd have the decency to leave you alone. Let me do it. Please. I'll get rid of him."

When she came back to the phone she said, "No, my husband says he wouldn't be interested in a job of that kind." Then she thanked me politely, said goodbye, and left me to climb guilty and sweating out of the phone booth.

— 1954

Fun with a Stranger

ALL that summer the children who were due to start third grade under Miss Snell had been warned about her. "Boy, you're gonna get it," the older children would say, distorting their faces with a wicked pleasure. "You're really gonna *get* it. Mrs. *Cleary's* all right" (Mrs. Cleary taught the other, luckier half of third grade) "— she's *fine*, but boy, that *Snell* — you better watch out." So it happened that the morale of Miss Snell's class was low even before school opened in September, and she did little in the first few weeks to improve it.

She was probably sixty, a big rawboned woman with a man's face, and her clothes, if not her very pores, seemed always to exude that dry essence of pencil shavings and chalk dust that is the smell of school. She was strict and humorless, preoccupied with rooting out the things she held intolerable: mumbling, slumping, daydreaming, frequent trips to the bathroom, and, the worst of all, "coming to school without proper supplies." Her small eyes were sharp, and when somebody sent out a stealthy alarm of whispers and nudges to try to borrow a pencil from somebody else, it almost never worked. "What's the trouble back there?" she would demand. "I mean you, John Gerhardt." And John Gerhardt — or Howard White or whoever it happened to be — caught in the middle of a whisper, could only turn red and say, "Nothing."

"Don't mumble. Is it a pencil? Have you come to school without a pencil again? Stand up when you're spoken to."

And there would follow a long lecture on Proper Supplies that ended only after the offender had come forward to receive a pencil from the small hoard on her desk, had been made to say, "Thank you, Miss Snell," and to repeat, until he said it loud enough for everyone to hear, a promise that he wouldn't chew it or break its point.

With erasers it was even worse because they were more often in short supply, owing to a general tendency to chew them off the ends of pencils. Miss Snell kept a big, shapeless old eraser on her desk, and she seemed very proud of it. "This is *my* eraser," she would say, shaking it at the class. "I've had this eraser for five years. Five years." (And this was not hard to believe, for the eraser looked as old and gray and worn-down as the hand that brandished it.) "I've never played with it because it's not a toy. I've never chewed it because it's not good to eat. And I've never lost it because I'm not foolish and I'm not careless. I need this eraser for my work and I've taken good care of it. Now, why can't you do the same with *your* erasers? I don't know what's the matter with this class. I've never had a class that was so foolish and so careless and so *childish* about its supplies."

She never seemed to lose her temper, but it would almost have been better if she did, for it was the flat, dry, passionless redundance of her scolding that got everybody down. When Miss Snell singled someone out for a special upbraiding it was an ordeal by talk. She would come up to within a foot of her victim's face, her eyes would stare unblinking into his, and the wrinkled gray flesh of her mouth would labor to pronounce his guilt, grimly and deliberately, until all the color faded from the day. She seemed to have no favorites; once she even picked on Alice Johnson, who always had plenty of supplies and did nearly everything right. Alice was mumbling while reading aloud, and when she continued to mumble after several warnings Miss Snell went over and took her book away and lectured her for several minutes running. Alice looked stunned at first; then her eyes filled up, her mouth twitched into terrible shapes, and she gave in to the ultimate humiliation of crying in class.

It was not uncommon to cry in Miss Snell's class, even among the boys. And ironically, it always seemed to be during the lull after one of these scenes — when the only sound in the room was somebody's slow, half-stifled sobbing, and the rest of the class stared straight ahead in an agony of embarrassment — that the noise of group laughter would float in from Mrs. Cleary's class across the hall.

Still, they could not hate Miss Snell, for children's villains must be all black, and there was no denying that Miss Snell was sometimes nice in an awkward, groping way of her own. "When we learn a new word it's like making a friend," she said once. "And we all like to make friends, don't we? Now, for instance, when school began this year you were all strangers to me, but I wanted very much to learn your names and remember your faces, and so I made the effort. It was confusing at first, but before long I'd made friends with all of you. And later on we'll have some good times together — oh, perhaps a little party at Christmastime, or something like that — and then I know I'd be very sorry if I hadn't made that effort, because you can't very well have fun with a stranger, can you?" She gave them a homely, shy smile. "And that's just the way it is with words."

When she said something like that it was more embarrassing than anything else, but it did leave the children with a certain vague sense of responsibility toward her, and often prompted them into a loyal reticence when children from other classes demanded to know how bad she really was. "Well, not too bad," they would say uncomfortably, and try to change the subject.

John Gerhardt and Howard White usually walked home from school together, and often as not, though they tried to avoid it, they were joined by two of the children from Mrs. Cleary's class who lived on their street — Freddy Taylor and his twin sister Grace. John and Howard usually got about as far as the end of the playground before the twins came running after them out of the crowd. "Hey, wait up!" Freddy would call. "Wait up!" And in a moment the twins would fall into step beside them, chattering, swinging their identical plaid canvas school-bags.

Guess what we're gonna do next week," Freddy said in his chirping voice one afternoon. "Our whole class, I mean. Guess. Come on, guess."

John Gerhardt had already made it plain to the twins once, in so many words, that he didn't like walking home with a girl, and now he very nearly said something to the effect that one girl was bad enough, but two were more than he could take. Instead he aimed a knowing glance at Howard White and they both walked on in silence, determined not to answer Freddy's insistent "Guess."

But Freddy didn't wait long for an answer. "We're gonna take a field trip," he said, "for our class in Transportation. We're gonna go to Harmon. You know what Harmon is?"

"Sure," Howard White said. "A town."

"No, but I mean, you know what they *do* there? What they do is, that's where they change all the trains coming into New York from steam locomotives to electric power. Mrs. Cleary says we're gonna watch 'em changing the locomotives and everything."

"We're gonna spend practically the whole day," Grace said.

"So what's so great about that?" Howard White asked. "I can go there *any* day, if I feel like it, on my bike." This was an exaggeration — he wasn't allowed out of a two-block radius on his bike — but it sounded good, especially when he added. "I don't need any Mrs. Cleary to take me," with a mincing, sissy emphasis on the "Cleary."

"On a school day?" Grace inquired. "Can you go on a *school* day?"

Lamely Howard murmured, "Sure, if I feel like it," but it was a clear point for the twins.

"Mrs. Cleary says we're gonna take a lotta field trips," Freddy said. "Later on, we're gonna go to the Museum of Natural History, in New York, and a whole lotta other places. Too bad you're not in Mrs. Cleary's class."

"Doesn't bother me any," John Gerhardt said. Then he came up with a direct quotation from his father that seemed appropriate: "Anyway, I don't *go* to school to fool around. I go to school to work. Come on, Howard."

A day or two later it turned out that both classes were scheduled to take the field trip together; Miss Snell had just neglected to tell her pupils about it. When she did tell them it was in one of her nice moods. "I think the trip will be especially valuable," she said, "because it will be instructive and at the same time it will be a real treat for all of us." That afternoon John Gerhardt and Howard White conveyed the news to the twins with studied carelessness and secret delight.

But the victory was short-lived, for the field trip itself only emphasized the difference between the two teachers. Mrs. Cleary ran everything with charm and enthusiasm; she was young and lithe and just about the prettiest woman Miss Snell's class had ever seen. It was she who arranged for the children to climb up and inspect the cab of a huge locomotive that stood idle on a siding, and she who found out where the public toilets were. The most tedious facts about trains came alive when she explained them; the most forbidding engineers and switchmen became jovial hosts when she smiled up at them, with her long hair blowing and her hands plunged jauntily in the pockets of her polo coat.

Through it all Miss Snell hung in the background, gaunt and sour, her shoulders hunched against the wind and her squinted eyes roving, alert for stragglers. At one point she made Mrs.

Cleary wait while she called her own class aside and announced that there would be no more field trips if they couldn't learn to stay together in a group. She spoiled everything, and by the time it was over the class was painfully embarrassed for her. She'd had every chance to give a good account of herself that day, and now her failure was as pitiful as it was disappointing. That was the worst part of it: she was pitiful — they didn't even want to look at her, in her sad, lumpy black coat and hat. All they wanted was to get her into the bus and back to school and out of sight as fast as possible.

The events of autumn each brought a special season to the school. First came Halloween, for which several art classes were devoted to crayoned jack-o'-lanterns and arching black cats. Thanksgiving was bigger; for a week or two the children painted turkeys and horns of plenty and brown-clad Pilgrim Fathers with high buckled hats and trumpet-barreled muskets, and in music class they sang "We Gather Together" and "America the Beautiful" again and again. And almost as soon as Thanksgiving was over the long preparations for Christmas began: red and green predominated, and carols were rehearsed for the annual Christmas Pageant. Every day the halls became more thickly festooned with Christmas trimmings, until finally it was the last week before vacation.

"You gonna have a party in your class?" Freddy Taylor inquired one day.

"Sure, prob'ly," John Gerhardt said, though in fact he wasn't sure at all. Except for that one vague reference, many weeks before, Miss Snell had said or hinted nothing whatever about a Christmas party.

"Miss Snell tell ya you're gonna have one, or what?" Grace asked.

"Well, she didn't exactly *tell* us," John Gerhardt said obscurely. Howard White walked along without a word, scuffing his shoes.

"Mrs. Cleary didn't tell us, either," Grace said, "because it's supposed to be a surprise, but we know we're gonna have one. Some of the kids who had her last year said so. They said she always has this big party on the last day, with a tree and everything, and favors and things to eat. You gonna have all that?"

"Oh, I don't know," John Gerhardt said. "Sure, prob'ly." But later, when the twins were gone, he got a little worried. "Hey, Howard," he said, "you think she *is* gonna have a party, or what?"

"Search *me*," Howard White said, with a careful shrug. "*I* didn't say anything." But he was uneasy about it too, and so was the rest of the class. As vacation drew nearer, and particularly during the few anticlimactic days of school left after the Christmas Pageant was over, it seemed less and less likely that Miss Snell was planning a party of any kind, and it preyed on all their minds.

It rained on the last day of school. The morning went by like any other morning, and after lunch, like any other rainy day, the corridors were packed with chattering children in raincoats and rubbers, milling around and waiting for the afternoon classes to begin. Around the third-grade classrooms there was a special tension, for Mrs. Cleary had locked the door of her room, and the word soon spread that she was alone inside making preparations for a party that would begin when the bell rang and last all afternoon. "I peeked," Grace Taylor was saying breathlessly to anyone who would listen. "She's got this little tree with all blue lights, and she's got the room all fixed up and all the desks moved away and everything."

Others from her class tagged after her with questions — "*What'd* you see?" "All blue lights?" — and still others jostled around the door, trying to get a look through the keyhole.

Miss Snell's class pressed self-consciously against the corridor wall, mostly silent, hands in their pockets. Their door was closed too, but nobody wanted to see if it was locked for fear it might swing open and reveal Miss Snell sitting sensibly at her desk, correcting papers. Instead they watched Mrs. Cleary's door, and when it opened at last they watched the other children flock in. All the girls yelled, "Ooh!" in chorus as they disappeared inside, and even from where Miss Snell's class stood they could see that the room was transformed. There *was* a tree with blue lights — the whole room glowed blue, in fact — and the floor was cleared. They could just see the corner of a table in the middle, bearing platters of bright candy and cake. Mrs. Cleary stood in the doorway, beautiful and beaming, slightly flushed with welcome. She gave a kindly, distracted smile to the craning faces of Miss Snell's class, then closed the door again.

A second later Miss Snell's door opened, and the first thing they saw was that the room was unchanged. The desks were all in place, ready for work; their own workaday Christmas paintings still spotted the walls, and there was no other decoration except for the grubby red cardboard letters spelling "Merry Christmas" that had hung over the blackboard all week. But then with a rush of relief they saw that on Miss Snell's desk lay a neat little pile of red-and-white-wrapped packages. Miss Snell stood unsmiling at the head of the room, waiting for the class to get settled. Instinctively, nobody lingered to stare at the gifts or to comment on them. Miss Snell's attitude made it plain that the party hadn't begun yet.

It was time for spelling, and she instructed them to get their pencils and paper ready. In the silences between her enunciation of each word to be spelled, the noise of Mrs. Cleary's class could be heard — repeated laughter and whoops of surprise. But the little pile of gifts made everything all right; the children had only to look at them to know that there was nothing to be embarrassed about, after all. Miss Snell had come through.

The gifts were all wrapped alike, in white tissue paper with red ribbon, and the few whose individual shapes John Gerhardt could discern looked like they might be jackknives. Maybe it would be jackknives for the boys, he thought, and little pocket flashlights for the girls. Or more likely, since jackknives were probably too expensive, it would be something well-meant and useless from the dime store, like individual lead soldiers for the boys and miniature dolls for the girls. But even that would be good enough — something hard and bright to prove that she was human after all, to pull out of a pocket and casually display to the Taylor twins. ("Well, no, not a *party*, exactly, but she gave us all these little presents. Look.")

"John Gerhardt," Miss Snell said, "if you can't give your attention to anything but the . . . things on my desk, perhaps I'd better put them out of sight." The class giggled a little, and she smiled. It was only a small, shy smile, quickly corrected before she turned back to her spelling book, but it was enough to break the tension. While the spelling papers were being collected Howard White leaned close to John Gerhardt and whispered, "Tie clips. Bet it's tie clips for the boys and some kinda jewelry for the girls."

"Sh-sh!" John told him, but then he added, "Too thick for tie clips." There was a general shifting around; everyone expected the party to begin as soon as Miss Snell had all the spelling papers. Instead she called for silence and began the afternoon class in Transportation.

The afternoon wore on. Every time Miss Snell glanced at the clock they expected her to say, "Oh, my goodness — I'd almost forgotten." But she didn't. It was a little after two, with less than an hour of school left, when Miss Snell was interrupted by a knock on the door. "Yes?" she said irritably. "What is it?"

Little Grace Taylor came in, with half a cupcake in her hand and the other half in her mouth. She displayed elaborate surprise at finding the class at work — backing up a step and putting her free hand to her lips.

"Well?" Miss Snell demanded. "Do you want something?"

"Mrs. Cleary wants to know if —"

"Must you talk with your mouth full?"

Grace swallowed. She wasn't the least bit shy. "Mrs. Cleary wants to know if you have any extra paper plates."

"I have no paper plates," Miss Snell said. "And will you kindly inform Mrs. Cleary that this class is in session?"

"All right," Grace took another bite of her cake and turned to leave. Her eyes caught the pile of gifts and she paused to look at them, clearly unimpressed.

"You're holding up the class," Miss Snell said. Grace moved on. At the door she gave the class a sly glance and a quick, silent giggle full of cake crumbs, and then slipped out.

The minute hand crept down to two-thirty, passed it, and inched toward two-forty-five. Finally, at five minutes of three, Miss Snell laid down her book. "All right," she said, "I think we may all put our books away now. This is the last day of school before the holidays, and I've prepared a — little surprise for you." She smiled again. "Now, I think it would be best if you all stay in your places, and I'll just pass these around. Alice Johnson, will you please come and help me? The rest of you stay seated." Alice went forward, and Miss Snell divided the little packages into two heaps, using two pieces of drawing paper as trays. Alice took one paperful, cradling it carefully, and Miss Snell the other. Before they started around the room Miss Snell said, "Now, I think the most courteous thing would be for each of you to wait until everyone is served, and then we'll all open the packages together. All right, Alice."

They started down the aisle, reading the labels and passing out the gifts. The labels were the familiar Woolworth kind with a picture of Santa Claus and "Merry Christmas" printed on them, and Miss Snell had filled them out in her neat blackboard lettering. John Gerhardt's read: "To John G., From Miss Snell." He picked it up, but the moment he felt the package he knew, with a little shock, exactly what it was. There was no surprise left by the time Miss Snell returned to the head of the class and said, "All right."

He peeled off the paper and laid the gift on his desk. It was an eraser, the serviceable ten-cent kind, half white for pencil and half gray for ink. From the corner of his eye he saw that Howard White, beside him, was unwrapping an identical one, and a furtive glance around the room confirmed that all the gifts had been the same. Nobody knew what to do, and for what seemed a full minute the room was silent except for the dwindling rustle of tissue paper. Miss Snell stood at the head of the class, her clasped fingers writhing like dry worms at her waist, her face melted into the soft, tremulous smile of a giver. She looked completely helpless.

At last one of the girls said, "Thank you, Miss Snell," and then the rest of the class said it in ragged unison: "Thank you, Miss Snell."

"You're all very welcome," she said, composing herself, "and I hope you all have a pleasant holiday."

Mercifully, the bell rang then, and in the jostling clamor of retreat to the cloakroom it was no longer necessary to look at Miss Snell. Her voice rose above the noise: "Will you all please dispose of your paper and ribbons in the basket before you leave?"

John Gerhardt yanked on his rubbers, grabbed his raincoat, and elbowed his way out of the cloakroom, out of the classroom and down the noisy corridor. "Hey, Howard, wait up!" he yelled to Howard White, and finally both of them were free of school, running, splashing through puddles on the playground. Miss Snell was left behind now, farther behind with every step; if they ran fast enough they could even avoid the Taylor twins, and then there would be no need to think about any of it any more. Legs pounding, raincoats streaming, they ran with the exhilaration of escape.

— 1952

The B.A.R. Man

Until he got his name on the police blotter, and in the papers, nobody had ever thought much about John Fallon. He was employed as a clerk in a big insurance company, where he hulked among the file cabinets with a conscientious frown, his white shirt cuffs turned back to expose a tight gold watch on one wrist and a loose serviceman's identification bracelet, the relic of a braver and more careless time, on the other. He was twenty-nine years old, big and burly, with neatly combed brown hair and a heavy white face. His eyes were kindly except when he widened them in bewilderment or narrowed them in menace, and his mouth was childishly slack except when he tightened it to say something tough. For street wear, he preferred slick, gas-blue suits with stiff shoulders and very low-set buttons, and he walked with the hard, ringing cadence of steel-capped heels. He lived in Sunnyside, Queens, and had been married for ten years to a very thin girl named Rose who suffered from sinus head-aches, couldn't have children, and earned more money than he did by typing eighty-seven words a minute without missing a beat on her chewing gum.

Five evenings a week, Sunday through Thursday, the Fallons sat at home playing cards or watching television, and sometimes she would send him out to buy sandwiches and potato salad for a light snack before they went to bed. Friday, being the end of the work week and the night of the fights on television, was his night with the boys at the Island Bar and Grill, just off Queens Boulevard. The crowd there were friends of habit rather than of choice, and for the first half hour they would stand around self-consciously, insulting one another and jeering at each new arrival ("Oh Jesus, looka what just come in!"). But by the time the fights were over they would usually have joked and drunk themselves into a high good humor, and the evening would often end in song and staggering at two or three o'clock. Fallon's Saturday, after a morning of sleep and an afternoon of helping with the housework, was devoted to the entertainment of his wife: they would catch the show at one of the neighborhood movies and go to an ice-cream parlor afterwards, and they were usually in bed by twelve. Then came the drowsy living-room clutter of newspapers on Sunday, and his week began again.

The trouble might never have happened if his wife had not insisted, that particular Friday, on breaking his routine: there was a Gregory Peck picture in its final showing that night, and she said she saw no reason why he couldn't do without his prize fight, for once in his life. She told him this on Friday morning, and it was the first of many things that went wrong with his day.

At lunch — the special payday lunch that he always shared with three fellow clerks from his office, in a German tavern downtown — the others were all talking about the fights, and Fallon took little part in the conversation. Jack Kopeck, who knew nothing about boxing (he had called the previous week's performance "a damn good bout" when in fact it had been fifteen rounds of clinches and cream-puff sparring, with the mockery of a decision at the end), told the party at some length that the best all-around bout he'd ever seen was in the Navy. And that led to a lot of Navy talk around the table, while Fallon squirmed in boredom.

"So here I was," Kopeck was saying, jabbing his breastbone with a manicured thumb in the windup of his third long story, "my first day on a new ship, and nothing but these tailor-made dress blues to stand inspection in. Scared? Jesus, I was shakin' like a leaf. Old man comes around, looks at me, says, 'Where d'ya think *you're* at, sailor? A fancy-dress ball?' "

"Talk about inspections," Mike Boyle said, bugging his round comedian's eyes. "Lemme tell ya, *we* had this commander, he'd take this white glove and wipe his finger down the bulkhead? And brother, if that glove came away with a specka dust on it, you were dead."

Then they started getting sentimental. "Ah, it's a good life, though, the Navy," Kopeck said. "A clean life. The best part about the Navy is, you're somebody, know what I mean? Every man's got his own individual job to do. And I mean what the hell, in the Army all you do is walk around and look stupid like everybody else."

"Brother," said little George Walsh, wiping mustard on his knockwurst, "you can say that again. I had four years in the Army and, believe me, you can say that again."

That was when John Fallon's patience ran out. "Yeah?" he said "What parta the Army was that?"

"What part?" Walsh said, blinking. "Well, I was in the ordnance for a while, in Virginia, and then I was in Texas, and Georgia — how d'ya mean, what part?"

Fallon's eyes narrowed and his lips curled tight. "You oughta tried an infantry outfit, Mac," he said.

"Oh, well," Walsh deferred with a wavering smile.

But Kopeck and Boyle took up the challenge, grinning at him.

"The *infantry?*" Boyle said. "Whadda they got — specialists in the infantry?"

"You betcher ass they got specialists," Fallon said. "Every son of a bitch *in* a rifle company's a specialist, if you wanna know something. And I'll tellya *one* thing, Mac — they don't worry about no silk gloves and no tailor-made clothes, you can betcher ass on that."

"Wait a second," Kopeck said. "I wanna know one thing, John. What was your specialty?"

"I was a B.A.R. man," Fallon said.

"What's that?"

And this was the first time Fallon realized how much the crowd in the office had changed over the years. In the old days, back around 'forty-nine or 'fifty, with the old crowd, anyone who didn't know what a B.A.R. was would almost certainly have kept his mouth shut.

"The B.A.R.," Fallon said, laying down his fork, "is the Browning Automatic Rifle. It's a thirty-caliber, magazine-fed, fully-automatic piece that provides the major firepower of a twelve-man rifle squad. That answer your question?"

"How d'ya mean?" Boyle inquired. "Like a tommy gun?"

And Fallon had to explain, as if he were talking to children or girls, that it was nothing at all like a tommy gun and that its tactical function was entirely different; finally he had to take out his mechanical pencil and draw, from memory and love, a silhouette of the weapon on the back of his weekly pay envelope.

"So okay," Kopeck said, "tell me one thing, John. Whaddya have to know to shoot this gun? You gotta have special training, or what?"

Fallon's eyes were angry slits as he crammed the pencil and envelope back into his coat. "Try it sometime," he said. "Try walkin' twenty miles on an empty stomach with that B.A.R. and a full ammo belt on your back, and then lay down in some swamp with the water up over your ass, and you're pinned down by machine-gun and mortar fire and your squad leader starts yellin', 'Get that B.A.R. up!' and you gotta cover the withdrawal of the whole platoon or the whole damn company. *Try* it sometime, Mac — *you'll* find out whatcha gotta have." And he took too deep a drink of his beer, which made him cough and sputter into his big freckled fist.

"Easy, easy," Boyle said, smiling. "Don't bust a gut, boy."

But Fallon only wiped his mouth and glared at them, breathing hard.

"Okay, so you're a hero," Kopeck said lightly. "You're a fighting man. Tell me one thing, though, John. Did you personally shoot this gun in combat?"

"Whadda you think?" Fallon said through thin, unmoving lips.

"How many times?"

The fact of the matter was that Fallon, as a husky and competent soldier of nineteen, many times pronounced "a damn good B.A.R. man" by the others in his squad, had carried his weapon on blistered feet over miles of road and field and forest in the last two months of the war, had lain with it under many artillery and mortar barrages and jabbed it at the chests of many freshly taken German prisoners; but he'd had occasion to fire it only twice, at vague areas rather than men, had brought down nothing either time, and had been mildly reprimanded the second time for wasting ammunition.

"Nunnya God damn business how many!" he said, and the others looked down at their plates with ill-concealed smiles. He glared at them, defying anyone to make a crack, but the worst part of it was that none of them said anything. They ate or drank their beer in silence, and after a while they changed the subject.

Fallon did not smile all afternoon, and he was still sullen when he met his wife at the supermarket, near home, for their weekend shopping. She looked tired, the way she always did when her sinus trouble was about to get worse, and while he ponderously wheeled the wire-mesh cart behind her he kept turning his head to follow the churning hips and full breasts of other young women in the store.

"Ow!" she cried once, and dropped a box of Ritz crackers to rub her heel in pain. "Can't you watch where you're *going* with that thing? You better let me push it."

"You shouldn't of stopped so sudden," he told her. "I didn't know you were gonna stop."

And thereafter, to make sure he didn't run the cart into her again, he had to give his full attention to her own narrow body and stick-thin legs. From the side view, Rose Fallon seemed always to be leaning slightly forward; walking, her buttocks seemed to float as an ungraceful separate entity in her wake. Some years ago, a doctor had explained her sterility with the fact that her womb was tipped, and told her it might be corrected by a course of exercises; she had done the exercises halfheartedly for a while and gradually given them up. Fallon could never remember whether her odd posture was supposed to be the cause or the result of the inner condition, but he did know for certain that, like her sinus trouble, it had grown worse in the years since their marriage; he could have sworn she stood straight when he met her.

"You want Rice Krispies or Post Toasties, John?" she asked him.

"Rice Krispies."

"Well, but we just had that last week. Aren't you tired of it?"

"Okay, the other, then."

"What are you mumbling for? I can't hear you."

"Post Toasties, I said!"

Walking home, he was puffing more than usual under the double armload of groceries. "What's the *matter?*" she asked, when he stopped to change his grip on the bags.

"Guess I'm outa shape," he said. "I oughta get out and play some handball."

"Oh, honestly," she said. "You're always saying that, and all you ever do is lie around and read the papers."

She took a bath before fixing the dinner, and then ate with a bulky housecoat roped around her in her usual state of post-bath dishevelment: hair damp, skin dry and porous, no lipstick and a smiling spoor of milk around the upper borders of her unsmiling mouth. "Where do you think you're going?" she said, when he had pushed his plate away and stood up. "Look at that — a full glass of milk on the table. Honestly, John, you're the one that makes me *buy* milk and then when I buy it you go and leave a full glass on the table. Now come back here and drink that up."

He went back and gulped the milk, which made him feel ill.

When her meal was over she began her careful preparations for the evening out; long after he had washed and dried the dishes she was still at the ironing board, pressing the skirt and blouse she planned to wear to the movies. He sat down to wait for her. "Be late to the show if you don't get a move on," he said.

"Oh, don't be silly. We've got practically a whole hour. What's the *matter* with you tonight, anyway?"

Her spike-heeled street shoes looked absurd under the ankle-length wrapper, particularly when she stooped over, splay-toed, to pull out the wall plug of the ironing cord.

"How come you quit those exercises?" he asked her.

"What exercises? What are you talking about?"

"You know," he said. "You know. Those exercises for your tipped utiyus."

"*Uterus*," she said. "You always say 'utiyus.' It's *uterus*."

"So what the hell's the difference? Why'd ya quit 'em?"

"Oh, honestly, John," she said, folding up the ironing board. "Why bring that up *now*, for heaven's sake?"

"So whaddya wanna do? Walk around with a tipped utiyus the resta ya life, or what?"

"Well," she said, "I certainly don't wanna get pregnant, if that's what you mean. May I ask where we'd be if I had to quit my job?"

He got up and began to stalk around the living room, glaring fiercely at the lamp shades, the watercolor flower paintings, and the small china figure of a seated, sleeping Mexican at whose back bloomed a dry cactus plant. He went to the bedroom, where her fresh underwear was laid out for the evening, and picked up a white brassiere containing the foam-rubber cups without which her chest was as meager as a boy's. When she came in he turned on her, waving it in her startled face, and said, "Why d'ya *wear* these God damn things?"

She snatched the brassiere from him and backed against the doorjamb, her eyes raking him up and down. "Now, *look*," she said. "I've had *enough* of this. Are you gonna start acting decent, or not? Are we going to the movies, or not?"

And suddenly she looked so pathetic that he couldn't stand it. He grabbed his coat and pushed past her. "Do whatcha like," he said. "I'm goin' out." And he slammed out of the apartment.

It wasn't until he swung onto Queens Boulevard that his muscles began to relax and his breathing to slow down. He didn't stop at the Island Bar and Grill — it was too early for the fights anyway, and he was too upset to enjoy them. Instead, he clattered down the stairs to the subway and whipped through the turnstile, headed for Manhattan.

He had set a vague course for Times Square, but thirst overcame him at Third Avenue; he went up to the street and had two shots with a beer chaser in the first bar he came to, a bleak place with stamped-tin walls and a urine smell. On his right, at the bar, an old woman was waving her cigarette like a baton and singing "Peg o' My Heart," and on his left one middle-aged man was saying to another, "Well, my point of view is this: maybe you can argue with McCarthy's methods, but son of a bitch, you can't argue with him on principle. Am I right?"

Fallon left the place and went to another near Lexington, a chrome-and-leather place where everyone looked bluish green in the subtle light. There he stood at the bar beside two young soldiers with divisional patches on their sleeves and infantry braid on the PX caps that lay folded under their shoulder tabs. They wore no ribbons — they were only kids — but Fallon could

tell they were no recruits: they knew how to wear their Eisenhower jackets, for one thing, short and skin-tight, and their
combat boots were soft and almost black with polish. Both
their heads suddenly turned to look past him, and Fallon, turning too, joined them in watching a girl in a tight tan skirt de-
tach herself from a party at one of the tables in a shadowy
corner. She brushed past them, murmuring, "Excuse me," and
all three of their heads were drawn to watch her buttocks shift
and settle, shift and settle until she disappeared in the ladies'
room.

"Man, that's rough," the shorter of the two soldiers said, and
his grin included Fallon, who grinned back.

"Oughta be a law against wavin' it around that way," the
tall soldier said. "Bad for the troops."

Their accents were Western, and they both had the kind of
blond, squint-eyed, country-boy faces that Fallon remembered
from his old platoon. "What outfit you boys in?" he inquired.
"I oughta reckanize that patch."

They told him, and he said, "Oh, yeah, sure — I remember.
They were in the Seventh Army, right? Back in 'forty-four
and -five?"

"Couldn't say for sure, sir," the short soldier said. "That was
a good bit before our time."

"Where the hellya get that 'sir' stuff?" Fallon demanded
heartily. "I wasn't no officer. I never made better'n pfc, except
for a couple weeks when they made me an acting buck sergeant, there in Germany. I was a B.A.R. man."

The short soldier looked him over. "That figures," he said.
"You got the build for a B.A.R. man. That old B.A.R.'s a heavy
son of a bitch."

"You're right," Fallon said. "It's heavy, but, I wanna tellya,
it's a damn sweet weapon in combat. Listen, what are you boys
drinking? My name's Johnny Fallon, by the way."

They shook hands with him, mumbling their names, and
when the girl in the tan skirt came out of the ladies' room they

all turned to watch her again. This time, watching until she had settled herself at her table, they concentrated on the wobbling fullness of her blouse.

"Man," the short soldier said, "I mean, that's a pair."

"Probably ain't real," the tall one said.

"They're real, son," Fallon assured him, turning back to his beer with a man-of-the-world wink. "They're real. I can spot a paira falsies a mile away."

They had a few more rounds, talking Army, and after a while the tall soldier asked Fallon how to get to the Central Plaza, where he'd heard about the Friday night jazz; then they were all three rolling down Second Avenue in a cab, for which Fallon paid. While they stood waiting for the elevator at the Central Plaza, he worked the wedding ring off his finger and stuck it in his watch pocket.

The wide, high ballroom was jammed with young men and girls; hundreds of them sat listening or laughing around pitchers of beer; another hundred danced wildly in a cleared space between banks of tables. On the bandstand, far away, a sweating group of colored and white musicians bore down, their horns gleaming in the smoky light.

Fallon, to whom all jazz sounded the same, took on the look of a connoisseur as he slouched in the doorway, his face tense and glazed under the squeal of clarinets, his gas-blue trousers quivering with the slight, rhythmic dip of his knees and his fingers snapping loosely to the beat of the drums. But it wasn't music that possessed him as he steered the soldiers to a table next to three girls, nor was it music that made him get up, as soon as the band played something slow enough, and ask the best-looking of the three to dance. She was tall and well-built, a black-haired Italian girl with a faint shine of sweat on her brow, and as she walked ahead of him toward the dance floor, threading her way between the tables, he reveled in the slow grace of her twisting hips and floating skirt. In his exultant, beer-blurred mind he already knew how it would be when he took her home — how she would feel to his exploring hands in the dark privacy of the taxi, and how she would be later, undulant and naked, in some ultimate vague bedroom at the end of the night. And as soon as they reached the dance floor, when she turned around and lifted her arms, he crushed her tight and warm against him.

"Now, *look*," she said, arching back angrily so that the cords stood out in her damp neck. "Is that what you call *dancing?*"

He relaxed his grip, trembling, and grinned at her. "Take it easy, honey," he said. "I won't bite."

"Never mind the 'honey,' either," she said, and that was all she said until the dance was over.

But she had to stay with him, for the two soldiers had moved in on her lively, giggling girl friends. They were all at the same table now, and for half an hour the six of them sat there in an uneasy party mood: one of the other girls (they were both small and blonde) kept shrieking with laughter at the things the short soldier was mumbling to her, and the other had the tall soldier's long arm around her neck. But Fallon's big brunette, who had reluctantly given her name as Marie, sat silent and primly straight beside him, snapping and unsnapping the clasp of the handbag in her lap. Fallon's fingers gripped the back of her chair with white-knuckled intensity, but whenever he let them slip tentatively to her shoulder she would shrug free.

"You live around here, Marie?" he asked her.

"The Bronx," she said.

"You come down here often?"

"Sometimes."

"Care for a cigarette?"

"I don't smoke."

Fallon's face was burning, the small curving vein in his right temple throbbed visibly, and sweat was sliding down his ribs. He was like a boy on his first date, paralyzed and stricken dumb by the nearness of her warm dress, by the smell of her perfume, by the way her delicate fingers worked on the handbag and the way the moisture glistened on her plump lower lip.

At the next table a young sailor stood up and bellowed something through cupped hands at the bandstand, and the cry was taken up elsewhere around the room. It sounded like "We want the saints!" but Fallon couldn't make sense of it. At least it gave him an opening. "What's that they're yellin'?" he asked her.

" 'The Saints,' " she told him, meeting his eyes just long enough to impart the information. "They wanna hear 'The Saints.' "

"Oh."

After that they stopped talking altogether for a long time until Marie made a face of impatience at the nearest of her girl friends. "Let's go, hey," she said. "C'mon. I wanna go home."

"Aw, *Marie*," the other girl said, flushed with beer and flirtation (she was wearing the short soldier's overseas cap now). "Don't be such a stupid." Then, seeing Fallon's tortured face, she tried to help him out. "Are you in the Army too?" she asked brightly, leaning toward him across the table.

"Me?" Fallon said, startled. "No, I — I used to be, though. I been outa the Army for quite a while now."

"Oh, yeah?"

"He used to be a B.A.R. man," the short soldier told her.

"Oh, yeah?"

"We want 'The Saints'!" "We want 'The Saints'!" They were yelling it from all corners of the enormous room now, with greater and greater urgency.

"C'mon, hey," Marie said again to her girl friend. "Let's go. I'm tired."

"So *go* then," the girl in the soldier's hat said crossly. "Go if you want to, Marie. Can'tcha go home by yourself?"

"No, wait, listen —" Fallon sprang to his feet. "Don't go yet,

Marie — I'll tell ya what. I'll go get some more beer, okay?" And he bolted from the table before she could refuse.

"No more for me," she called after him, but he was already three tables away, walking fast toward the little ell of the room where the bar was. "Bitch," he was whispering. "Bitch. Bitch." And the images that tortured him now, while he stood in line at the makeshift bar, were intensified by rage: there would be struggling limbs and torn clothes in the taxi; there would be blind force in the bedroom, and stifled cries of pain that would turn to whimpering and finally to spastic moans of lust. Oh, he'd loosen her up! He'd loosen her up!

"C'mon, c'mon," he said to the men who were fumbling with pitchers and beer spigots and wet dollar bills behind the bar.

"We — want — 'The Saints'!" "We — want — 'The Saints'!" The chant in the ballroom reached its climax. Then, after the drums built up a relentless, brutal rhythm that grew all but intolerable until it ended in a cymbal smash and gave way to the blare of the brass section, the crowd went wild. It took some seconds for Fallon to realize, getting his pitcher of beer at last and turning away from the bar, that the band was playing "When the Saints Go Marching In."

The place was a madhouse. Girls screamed and boys stood yelling on chairs, waving their arms; glasses were smashed and chairs sent spinning, and four policemen stood alert along the walls, ready for a riot as the band rode it out.

> *When the saints*
> *Go marching in*
> *Oh, when the saints go marching in . . .*

Fallon moved in jostled bewilderment through the noise, trying to find his party. He found their table, but couldn't be sure it was theirs — it was empty except for a crumpled cigarette package and a wet stain of beer, and one of its chairs lay overturned on the floor. He thought he saw Marie among the frantic dancers, but it turned out to be another big brunette in the same kind of dress. Then he thought he saw the short soldier gesturing wildly across the room, and made his way over to him, but it was another soldier with a country-boy face. Fallon turned around and around, sweating, looking everywhere in the dizzy crowd. Then a boy in a damp pink shirt reeled heavily against his elbow and the beer spilled in a cold rush on his hand and sleeve, and that was when he realized they were gone. They had ditched him.

He was out on the street and walking, fast and hard on his steel-capped heels, and the night traffic noises were appallingly quiet after the bedlam of shouting and jazz. He walked with no idea of direction and no sense of time, aware of nothing beyond the pound of his heels, the thrust and pull of his muscles, the quavering intake and sharp outward rush of his breath and the pump of his blood.

He didn't know if ten minutes or an hour passed, twenty blocks or five, before he had to slow down and stop on the fringe of a small crowd that clustered around a lighted doorway where policemen were waving the people on.

"Keep moving," one of the policemen was saying. "Move along, please. Keep moving."

But Fallon, like most of the others, stood still. It was the doorway to some kind of lecture hall — he could tell that by the bulletin board that was just visible under the yellow lights inside, and by the flight of marble stairs that led up to what must have been an auditorium. But what caught most of his attention was the picket line: three men about his own age, their eyes agleam with righteousness, wearing the blue-and-gold overseas caps of some veterans' organization and carrying placards that said:

SMOKE OUT THIS FIFTH AMENDMENT COMMIE
PROF. MITCHELL GO BACK TO RUSSIA
AMERICA'S FIGHTING SONS PROTEST MITCHELL

"Move along," the police were saying. "Keep moving."

"Civil rights, my ass," said a flat muttering voice at Fallon's elbow. "They oughta lock this Mitchell up. You read what he said in the Senate hearing?" And Fallon, nodding, recalled a fragile, snobbish face in a number of newspaper pictures.

"Look at there —" the muttering voice said. "Here they come. They're comin' out now."

And they were. Down the marble steps they came, past the bulletin board and out onto the sidewalk: men in raincoats and greasy tweeds, petulant, Greenwich-Village-looking girls in tight pants, a few Negroes, a few very clean, self-conscious college boys.

The pickets were backed off and standing still now, holding their placards high with one hand and curving the other around their mouths to call, "Boo-oo! Boo-oo!"

The crowd picked it up: "Boo-oo!" "Boo-oo!" And somebody called, "Go back to Russia!"

"Keep moving," the cops were saying. "Move along, now. Keep moving."

"There he is," said the muttering voice. "There he comes now — that's Mitchell."

And Fallon saw him: a tall, slight man in a cheap double-breasted suit that was too big for him, carrying a briefcase and flanked by two plain women in glasses. There was the snobbish face of the newspaper pictures, turning slowly from side to side now, with a serene, superior smile that seemed to be saying, to everyone it met: *Oh, you poor fool. You poor fool.*

"KILL *that bastard!*"

Not until several people whirled to look at him did Fallon realize he was yelling; then all he knew was that he had to yell again and again until his voice broke, like a child in tears: "KILL *that bastard! KILL 'im! KILL 'im!*"

In four bucking, lunging strides he was through to the front of the crowd; then one of the pickets dropped his placard and rushed him, saying, "Easy, Mac! Take it *easy* —" But Fallon threw him off, grappled with another man and wrenched free again, got both hands on Mitchell's coat front and tore him down like a crumpled puppet. He saw Mitchell's face recoil in wet-mouthed terror on the sidewalk, and the last thing he knew, as the cop's blue arm swung high over his head, was a sense of absolute fulfillment and relief.

— 1954

A Really Good Jazz Piano

Because of the midnight noise on both ends of the line there was some confusion at Harry's New York Bar when the call came through. All the bartender could tell at first was that it was a long-distance call from Cannes, evidently from some kind of nightclub, and the operator's frantic voice made it sound like an emergency. Then at last, by plugging his free ear and shouting questions into the phone, he learned that it was only Ken Platt, calling up to have an aimless chat with his friend Carson Wyler, and this made him shake his head in exasperation as he set the phone on the bar beside Carson's glass of Pernod.

"Here," he said. "It's for you, for God's sake. It's your buddy." Like a number of other Paris bartenders he knew them both pretty well: Carson was the handsome one, the one with the slim, witty face and the English-sounding accent; Ken was the fat one who laughed all the time and tagged along. They were both three years out of Yale and trying to get all the fun they could out of living in Europe.

"Carson?" said Ken's eager voice, vibrating painfully in the receiver. "This is Ken — I knew I'd find you there. Listen, when you coming down, anyway?"

Carson puckered his well-shaped brow at the phone. "You know when I'm coming down," he said. "I wired you, I'm coming down Saturday. What's the matter with you?"

"Hell, nothing's the matter with me — maybe a little drunk, is all. No, but listen, what I really called up about, there's a man here named Sid plays a really good jazz piano, and I want you to hear him. He's a friend of mine. Listen, wait a minute, I'll get the phone over close so you can hear. Listen to this, now. Wait a minute."

There were some blurred scraping sounds and the sound of Ken laughing and somebody else laughing, and then the piano came through. It sounded tinny in the telephone, but Carson could tell it was good. It was "Sweet Lorraine," done in a rich traditional style with nothing commercial about it, and this surprised him, for Ken was ordinarily a poor judge of music. After a minute he handed the phone to a stranger he had been drinking with, a farm machinery salesman from Philadelphia. "Listen to this," he said. "This is first-rate."

The farm machinery salesman held his ear to the phone with a puzzled look. "What is it?"

" 'Sweet Lorraine.' "

"No, but I mean what's the deal? Where's it coming from?"

"Cannes. Somebody Ken turned up down there. You've met Ken, haven't you?"

"No, I haven't," the salesman said, frowning into the phone. "Here, it's stopped now and somebody's talking. You better take it."

"Hello? Hello?" Ken's voice was saying. "Carson?"

"Yes, Ken. I'm right here."

"Where'd you go? Who was that other guy?"

"That was a gentleman from Philadelphia named —" he looked up questioningly.

"Baldinger," said the salesman, straightening his coat.

"Named Mr. Baldinger. He's here at the bar with me."

"Oh. Well listen, how'd you like Sid's playing?"

"Fine, Ken. Tell him I said it was first-rate."

"You want to talk to him? He's right here, wait a minute."

There were some more obscure sounds and then a deep middle-aged voice said, "Hello there."

"How do you do, Sid. My name's Carson Wyler, and I enjoyed your playing very much."

"Well," the voice said. "Thank you, thank you a lot. I appreciate it." It could have been either a colored or a white man's voice, but Carson assumed he was colored, mostly from the slight edge of self-consciousness or pride in the way Ken had said, "He's a friend of mine."

"I'm coming down to Cannes this weekend, Sid," Carson said, "and I'll be looking forward to —"

But Sid had evidently given back the phone, for Ken's voice cut in. "Carson?"

"What?"

"Listen, what time you coming Saturday? I mean what train and everything?" They had originally planned to go to Cannes together, but Carson had become involved with a girl in Paris, and Ken had gone on alone, with the understanding that Carson would join him in a week. Now it had been nearly a month.

"I don't know the exact train," Carson said, with some impatience. "It doesn't matter, does it? I'll see you at the hotel sometime Saturday."

"Okay. Oh and wait, listen, the other reason I called, I want to sponsor Sid here for the IBF, okay?"

"Right. Good idea. Put him back on." And while he was waiting he got out his fountain pen and asked the bartender for the IBF membership book.

"Hello again," Sid's voice said. "What's this I'm supposed to be joining here?"

"The IBF," Carson said. "That stands for International Bar Flies, something they started here at Harry's back in — I don't know. Long time ago. Kind of a club."

"Very good," Sid said, chuckling.

"Now, what it amounts to is this," Carson began, and even the bartender, for whom the IBF was a bore and a nuisance, had to smile with pleasure at the serious, painstaking way he told about it — how each member received a lapel button bearing the insignia of a fly, together with a printed booklet that contained the club rules and a listing of all other IBF bars in the world; how the cardinal rule was that when two members met they were expected to greet one another by brushing the fingers of their right hands on each other's shoulders and saying, "*Bzz-z-z, bzz-z-z!*"

This was one of Carson's special talents, the ability to find and convey an unashamed enjoyment in trivial things. Many people could not have described the IBF to a jazz musician without breaking off in an apologetic laugh to explain that it was, of course, a sort of sad little game for lonely tourists, a square's thing really, and that its very lack of sophistication was what made it fun; Carson told it straight. In much the same way he had once made it fashionable among some of the more literary undergraduates at Yale to spend Sunday mornings respectfully absorbed in the funny papers of the *New York Mirror*; more recently the same trait had rapidly endeared him to many chance acquaintances, notably to his current girl, the young Swedish art student for whom he had stayed in Paris. "You have beautiful taste in everything," she had told him on their first memorable night together. "You have a truly educated, truly original mind."

"Got that?" he said into the phone, and paused to sip his Pernod. "Right. Now if you'll give me your full name and address, Sid, I'll get everything organized on this end." Sid spelled it out and Carson lettered it carefully into the membership book, with his own name and Ken's as co-sponsors, while Mr. Baldinger watched. When they were finished Ken's voice came back to say a reluctant goodbye, and they hung up.

"That must've been a pretty expensive telephone call," Mr. Baldinger said, impressed.

"You're right," Carson said. "I guess it was."

"What's the deal on this membership book, anyway? All this barfly business?"

Oh, aren't you a member, Mr. Baldinger? I thought you were a member. Here, I'll sponsor you, if you like."

Mr. Baldinger got what he later described as an enormous kick out of it: far into the early morning he was still sidling up to everyone at the bar, one after another, and buzzing them.

Carson didn't get to Cannes on Saturday, for it took him longer than he'd planned to conclude his affair with the Swedish girl. He had expected a tearful scene, or at least a brave exchange of tender promises and smiles, but instead she was surprisingly casual about his leaving — even abstracted, as if already concentrating on her next truly educated, truly original mind — and this forced him into several uneasy delays that accomplished nothing except to fill her with impatience and him with a sense of being dispossessed. He didn't get to Cannes until the following Tuesday afternoon, after further telephone talks with Ken, and then, when he eased himself onto the station platform, stiff and sour with hangover, he was damned if he knew why he'd come at all. The sun assaulted him, burning deep into his gritty scalp and raising a quick sweat inside his rumpled suit; it struck blinding glints off the chromework of parked cars and motor scooters and made sickly blue vapors of exhaust rise up against pink buildings; it played garishly among the swarm of tourists who jostled him, showing him all their pores, all the tension of their store-new sports clothes, their clutched suitcases and slung cameras, all the anxiety of their smiling, shouting mouths. Cannes would be like any other resort town in the world, all hurry and disappointment, and why hadn't he stayed where he belonged, in a high cool room with a long-legged girl? Why the hell had he let himself be coaxed and wheedled into coming here?

But then he saw Ken's happy face bobbing in the crowd — "Carson!" — and there he came, running in his overgrown fat boy's thigh-chafing way, clumsy with welcome. "Taxi's over here, take your bag — boy, do you look beat! Get you a shower and a drink first, okay? How the hell are you?"

And riding light on the taxi cushions as they swung onto the Croisette, with its spectacular blaze of blue and gold and its blood-quickening rush of sea air, Carson began to relax. Look at the girls! There were acres of them; and besides, it was good to be with old Ken again. It was easy to see, now, that the thing in Paris could only have gotten worse if he'd stayed. He had left just in time.

Ken couldn't stop talking. Pacing in and out of the bathroom while Carson took his shower, jingling a pocketful of coins, he talked in the laughing, full-throated joy of a man who has gone for weeks without hearing his own voice. The truth was that Ken never really had a good time away from Carson. They were each other's best friends, but it had never been an equal friendship, and they both knew it. At Yale Ken would probably have been left out of everything if it hadn't been for his status as Carson's dull but inseparable companion, and this was a pattern that nothing in Europe had changed. What *was* it about Ken that put people off? Carson had pondered this question for years. Was it just that he was fat and physically awkward, or that he could be strident and silly in his eagerness to be liked? But weren't these essentially likable qualities? No, Carson guessed the closest he could come to a real explanation was the fact that when Ken smiled his upper lip slid back to reveal a small moist inner lip that trembled against his gum. Many people with this kind of mouth may find it no great handicap — Carson was willing to admit that — but it did seem to be the thing everyone remembered most vividly about Ken Platt, whatever more substantial-sounding reasons one might give for avoiding him; in any case it was what Carson himself was always most aware of, in moments of irritation. Right now, for example, in the simple business of trying to dry himself and comb his hair and put on fresh clothes, this wide, moving, double-lipped smile kept getting in his way. It was everywhere, blocking his reach for the towel rack, hovering too close over his jumbled suitcase, swimming in the mirror to eclipse the tying of his tie, until Carson had to clamp his jaws tight to keep from yelling, "All *right*, Ken — shut *up* now!"

But a few minutes later they were able to compose themselves in the shaded silence of the hotel bar. The bartender was peeling a lemon, neatly pinching and pulling back a strip of its bright flesh between thumb and knife blade, and the fine citric smell of it, combining with the scent of gin in the faint smoke of crushed ice, gave flavor to a full restoration of their ease. A couple of cold martinis drowned the last of Carson's pique, and by the time they were out of the place and swinging down the sidewalk on their way to dinner he felt strong again with a sense of the old camaraderie, the familiar, buoyant wealth of Ken's admiration. It was a feeling touched with sadness, too, for Ken would soon have to go back to the States. His father in Denver, the author of sarcastic weekly letters on business stationery, was holding open a junior partnership for him, and Ken, having long since completed the Sorbonne courses that were his ostensible reason for coming to France, had no further excuse for staying. Carson, luckier in this as in everything else, had no need of an excuse: he had an adequate private income and no family ties; he could afford to browse around Europe for years, if he felt like it, looking for things that pleased him.

"You're still white as a sheet," he told Ken across their restaurant table. "Haven't you been going to the beach?"

"Sure." Ken looked quickly at his plate. "I've been to the beach a few times. The weather hasn't been too good for it lately, is all."

But Carson guessed the real reason, that Ken was embarrassed to display his body, so he changed the subject. "Oh, by the way," he said. "I brought along the IBF stuff, for that piano player friend of yours."

"Oh, swell." Ken looked up in genuine relief. "I'll take you over there soon as we're finished eating, okay?" And as if to hurry this prospect along he forked a dripping load of salad into his mouth and tore off too big a bite of bread to chew with it, using the remaining stump of bread to mop at the oil and vinegar in his plate. "You'll like him, Carson," he said soberly around his chewing. "He's a great guy. I really admire him a lot." He swallowed with effort and hurried on: "I mean hell, with talent like that he could go back to the States tomorrow and make a fortune, but he likes it here. One thing, of course, he's got a girl here, this really lovely French girl, and I guess he couldn't very well take her back with him — no, but really, it's more than that. People accept him here. As an artist, I mean, as well as a man. Nobody condescends to him, nobody tries to interfere with his music, and that's all he wants out of life. Oh, I mean he doesn't tell you all this — probably be a bore if he did — it's just a thing you sense about him. Comes out in everything he says, his whole mental attitude." He popped the soaked bread into his mouth and chewed it with authority. "I mean the guy's got *authentic* integrity," he said. "Wonderful thing."

"Did sound like a damn good piano," Carson said, reaching for the wine bottle, "what little I heard of it."

"Wait'll you really hear it, though. Wait'll he really gets going."

They both enjoyed the fact that this was Ken's discovery. Always before it had been Carson who led the way, who found the girls and learned the idioms and knew how best to spend each hour; it was Carson who had tracked down all the really colorful places in Paris where you never saw Americans, and who then, just when Ken was learning to find places of his own, had paradoxically made Harry's Bar become the most colorful place of all. Through all this, Ken had been glad enough to follow, shaking his grateful head in wonderment; but it was no small thing to have turned up an incorruptible jazz talent in the back streets of a foreign city, all alone. It proved that Ken's dependence could be less than total after all, and this reflected credit on them both.

The place where Sid played was more of an expensive bar than a nightclub, a small carpeted basement several streets back from the sea. It was still early, and they found him having a drink alone at the bar.

"Well," he said when he saw Ken. "Hello there." He was stocky and well-tailored, a very dark Negro with a pleasant smile full of strong white teeth.

"Sid, I'd like you to meet Carson Wyler. You talked to him on the phone that time, remember?"

"Oh yes," Sid said, shaking hands. "Oh yes. Very pleased to meet you, Carson. What're you gentlemen drinking?"

They made a little ceremony of buttoning the IBF insignia into the lapel of Sid's tan gabardine, of buzzing his shoulder and offering the shoulders of their own identical seersucker jackets to be buzzed in turn. "Well, this is fine," Sid said, chuckling and leafing through the booklet. "Very good." Then he put the booklet in his pocket, finished his drink and slid off the barstool. "And now if you'll excuse me, I got to go to work."

"Not much of an audience yet," Ken said.

Sid shrugged. "Place like this, I'd just as soon have it that way. You get a big crowd, you always get some square asking for 'Deep in the Heart of Texas,' or some damn thing."

Ken laughed and winked at Carson, and they both turned to watch Sid take his place at the piano, which stood on a low spotlighted dais across the room. He fingered the keys idly for a while to make stray phrases and chords, a craftsman fondling his tools, and then he settled down. The compelling beat emerged, and out of it the climb and waver of the melody, an arrangement of "Baby, Won't You Please Come Home."

They stayed for hours, listening to Sid play and buying him drinks whenever he took a break, to the obvious envy of other customers. Sid's girl came in, tall and brown-haired, with a bright, startled-looking face that was almost beautiful, and Ken introduced her with a small uncontrollable flourish: "This is Jaqueline." She whispered something about not speaking English very well, and when it was time for Sid's next break — the place was filling up now and there was considerable applause when he finished — the four of them took a table together.

Ken let Carson do most of the talking now; he was more than content just to sit there, smiling around this tableful of friends with all the serenity of a well-fed young priest. It was the happiest evening of his life in Europe, to a degree that even Carson would never have guessed. In the space of a few hours it filled all the emptiness of his past month, the time that had begun with Carson's saying "Go, then. Can't you go to Cannes by yourself?" It atoned for all the hot miles walked up and down the Croisette on blistered feet to peek like a fool at girls who lay incredibly near naked in the sand; for the cramped, boring bus rides to Nice and Monte Carlo and St. Paul-de-Vence; for the day he had paid a sinister druggist three times too much for a pair of sunglasses only to find, on catching sight of his own image in the gleam of a passing shop window, that they made him look like a great blind fish; for the terrible daily, nightly sense of being young and rich and free on the Riviera — the Riviera! — and of having nothing to do. Once in the first week he had gone with a prostitute whose canny smile, whose shrill insistence on a high price and whose facial flicker of distaste at the sight of his body had frightened him into an agony of impotence; most other nights he had gotten drunk or sick from bar to bar, afraid of prostitutes and of rebuffs from other girls, afraid even of striking up conversations with men lest they mistake him for a fairy. He had spent a whole afternoon in the French equivalent of a dime store, feigning a shopper's interest in padlocks and shaving cream and cheap tin toys, moving through the bright stale air of the place with a throatful of longing for home. Five nights in a row he had hidden himself in the protective darkness of American movies, just as he'd done years ago in Denver to get away from boys who called him Lard-Ass Platt, and after the last of these entertainments, back in the hotel with the taste of chocolate creams still cloying his mouth, he had cried himself to sleep. But all this was dissolving now under the fine reckless grace of Sid's piano, under the spell of Carson's intelligent smile and the way Carson raised his hands to clap each time the music stopped.

Sometime after midnight, when everyone but Sid had drunk too much, Carson asked him how long he had been away from the States. "Since the war," he said. "I came over in the Army and I never did go back."

Ken, coated with a film of sweat and happiness, thrust his glass high in the air for a toast. "And by God, here's hoping you never have to, Sid."

"Why is that, 'have to'?" Jaqueline said. Her face looked harsh and sober in the dim light. "Why do you say that?"

Ken blinked at her. "Well, I just mean — you know — that he never has to sell out, or anything. He never would, of course."

"What does this mean, 'sell out'?" There was an uneasy silence until Sid laughed in his deep, rumbling way. "Take it easy, honey," he said, and turned to Ken. "We don't look at it that way, you see. Matter of fact, I'm working on angles all the time to get back to the States, make some money there. We both feel that way about it."

"Well, but you're doing all right here, aren't you?" Ken said, almost pleading with him. "You're making enough money and everything, aren't you?"

Sid smiled patiently. "I don't mean a job like this, though, you see. I mean real money."

"You know who is Murray Diamond?" Jacqueline inquired, holding her eyebrows high. "The owner of nightclubs in Las Vegas?"

But Sid was shaking his head and laughing. "Honey, wait a minute — I keep telling you, that's nothing to count on. Murray

Diamond happened to be in here the other night, you see," he explained. "Didn't have much time, but he said he'd try to drop around again some night this week. Be a big break for me. 'Course, like I say, that's nothing to count on."

"Well but *Jesus*, Sid —" Ken shook his head in bafflement; then, letting his face tighten into a look of outrage, he thumped the table with a bouncing fist. "Why prostitute yourself?" he demanded. "I mean damn it, you *know* they'll make you prostitute yourself in the States!"

Sid was still smiling, but his eyes had narrowed slightly. "I guess it's all in the way you look at it," he said.

And the worst part of it, for Ken, was that Carson came so quickly to his rescue. "Oh, I'm sure Ken doesn't mean that the way it *sounds*," he said, and while Ken was babbling quick apologies of his own ("No, of course not, all I meant was — *you* know. . . .") he went on to say other things, light, nimble things that only Carson could say, until the awkwardness was gone. When the time came to say goodnight there were handshakes and smiles and promises to see each other soon.

But the minute they were out on the street, Carson turned on Ken. "Why did you have to get so damned sophomoric about that? Couldn't you see how embarrassing it was?"

"I know," Ken said, hurrying to keep pace with Carson's long legs, "I know. But hell, I *was* disappointed in him, Carson. The point is I never heard him *talk* like that before." What he omitted here, of course, was that he had never really heard him talk at all, except in the one shy conversation that had led to the calling-up of Harry's Bar that other night, after which Ken had fled back to the hotel in fear of overstaying his welcome.

"Well, but even so," Carson said. "Don't you think it's the man's own business what he wants to do with his life?"

"Okay," Ken said, "*okay*. I *told* him I was sorry, didn't I?" He felt so humble now that it took him some minutes to realize that, in a sense, he hadn't come off too badly. After all, Carson's only triumph tonight had been that of the diplomat, the soother of feelings; it was he, Ken, who had done the more dramatic thing. Sophomoric or not, impulsive or not, wasn't there a certain dignity in having spoken his mind that way? Now, licking his lips and glancing at Carson's profile as they walked, he squared his shoulders and tried to make his walk less of a waddle and more of a headlong, manly stride. "It's just that I can't help how I feel, that's all," he said with conviction. "When I'm disappointed in a person I show it, that's all."

"All right. Let's forget it."

And Ken was almost sure, though he hardly dared believe it, that he could detect a grudging respect in Carson's voice.

Everything went wrong the next day. The fading light of afternoon found the two of them slumped and staring in a bleak workingman's café near the railroad station, barely speaking to each other. It was a day that had started out unusually well, too — that was the trouble.

They had slept till noon and gone to the beach after lunch, for Ken didn't mind the beach when he wasn't alone, and before long they had picked up two American girls in the easy, graceful way that Carson always managed such things. One minute the girls were sullen strangers, wiping scented oil on their bodies and looking as if any intrusion would mean a call for the police, the next minute they were weak with laughter at the things Carson was saying, moving aside their bottles and their zippered blue TWA satchels to make room for unexpected guests. There was a tall one for Carson with long firm thighs, intelligent eyes and a way of tossing back her hair that gave her a look of real beauty, and a small one for Ken — a cute, freckled good-sport of a girl whose every cheerful glance and gesture showed she was used to taking second best. Ken, bellying deep into the sand with his chin on two stacked fists, smiling up very close to her warm legs, felt almost none of the conversational tension that normally hampered him at times like this. Even when Carson and the tall girl got up to run splashing into the water he was able to hold her interest: she said several times that the Sorbonne "must have been fascinating," and she sympathized with his having to go back to Denver, though she said it was "probably the best thing."

"And your friend's just going to stay over here indefinitely, then?" she asked. "Is it really true what he said? I mean that he isn't studying or working or anything? Just sort of floating around?"

"Well — yeah, that's right." Ken tried a squinty smile like Carson's own. "Why?"

"It's interesting, that's all. I don't think I've ever met a person like that before."

That was when Ken began to realize what the laughter and the scanty French bathing suits had disguised about these girls, that they were girls of a kind neither he nor Carson had dealt with for a long time — suburban, middle-class girls who had dutifully won their parents' blessing for this guided tour; girls who said "golly Moses," whose campus-shop clothes and hockey-field strides would have instantly betrayed them on the street. They were the very kind of girls who had gathered at the punch bowl to murmur "Ugh!" at the way he looked in his first tuxedo, whose ignorant, maddeningly bland little stares of rejection had poisoned all his aching years in Denver and New Haven. They were squares. And the remarkable thing was that he felt so good. Rolling his weight to one elbow, clutching up slow, hot handfuls of sand and emptying them, again and again, he found his flow of words coming quick and smooth:

". . . no, really, there's a lot to see in Paris; shame you couldn't spend more time there; actually most of the places I like best are more or less off the beaten track; of course I was lucky in having a fairly good grasp of the language, and then I met so many congenial. . . ."

He was holding his own; he was making out. He hardly even noticed when Carson and the tall girl came trotting back from their swim, as lithe and handsome as a couple in a travel poster, to drop beside them in a bustle of towels and cigarettes and shuddering jokes about how cold the water was. His only mounting worry was that Carson, who must by now have made his own discovery about these girls, would decide they weren't worth bothering with. But a single glance at Carson's subtly smiling, talking face reassured him: sitting tense at the tall girl's feet while she stood to towel her back in a way that made her breasts sway delightfully, Carson was plainly determined to follow through. "Look," he said. "Why don't we all have dinner together? Then afterwards we might —"

Both girls began chattering their regrets: they were afraid not, thanks anyway, they were meeting friends at the hotel for dinner and actually ought to be starting back now, much as they hated to — "God, look at the time!" And they really did sound sorry, so sorry that Ken, gathering all his courage, reached out and held the warm, fine-boned hand that swung at the small girl's thigh as the four of them plodded back toward the bathhouses. She even squeezed his heavy fingers, and smiled at him.

"Some other night, then?" Carson was saying. "Before you leave?"

"Well, actually," the tall girl said, "our evenings do seem to be pretty well booked up. Probably run into you on the beach again though. It's been fun."

"God damn little snot-nosed New Rochelle bitch," Carson said when they were alone in the men's bathhouse.

"*Sh-h-h!* Keep your *voice* down, Carson. They can *hear* you in there."

"Oh, don't be an idiot." Carson flung his trunks on the duckboards with a sandy slap. "I hope they do hear me — what the hell's the matter with you?" He looked at Ken as if he hated him. "Pair of God damn teasing little professional virgins. *Christ,* why didn't I stay in Paris?"

And now here they were, Carson glowering, Ken sulking at

the sunset through flyspecked windows while a pushing, garlic-smelling bunch of laborers laughed and shouted over the pinball machine. They went on drinking until long past the dinner hour; then they ate a late, upleasant meal together in a restaurant where the wine was corky and there was too much grease on the fried potatoes. When the messy plates were cleared away Carson lit a cigarette. "What do you want to do tonight?" he said.

There was a faint shine of grease around Ken's mouth and cheeks. "I don't know," he said. "Lot of good places to go, I guess."

"I suppose it would offend your artistic sensibilities to go and hear Sid's piano again?"

Ken gave him a weak, rather testy smile. "You still harping on that?" he said. "Sure I'd like to go."

"Even though he may prostitute himself?"

"Why don't you lay off that, Carson?"

They could hear the piano from the street, even before they walked into the square of light that poured up from the doorway of Sid's place. On the stairs the sound of it grew stronger and richer, mixed now with the sound of a man's hoarse singing, but only when they were down in the room, squinting through the blue smoke, did they realize the singer was Sid himself. Eyes half closed, head turned to smile along his shoulder into the crowd, he was singing as he swayed and worked at the keys.

> *"Man, she got a pair of eyes. . . ."*

The blue spotlight struck winking stars in the moisture of his teeth and the faint thread of sweat that striped his temple.

> *"I mean they're brighter than the summer skies*
> *And when you see them you gunna realize*
> *Just why I love my sweet Lorraine. . . ."*

"Damn place is packed," Carson said. There were no vacancies at the bar, but they stood uncertainly near it for a while, watching Sid perform, until Carson found that one of the girls on the barstools directly behind him was Jaqueline. "Oh," he said, "Hi. Pretty good crowd tonight."

She smiled and nodded and then craned past him to watch Sid.

"I didn't know he sang too," Carson said. "This something new?"

Her smile gave way to an impatient little frown and she put a forefinger against her lips. Rebuffed, he turned back and moved heavily from one foot to the other. Then he nudged Ken. "You want to go or stay? If you want to stay let's at least sit down."

"*Sh-h-h!*" Several people turned in their chairs to frown at him. "*Sh-h-h!*"

"Come on, then," he said, and he led Ken sidling and stumbling through the ranks of listeners to the only vacant table in the room, a small one down in front, too close to the music and wet with spilled drink, that had been pushed aside to make room for larger parties. Settled there, they could see now that Sid wasn't looking into the crowd at large. He was singing directly to a bored-looking couple in evening clothes who sat a few tables away, a silver-blonde girl who could have been a movie starlet and a small, chubby bald man with a deep tan, a man so obviously Murray Diamond that a casting director might have sent him here to play the part. Sometimes Sid's large eyes would stray to other parts of the room or to the smoke-hung ceiling, but they seemed to come into focus only when he looked at these two people. Even when the song ended and the piano took off alone on a long, intricate variation, even then he kept glancing up to see if they were watching. When he finished, to a small thunderclap of applause, the bald man lifted his face, closed it around an amber cigarette holder and clapped his hands a few times.

"Very nice, Sam," he said.

"My name's Sid, Mr. Diamond," Sid said, "but I thank you

a lot just the same. Glad y'enjoyed it, sir." He was leaning back, grinning along his shoulder while his fingers toyed with the keys. "Anything special you'd like to hear, Mr. Diamond? Something old-time? Some more of that real old Dixieland? Maybe a little boogie, maybe something a little on the sweet side, what we call a commercial number? Got all kind of tunes here, waitin' to be played."

"Anything at all, uh, Sid," Murray Diamond said, and then the blonde leaned close and whispered something in his ear. "How about 'Stardust,' there, Sid?" he said. "Can you play 'Stardust'?"

"Well, now, Mr. Diamond. If I couldn't play 'Stardust' I don't guess I'd be in business very long, France or any other country." His grin turned into a deep false laugh and his hands slid into the opening chords of the song.

That was when Carson made his first friendly gesture in hours, sending a warm blush of gratitude into Ken's face. He hitched his chair up close to Ken's and began to speak in a voice so soft that no one could have accused him of making a disturbance. "You know something?" he said. "This is disgusting. My God, *I* don't care if he wants to go to Las Vegas. I don't even care if he wants to suck *around* for it. This is something else. This is something that turns my stomach." He paused, frowning at the floor, and Ken watched the small wormlike vein moving in his temple. "Putting on this phony accent," Carson said. "All this big phony Uncle Remus routine." And then he went into a little popeyed, head-tossing, hissing parody of Sid. "Yassuh, Mr. Dahmon' suh. Wudg'all lak t'heah, Mr. Dahmon' suh? Got awl *kine* a toons heah, jes' waitin' to be played, and yok, yok, yok, and shet ma mouf!" He finished his drink and set the glass down hard. "You know damn well he doesn't have to talk that way. You know damn well he's a perfectly bright, educated guy. My God, on the phone I couldn't even tell he was colored."

"Well, yeah," Ken said. "It is sort of depressing."

"Depressing? It's degrading." Carson curled his lip. "It's degenerate."

"I know," Ken said. "I guess that may be partly what I meant about prostituting himself."

"You were certainly right, then. This is damn near enough to make you lose faith in the Negro race."

Being told he was right was always a tonic to Ken, and it was uncommonly bracing after a day like this. He knocked back his drink, straightened his spine and wiped the light mustache of sweat from his upper lip, pressing his mouth into a soft frown to show that his faith, too, in the Negro race was badly shaken. "Boy," he said. "I sure had him figured wrong."

"No," Carson assured him, "you couldn't have known."

"Listen, let's go, then, Carson. The hell with him." And Ken's mind was already full of plans: they would stroll in the cool of the Croisette for a long, serious talk on the meaning of integrity, on how rare it was and how easily counterfeited, how its pursuit was the only struggle worthy of a man's life, until all the discord of the day was erased.

But Carson moved his chair back, smiling and frowning at the same time. "Go?" he said. "What's the matter with you? Don't you want to stay and watch the spectacle? I do. Doesn't it hold a certain horrible fascination for you?" He held up his glass and signaled for two more cognacs.

"Stardust" came a graceful conclusion and Sid stood up, bathed in applause, to take his break. He loomed directly over their table as he came forward and stepped down off the dais, his big face shining with sweat; he brushed past them, looking toward Diamond's table, and paused there to say, "Thank you, sir," though Diamond hadn't spoken to him, before he made his way back to the bar.

"I suppose he thinks he didn't see us," Carson said.

"Probably just as well," Ken said. "I wouldn't know what to say to him."

"Wouldn't you? I think I would."

The room was stifling, and Ken's cognac had taken on a faintly repellent look and smell in his hand. He loosened his collar and tie with moist fingers. "Come on, Carson," he said. "Let's get out of here. Let's get some air."

Carson ignored him, watching what went on at the bar. Sid drank something Jaqueline offered and then disappeared into the men's room. When he came out a few minutes later, his face dried and composed, Carson turned back and studied his glass. "Here he comes. I think we're going to get the big hello, now, for Diamond's benefit. Watch."

An instant later Sid's fingers brushed the cloth of Carson's shoulder. "*Bzz-z-z, bzz-z-z!*" he said. "How're you tonight?"

Very slowly, Carson turned his head. With heavy eyelids he met Sid's smile for a split second, the way a man might look at a waiter who had accidentally touched him. Then he turned back to his drink.

"Oh-oh," Sid said. "Maybe I didn't do that right. Maybe I got the wrong shoulder here. I'm not too familiar with the rules and regulations yet." Murray Diamond and the blonde were watching, and Sid winked at them, thumbing out the IBF button in his lapel as he moved in sidling steps around the back of Carson's chair. "This here's a club we belong to, Mr. Diamond," he said. "Barflies club. Only trouble is, I'm not very familiar with the rules and regulations yet." He held the attention of nearly everyone in the room as he touched Carson's other shoulder. "*Bzz-z-z, bzz-z-z!*" This time Carson winced and drew his jacket away, glancing at Ken with a perplexed little shrug as if to say, Do you know what this man wants?

Ken didn't know whether to giggle or vomit; both desires were suddenly strong in him, though his face held straight. For a long time afterwards he would remember how the swabbed black plastic of the table looked between his two unmoving hands, how it seemed the only steady surface in the world.

"Say," Sid said, backing away toward the piano with a glazed smile. "What *is* this here? Some kinda conspiracy here?"

Carson allowed a heavy silence to develop. Then with an air of sudden, mild remembrance, seeming to say, Oh yes, of course, he rose and walked over to Sid, who backed up confusedly into the spotlight. Facing him, he extended one limp finger and touched him on the shoulder. "Buzz," he said. "Does that take care of it?" He turned and walked back to his seat.

Ken prayed for someone to laugh — anyone — but no one did. There was no movement in the room but the dying of Sid's smile as he looked at Carson and at Ken, the slow fleshy enclosing of his teeth and the widening of his eyes.

Murray Diamond looked at them too, briefly — a tough, tan little face — then he cleared his throat and said, "How about 'Hold Me,' there, Sid? Can you play 'Hold Me'?" And Sid sat down and began to play, looking at nothing.

With dignity, Carson nodded for the check and laid the right number of thousand- and hundred-franc notes on the saucer. It seemed to take him no time at all to get out of the place, sliding expertly between the tables and out to the stairs, but it took Ken much longer. Lurching, swaying in the smoke like a great imprisoned bear, he was caught and held by Jaqueline's eyes even before he had cleared the last of the tables. They stared relentlessly at the flabby quaver of his smile, they drilled into his back and sent him falling upstairs. And as soon as the sobering night air hit him, as soon as he saw Carson's erect white suit retreating several doors away, he knew what he wanted to do. He wanted to run up and hit him with all his strength between the shoulder blades, one great chopping blow that would drop him to the street, and then he would hit him again, or kick him — yes, kick him — and he'd say, God damn you! God damn you, Carson! The words were already in his mouth and he was ready to swing when Carson stopped and turned to face him under a streetlamp.

"What's the trouble, Ken?" he said. "Don't you think that was funny?"

It wasn't what he said that mattered — for a minute it seemed that nothing Carson said would ever matter again — it was that his face was stricken with the uncannily familiar look of his own heart, the very face he himself, Lard-Ass Platt, had shown all his life to others: haunted and vulnerable and terribly dependent, trying to smile, a look that said Please don't leave me alone.

Ken hung his head, either in mercy or shame. "Hell, I don't know, Carson," he said. "Let's forget it. Let's get some coffee somewhere."

"Right." And they were together again. The only problem now was that they had started out in the wrong direction: in order to get to the Croisette they would have to walk back past the lighted doorway of Sid's place. It was like walking through fire, but they did it quickly and with what anyone would have said was perfect composure, heads up, eyes front, so that the piano only came up loud for a second or two before it diminished and died behind them under the rhythm of their heels.

— 1951-58

Out with the Old

Building Seven, the TB building, had grown aloof from the rest of Mulloy Veterans' Hospital in the five years since the war. It lay less than fifty yards from Building Six, the paraplegic building — they faced the same flagpole on the same wind-swept Long Island plain — but there had been no neighborliness between them since the summer of 1948, when the paraplegics got up a petition demanding that the TB's be made to stay on their own lawn. This had caused a good deal of resentment at the time ("Those paraplegic bastards think they *own* the God damn place"), but it had long since ceased to matter very much; nor did it matter that nobody from Building Seven was allowed in the hospital canteen unless he hid his face in a sterile paper mask.

Who cared? After all, Building Seven was different. The hundred-odd patients of its three yellow wards had nearly all escaped the place at least once or twice over the years, and had every hope of escaping again, for good, as soon as their X rays cleared up or as soon as they had recovered from various kinds of surgery; meanwhile, they did not think of it as home or even as life, exactly, but as a timeless limbo between spells of what, like prisoners, they called "the outside." Another thing: owing to the unmilitary nature of their ailment, they didn't think of themselves primarily as "veterans" anyway (except perhaps at Christmastime, when each man got a multigraphed letter of salutation from the President and a five-dollar bill from the *New York Journal-American*) and so felt no real bond with the wounded and maimed.

Building Seven was a world of its own. It held out a daily choice between its own kind of virtue — staying in bed — and its own kind of vice: midnight crap games, AWOL, and the smuggling of beer and whiskey through the fire-exit doors of its two latrines. It was the stage for its own kind of comedy — the night Snyder chased the charge nurse into the fluoroscopy room with a water pistol, for instance, or the time the pint of bourbon slipped out of old Foley's bathrobe and smashed at Dr. Resnick's feet — and once in a while its own kind of tragedy — the time Jack Fox sat up in bed to say, "Chrissake, open the *window*," coughed, and brought up the freak hemorrhage that killed him in ten minutes, or the other times, two or three times a year, when one of the men who had been wheeled away to surgery, smiling and waving to cries of "Take it easy!" and "Good luck t'ya, boy!" would never come back. But mostly it was a world consumed by its own kind of boredom, where everyone sat or lay amid the Kleenex and the sputum cups and the clangor of all-day radios. That was the way things were in "C" Ward on the afternoon of New Year's Eve, except that the radios were swamped under the noise of Tiny Kovacs's laughter.

He was an enormous man of thirty, six and a half feet tall and broad as a bear, and that afternoon he was having a private talk with his friend Jones, who looked comically small and scrawny beside him. They would whisper together and then laugh — Jones with a nervous giggle, repeatedly scratching his belly through the pajamas, Tiny with his great guffaw. After a while they got up, still flushed with laughter, and made their way across the ward to McIntyre's bed.

"Hey, Mac, listen," Jones began, "Tiny'n I got an idea." Then he got the giggles and said, "Tell him, Tiny."

The trouble was that McIntyre, a fragile man of forty-one

with a lined, sarcastic face, was trying to write an important letter at the time. But they both mistook his grimace of impatience for a smile, and Tiny began to explain the idea in good faith.

"Listen, Mac, tonight around twelve I'm gonna get all undressed, see?" He spoke with some difficulty because all his front teeth were missing; they had gone bad soon after his lungs, and the new plate the hospital had ordered for him was long overdue. "I'll be all naked except I'm gonna wear this towel, see? Like a diper? And then look, I'm gonna put this here acrost my chest." He unrolled a strip of four-inch bandage, a yard long, on which he or Jones had written "1951" in big block numerals, with marking ink. "Get it?" he said. "A big fat baby? No teef? And then listen, Mac, you can be the old year, okay? You can put this here on, and this here. You'll be perfect." The second bandage said "1950," and the other item was a false beard of white cotton wool that they'd dug up from a box of Red Cross supplies in the dayroom — it had evidently belonged to an old Santa Claus costume.

"No, thanks," McIntyre said. "Find somebody else, okay?"

"Aw, jeez, you gotta do it, Mac," Tiny said. "Listen, we thought evvybody else in the building and you're the only one — don'tcha see? Skinny, bald, a little gray hair? And the best part is you're like me — you got no teef *eiver*." Then, to show no offense was meant, he added, "Well, I mean, at lease you could take 'em out, right? You could take 'em out for a couple minutes and put 'em back in *after* — right?"

"Look, Kovacs," McIntyre said, briefly closing his eyes, "I already said no. Now will the both a you please take off?"

Slowly Tiny's face reshaped itself into a pout, blotched red in the cheeks as if he'd ben slapped. "Arright," he said with self-control, grabbing the beard and the bandages from McIntyre's bed. "Arright, the hell wiv it." He swung around and strode back to his own side of the ward, and Jones trotted after him, smiling in embarrassment, his loose slippers flapping on the floor.

McIntyre shook his head. "How d'ya like them two for a paira idiot bastards?" he said to the man in the next bed, a thin and very ill Negro named Vernon Sloan. "You hear all that, Vernon?"

"I got the general idea," Sloan said. He started to say something else but began coughing instead, reaching out a long brown hand for his sputum cup, and McIntyre went to work on his letter again.

Back at his own bed, Tiny threw the beard and the bandages in his locker and slammed it shut. Jones hurried up beside him, pleading. "Listen, Tiny, we'll get another guy, is all. We'll get Shulman, or —"

"Ah, Shulman's too fat."

"Well, or Johnson, then, or —"

"Look, forget it, willya, Jones?" Tiny exploded. "Piss on it. I'm through. Try thinkin' up somethin' to give the guys a little laugh on New Year's, and that's whatcha get."

Jones sat down on Tiny's bedside chair. "Well, hell," he said after a pause, "it's still a good idea, isn't it?"

"Ah!" Tiny pushed one heavy hand away in disgust. "Ya think any a these bastids 'ud appreciate it? Ya think there's one sunuvabitchin' bastid in this building 'ud appreciate it? Piss on 'em all."

It was no use arguing; Tiny would sulk for the rest of the day now. This always happened when his feelings were hurt, and they were hurt fairly often, for his particular kind of jollity was apt to get on the other men's nerves. There was, for instance, the business of the quacking rubber duck he had bought in the hospital canten shortly before Christmas, as a gift for one of his nephews. The trouble that time was that in the end he had decided to buy something else for the child, and keep the duck for himself; quacking it made him laugh for hours on end. After the lights were out at night he would creep up on the other patients and quack the duck in their faces, and it wasn't long before nearly everyone told him to cut it out and shut up. Then somebody — McIntyre, in fact — had swiped the duck from Tiny's bed and hidden it, and Tiny had sulked for three days. "You guys think you're so smart," he had grumbled to the ward at large. "Actin' like a buncha kids."

It was Jones who found the duck and returned it to him; Jones was about the only man left who thought the things Tiny did were funny. Now his face brightened a little as he got up to leave. "Anyway, I got my bottle, Tiny," he said. "You'n *me'll* have some fun tonight." Jones was not a drinking man, but New Year's Eve was special and smuggling was a challenge: a few days earlier he had arranged to have a pint of rye brought in and had hidden it, with a good deal of giggling, under some spare pajamas in his locker.

"Don't tell nobody *else* you got it," Tiny said. "I wouldn't tell these bastids the time a day." He jerked a cigarette into his lips and struck the match savagely. Then he got his new Christmas robe off the hanger and put it on — careful, for all his temper, to arrange the fit of the padded shoulders and the sash just right. It was a gorgeous robe, plum-colored satin with contrasting red lapels, and Tiny's face and manner assumed a strange dignity whenever he put it on. This look was as new, or rather, as seasonal, as the robe itself: it dated back to the week before, when he'd gotten dressed to go home for his Christmas pass.

Many of the men were a revelation in one way or another when they appeared in their street clothes. McIntyre had grown surprisingly humble, incapable of sarcasm or pranks, when he put on his scarcely worn accounting clerk's costume of blue serge, and Jones had grown surprisingly tough in his old Navy foul-weather jacket. Young Krebs, whom everybody called "Junior," had assumed a portly maturity with his double-breasted business suit, and Travers, who most people had forgotten was a Yale man, looked oddly effete in his J. Press flannels and his button-down collar. Several of the Negroes had suddenly become Negroes again, instead of ordinary men, when they appeared in their sharply pegged trousers, draped coats and huge Windsor knots, and they even seemed embarrassed to be talking to the white men on the old familiar terms. But possibly the biggest change of all had been Tiny's. The clothes themselves were no surprise — his family ran a prosperous restaurant in Queens, and he was appropriately well-turned-out in a rich black overcoat and silk scarf — but the dignity they gave him was remarkable. The silly grin was gone, the laugh silenced, the clumsy movements overcome. The eyes beneath his snap-brim hat were not Tiny's eyes at all, but calm and masterful. Even his missing teeth didn't spoil the effect, for he kept his mouth shut except to mutter brief, almost curt Christmas wishes. The other patients looked up with a certain shy respect at this new man, this dramatic stranger whose hard heels crashed on the marble floor as he strode out of the building — and later, when he swung along the sidewalks of Jamaica on his way home, the crowds instinctively moved aside to make way for him.

Tiny was aware of the splendid figure he cut, but by the time he was home he'd stopped thinking about it; in the circle of his family it was real. Nobody called him Tiny there — he was Harold, a gentle son, a quiet hero to many round-eyed children, a rare and honored visitor. At one point, in the afterglow of a great dinner, a little girl was led ceremoniously up to his chair, where she stood shyly, not daring to meet his eyes, her fingers clasping the side seams of her party dress. Her mother urged her to speak: "Do you want to tell Uncle Harold what you say in your prayers every night, Irene?"

"Yes," the little girl said. "I tell Jesus please to bless Uncle Harold and make him get well again soon."

Uncle Harold smiled and took hold of both her hands. "That's swell, Irene," he said huskily. "But you know, you shunt *tell* Him. You should *ask* Him."

She looked into his face for the first time. "That's what I mean," she said. "I ask Him."

And Uncle Harold gathered her in his arms, putting his big face over her shoulder so she couldn't see that his eyes were blurred with tears. "That's a good girl," he whispered. It was a scene nobody in Building Seven would have believed.

He remained Harold until the pass was over and he strode away from a clinging family farewell, shrugging the great overcoat around his shoulders and squaring the hat. He was Harold all the way to the bus terminal and all the way back to the hospital, and the other men still looked at him oddly and greeted him a little shyly when he pounded back into "C" Ward. He went to his bed and put down his several packages (one of which contained the new robe), then headed for the latrine to get undressed. That was the beginning of the end, for when he came out in the old faded pajamas and scuffed slippers there was only a trace of importance left in his softening face, and even that disappeared in the next hour or two, while he lay on his bed and listened to the radio. Later that evening, when most of the other returning patients had settled down, he sat up and looked around in the old, silly way. He waited patiently for a moment of complete silence, then thrust his rubber duck high in the air and quacked it seven times to the rhythm of "shave-and-a-haircut, two-bits," while everybody groaned and swore. Tiny was back, ready to start a new year.

Now, less than a week later, he could still recapture his dignity whenever he needed it by putting on the robe, striking a pose and thinking hard about his home. Of course, it was only a question of time before the robe grew rumpled with familiarity, and then it would all be over, but meanwhile it worked like a charm.

Across the aisle, McIntyre sat brooding over his unfinished letter. "I don't know, Vernon," he said to Sloan. "I felt sorry for you last week, having to stay in this dump over Christmas, but you know something? You were lucky. I wish they wouldn't of let me go home, either."

"That so?" Sloan said. "How do you mean?"

"Ah, I don't know," McIntyre said, wiping his fountain pen with a piece of Kleenex. "I don't know. Just that it's a bitch having to come back afterwards, I guess." But that was only part of it; the other part, like the letter he'd been trying to write all week, was his own business.

McIntyre's wife had grown fat and bewildered in the last year or two. On the alternate Sunday afternoons when she came out to visit him she never seemed to have much on her mind but the movies she had seen, or the television shows, and she gave him very little news of their two children, who almost never came out. "Anyway, you'll be seein' them Christmas," she would say. We'll have a lot of fun. Only listen, Dad, are you sure that bus trip isn't gonna tire you out?"

"'Course not," he had said, a number of times. "I didn't have no trouble last year, did I?"

Nevertheless he was breathing hard when he eased himself off the bus at last, carrying the packages he had bought in the hospital canteen, and he had to walk very slowly up the snow-crusted Brooklyn street to his home.

His daughter Jean, who was eighteen now, was not there when he came in.

"Oh, sure," his wife explained, "I thought I told you she'd prob'ly be out tonight."

"No," he said. "You didn't tell me. Where'd she go?"

"Oh, out to the movies is all, with her girlfriend Brenda. I didn't think you'd mind, Dad. Fact, I told her to go. She needs a little night off once in a while. You know, she's kind of run-down. She gets nervous and everything."

"What's she get nervous about?"

"Well, *you* know. One thing, this job she's got now's very tiring. I mean she likes the work and everything, but she's not used to the full eight hours a day, you know what I mean?

She'll settle down to it. Come on, have a cuppa coffee, and then we'll put the tree up. We'll have a lot of fun."

On his way to wash up he passed her empty room, with its clean cosmetic smell, its ragged teddy bear and framed photographs of singers, and he said, "It sure seems funny to be home."

His boy Joseph had still been a kid fooling around with model airplanes the Christmas before; now he wore his hair about four inches too long and spent a great deal of time working on it with his comb, shaping it into a gleaming pompadour with upswept sides. He was a heavy smoker, too, pinching the cigarette between his yellow-stained thumb and forefinger and cupping the live end in his palm. He hardly moved his lips when he spoke, and his only way of laughing was to make a brief snuffling sound in his nose. He gave one of these little snorts during the trimming of the Christmas tree, when McIntyre said something about a rumor that the Veterans' Administration might soon increase disability pensions. It might have meant nothing, but to McIntyre it was the same as if he had said, "Who you tryna kid, Pop? We know where the money's coming from." It seemed an unmistakable, wise-guy reference to the fact that McIntyre's brother-in-law, and not his pension, was providing the bulk of the family income. He resolved to speak to his wife about it at bedtime that night, but when the time came all he said was, "Don't he ever get his hair cut any more?"

"All the kids are wearing it that way now," she said. "Why do you have to criticize him all the time?"

Jean was there in the morning, slow and rumpled in a loose blue wrapper. "Hi, sweetie," she said, and gave him a kiss that smelled of sleep and stale perfume. She opened her presents quietly and then lay for a long time with one leg thrown over the arm of a deep upholstered chair, her foot swinging, her fingers picking at a pimple on her chin.

McIntyre couldn't take his eyes off her. It wasn't just that she was a woman — the kind of withdrawn, obliquely smiling woman that had filled him with intolerable shyness and desire in his own youth — it was something more disturbing even than that.

"Whaddya looking at, Dad?" she said, smiling and frowning at once. "You keep *lookin'* at me all the time."

He felt himself blushing. "I always like to look at pretty girls. Is that so terrible?"

"'Course not." She began intently plucking at the broken edge of one of her fingernails, frowning down at her hands in a way that made her long eyelashes fall in delicate curves against her cheeks. "It's just — you know. When a person keeps looking at you all the time it makes you nervous, that's all."

"Honey, listen." McIntyre leaned forward with both elbows on his skinny knees. "Can I ask you something? What's all this business about being nervous? Ever since I come home, that's all I heard. 'Jean's very nervous. Jean's very nervous.' So listen, will you please tell me something? What's there to be so nervous about?"

"Nothing," she said. "I don't know, Dad. Nothing, I guess."

"Well, because the reason I ask —" he was trying to make his voice deep and gentle, the way he was almost sure it had sounded long ago, but it came out scratchy and querulous, short of breath — "the reason I ask is, if there's something bothering you or anything, don't you think you ought to tell your dad about it?"

Her fingernail tore deep into the quick, which caused her to shake it violently and pop it into her mouth with a little whimper of pain, and suddenly she was on her feet, red-faced and crying. "Dad, willya lea' me alone? Willya just please lea' me *alone?*" She ran out of the room and upstairs and slammed her door.

McIntyre had started after her, but instead he stood swaying and glared at his wife and son, who were examining the carpet at opposite ends of the room.

"What's the matter with her, anyway?" he demanded. "Huh? What the hell's going on around here?" But they were as silent as two guilty children. "C'mon," he said. His head made a slight involuntary movement with each suck of air into his frail chest. "C'mon, God damn it, *tell* me."

With a little wet moan his wife sank down and spread herself among the sofa cushions, weeping, letting her face melt. "All right," she said. "All right, you asked for it. We all done our best to give you a nice Christmas, but if you're gonna come home and snoop around and drive everybody crazy with your questions, all right — it's your funeral. She's four months pregnant — there, now are you satisfied? Now willya please quit bothering everybody?"

McIntyre sat down in an easy chair that was full of rattling Christmas paper, his head still moving with each breath.

"Who was it?" he said at last. "Who's the boy?"

"*Ask* her," his wife said. "Go on, ask her and see. She won't tell you. She won't tell anybody — that's the whole trouble. She wouldn't even of let on about the *baby* if I hadn't found out, and now she won't even tell her own mother the boy's name. She'd rather break her mother's heart — yes, she would, and her brother's too."

Then he heard it again, a little snuffle across the room. Joseph was standing there smirking as he stubbed out a cigarette. His lower lip moved slightly and he said, "Maybe she don't *know* the guy's name."

McIntyre rose very slowly out of the rattling paper, walked over to his son and hit him hard across the face with the flat of his hand, making the long hair jump from his skull and fall around his ears, making his face wince into the face of a hurt, scared little boy. Then blood began to run from the little boy's nose and dribble on the nylon shirt he had gotten for Christmas, and McIntyre hit him again, and that was when his wife screamed.

A few hours later he was back in Building Seven with nothing to do. All week he ate poorly, talked very little, except to Vernon Sloan, and spent a great deal of time working on a letter to his daughter that was still unfinished on the afternoon of New Year's Eve.

After many false starts, which had ended up among the used Kleenex tissues in the paper bag that hung beside his bed, this was what he had written:

JEAN HONEY,

I guess I got pretty excited and made a lot of trouble when I was home. Baby it was only that I have been away so long it is hard for me to understand that your a grown up woman and that is why I kind of went crazy that day. Now Jean I have done some thinking since I got back here and I want to write you a few lines.

The main thing is try not to worry. Remember your not the first girl that's made a mistake and

(*p. 2*)

gotten into trouble of this kind. Your mom is all upset I know but do not let her get you down. Now Jean it may seem that you and I don't know each other very well any more but this is not so. Do you remember when I first come out of the army and you were about 12 then and we used to take a walk in Prospect Pk. sometimes and talk things over. I wish I could have a talk like that

(*p. 3*)

with you now. Your old dad may not be good for much any more but he does know a thing or two about life and especially one important thing, and that is

That was as far as the letter went.

Now that Tiny's laughter was stilled, the ward seemed unnaturally quiet. The old year faded in a thin yellow sunset behind the west windows; then darkness fell, the lights came on and shuddering rubber-wheeled wagons of dinner trays were rolled in by masked and gowned attendants. One of them, a gaunt, bright-eyed man named Carl, went through his daily routine.

"Hey, you guys heard about the man that ran over himself?" he asked, stopping in the middle of the aisle with a steaming pitcher of coffee in his hand.

"Just pour the coffee, Carl," somebody said.

Carl filled a few cups and started across the aisle to fill a few more, but midway he stopped again and bugged his eyes over the rim of his sterile mask. "No, but listen — you guys heard about the man that ran over himself? This is a new one." He looked at Tiny, who usually was more than willing to play straight man for him, but Tiny was moodily buttering a slice of bread, his cheeks wobbling with each stroke of the knife. "Well, anyways," Carl said at last, "this man says to this kid, 'Hey kid, run acrost the street and get me a packa cigarettes, willya?' Kid says, 'No,' see? So the man ran over him*self!*" He doubled up and pounded his thigh. Jones groaned appreciatively; everyone else ate in silence.

When the meal was over and the trays cleared away, McIntyre tore up the old beginning of page 3 and dropped it in the waste bag. He resettled his pillows, brushed some food crumbs off the bed, and wrote this:

(*p.* 3)
with you now.

So Jean please write and tell me the name of this boy. I promise I

But he threw that page away too, and sat for a long time writing nothing, smoking a cigarette with his usual careful effort to avoid inhaling. At last he took up his pen again and cleaned its point very carefully with a leaf of Kleenex. Then he began a new page:

(*p.* 3)
with you now.

Now baby I have got an idea. As you know I am now waiting to have another operation on the left side in February but if all goes well maybe I could take off out of this place by April 1. Of course I would not get a discharge but I could take a chance like I did in

1947 and hope for better luck this time. Then we could go away to the country someplace just you and I and I could take a part time job and we could

The starched rustle and rubber-heeled thump of a nurse made him look up; she was standing beside his bed with a bottle of rubbing alcohol. "How about you, McIntyre?" she said. "Back rub?"

"No thanks," he said. "Not tonight."

"My goodness." She peered just a little at the letter, which he shielded just a little with his hand. "You still writing letters? Every time I come past here you're writing letters. You must have a lot of people to write to. I wish I had the time to catch up on my letters."

"Yeah," he said. "Well, that's the thing, see. I got plenty of time."

"Well, but how can you think of so many things to write about?" she said. "That's my trouble. I sit down and I get all ready to write a letter and then I can't think of a single thing to write about. It's terrible."

He watched the shape of her buttocks as she moved away down the aisle. Then he read over the new page, crumpled it, and dropped it in the bag. Closing his eyes and massaging the bridge of his nose with thumb and forefinger, he tried to remember the exact words of the first version. At last he wrote it out again as well as he could:

(*p.* 3)
with you now.

Baby Jean your old dad may not be good for much any more but he does know a thing or two about life and especially one important thing, and that is

But from there on, the pen lay dead in his cramped fingers. It was as if all the letters of the alphabet, all the combinations of letters into words, all the infinite possibilities of handwritten language had ceased to exist.

He looked out the window for help, but the window was a black mirror now and gave back only the lights, the bright bed sheets and pajamas of the ward. Pulling on his robe and slippers, he went over to stand with his forehead and cupped hands against the cold pane. Now he could make out the string of highway lights in the distance and, beyond that, the horizon of black trees between the snow and the sky. Just above the horizon, on the right, the sky was suffused with a faint pink blur from the lights of Brooklyn and New York, but this was partly hidden from view by a big dark shape in the foreground that was a blind corner of the paraplegic building, a world away.

When McIntyre turned back from the window to blink in the yellow light, leaving a shriveling ghost of his breath on the glass, it was with an oddly shy look of rejuvenation and relief. He walked to his bed, stacked the pages of his manuscript neatly, tore them in halves and in quarters and dropped them into the waste bag. Then he got his pack of cigarettes and went over to stand beside Vernon Sloan, who was blinking through his reading glasses at *The Saturday Evening Post*.

"Smoke, Vernon?" he said.

"No thanks, Mac. I smoke more'n one or two a day, it only makes me cough."

"Okay," McIntyre said, lighting one for himself. "Care to play a little checkers?"

"No thanks, Mac, not right now. I'm a little tired — think I'll just read awhile."

"Any good articles in there this week, Vernon?"

"Oh, pretty good," he said. "Couple pretty good ones." Then his mouth worked into a grin that slowly disclosed nearly all of his very clean teeth. "Say, what's the matter with you, man? You feelin' good or somethin'?"

"Oh, not too bad, Vernon," he said, stretching his skinny arms and his spine. "Not too bad."

"You finish all your writin' finally? Is that it?"

"Yeah, I guess so," he said. "My trouble is, I can't think of anythink to write about."

Looking across the aisle to where Tiny Kovacs's wide back sat slumped in the purple amplitude of the new robe, he walked over and laid a hand on one of the enormous satin shoulders. "So?" he said.

Tiny's head swung around to glare at him, immediately hostile. "So what?"

"So where's that beard?"

Tiny wrenched open his locker, grabbed out the beard and thrust it roughly into McIntyre's hands. "Here," he said. "You want it? Take it."

McIntyre held it up to his ears and slipped the string over his head. "String oughta be a little tighter," he said. "There, how's that? Prob'ly look better when I get my teeth out."

But Tiny wasn't listening. He was burrowing in his locker for the strips of bandage. "Here," he said. "Take this stuff too. I don't want no part of it. You wanna do it, you get somebody else."

At that moment Jones came padding over, all smiles. "Hey, you gonna do it, Mac? You change your mind?"

"Jones, talk to this big son of a bitch," McIntyre said through the wagging beard. "He don't wanna cooperate."

"Aw, *jeez*, Tiny," Jones implored. "The whole *thing* depends on you. The whole *thing* was your idea."

"I already told ya," Tiny said. "I don't want no part of it. You wanna do it, you find some other sucker."

After the lights went out at ten nobody bothered much about hiding their whiskey. Men who had been taking furtive nips in the latrines all evening now drank in quietly jovial groups around the wards, with the unofficial once-a-year blessing of the charge nurse. Nobody took particular notice when, a little before midnight, three men from "C" Ward slipped out to the linen closet to get a sheet and a towel, then to the kitchen to get a mop handle, and then walked the length of the building and disappeared into the "A" Ward latrine.

There was a last-minute flurry over the beard: it hid so much of McIntyre's face that the effect of his missing teeth was spoiled. Jones solved the problem by cutting away all of it but the chin whiskers, which he fastened in place with bits of adhesive tape. "There," he said, "that does it. That's perfect. Now roll up your pajama pants, Mac, so just your bare legs'll show under the sheet? Get it? Now where's your mop handle?"

"Jones, it don't *work!*" Tiny called tragically. He was standing naked except for a pair of white woolen socks, trying to pin the folded towel around his loins. "The son of à bitch won't stay *up!*"

Jones hurried over to fix it, and finally everything was ready. Nervously, they killed the last of Jones's rye and dropped the empty bottle into a laundry hamper; then they slipped outside and huddled in the darkness at the head of "A" Ward.

"Ready?" Jones whispered. "Okay. . . . Now." He flicked on the overhead lights, and thirty startled faces blinked in the glare.

First came 1950, a wasted figure crouched on a trembling staff, lame and palsied with age; behind him, grinning and flexing his muscles, danced the enormous diapered baby of the New Year. For a second or two there was silence except for the unsteady tapping of the old man's staff, and then the laughter and the cheers began.

"*Out wivvie old!*" the baby bellowed over the noise, and he made an elaborate burlesque of hauling off and kicking the old man in the seat of the pants, which caused the old man to stagger weakly and rub one buttock as they moved up the aisle. "*Out wivvie old! In wivva new!*"

Jones ran on ahead to turn on the lights of "B" Ward, where the ovation was even louder. Nurses clustered helplessly in the doorway to watch, frowning or giggling behind their sterile masks as the show made its way through cheers and catcalls.

"Out wivvie old! In wivva new!"

In one of the private rooms a dying man blinked up through the window of his oxygen tent as his door was flung open and his light turned on. He stared bewildered at the frantic toothless clowns who capered at the foot of his bed; finally he understood and gave them a yellow smile, and they moved on to the next private room and the next, arriving at last in "C" Ward, where their friends stood massed and laughing in the aisle.

There was barely time for the pouring of fresh drinks before all the radios blared up at once and Guy Lombardo's band broke into "Auld Lang Syne"; then all the shouts dissolved into a great off-key chorus in which Tiny's voice could be heard over all the others:

> *Should old acquaintance be forgot*
> *And never brought to mind? . . .*

Even Vernon Sloan was singing, propped up in bed and holding a watery highball, which he slowly waved in time to the music. They were all singing.

> *For o-o-old lang syne, my boys,*
> *For o-o-old lang syne . . .*

And when the song was over the handshaking began.

"Good luck t'ya, boy."

"Same to you, boy — hope you make it this year."

All over Building Seven men wandered in search of hands to shake; under the noise of shouts and radios the words were repeated again and again: "Good luck t'ya . . ." "Hope you make it this year, boy . . ." And standing still and tired by Tiny Kovacs's bed, where the purple robe lay thrown in careless wads and wrinkles, McIntyre raised his glass and his bare-gummed smile to the crowd, with Tiny's laughter roaring in his ear and Tiny's heavy arm around his neck.

— 1953-57

Builders

WRITERS who write about writers can easily bring on the worst kind of literary miscarriage; everybody knows that. Start a story off with "Craig crushed out his cigarette and lunged for the typewriter," and there isn't an editor in the United States who'll feel like reading your next sentence.

So don't worry: this is going to be a straight, no-nonsense piece of fiction about a cab driver, a movie star, and an eminent child psychologist, and that's a promise. But you'll have to be patient for a minute, because there's going to be a writer in it too. I won't call him "Craig," and I can guarantee that he won't get away with being the only Sensitive Person among the characters, but we're going to be stuck with him right along and you'd better count on his being as awkward and obtrusive as writers nearly always are, in fiction or in life.

Thirteen years ago, in 1948, I was twenty-two and employed as a rewrite man on the financial news desk of the United Press. The salary was fifty-four dollars a week and it wasn't much of a job, but it did give me two good things. One was that whenever anybody asked me what I did I could say, "Work for the UP," which had a jaunty sound; the other was that every morning I could turn up at the *Daily News* building wearing a jaded look, a cheap trench coat that had shrunk a size too small for me, and a much-handled brown fedora ("Battered" is the way I would have described it then, and I'm grateful that I know a little more now about honesty in the use of words. It was a handled hat, handled by endless nervous pinchings and shapings and reshapings; it wasn't battered at all). What I'm getting at is that just for those few minutes each day, walking up the slight hill of the last hundred yards between the subway exit and the *News* building, I was Ernest Hemingway reporting for work at the *Kansas City Star*.

Had Hemingway been to the war and back before his twentieth birthday? Well, so had I; and all right, maybe there were no wounds or medals for valor in my case, but the basic fact of the matter was there. Had Hemingway bothered about anything as time-wasting and career-delaying as going to college? Hell, no; and me neither. Could Hemingway ever really have cared very much about the newspaper business? Of course not; so there was only a marginal difference, you see, between his lucky break at the *Star* and my own dismal stint on the financial desk. The important thing, as I knew Hemingway would be the first to agree, was that a writer had to begin somewhere.

"Domestic corporate bonds moved irregularly higher in moderately active trading today . . ." That was the kind of prose I wrote all day long for the UP wire, and "Rising oil shares paced a lively curb market," and "Directors of Timken Roller Bearing today declared" — hundreds on hundreds of words that I never really understood (What in the name of God are puts and calls, and what is a sinking fund debenture? I'm still damned if I know), while the teletypes chugged and rang and the Wall Street tickers ticked and everybody around me argued baseball, until it was mercifully time to go home.

It always pleased me to reflect that Hemingway had married young; I could go right along with him there. My wife Joan and I lived as far west as you can get on West Twelfth Street, in a big three-window room on the third floor, and if it wasn't the Left Bank it certainly wasn't our fault. Every evening after dinner, while Joan washed the dishes, there would be a respectful, almost reverent hush in the room, and this was the time for me to retire behind a three-fold screen in the corner where a table, a student lamp and a portable typewriter were set up. But it was here, of course, under the white stare of that lamp, that the tenuous parallel between Hemingway and me endured its heaviest strain. Because it wasn't any "Up in Michigan" that came out of my machine; it wasn't any "Three Day Blow," or "The Killers"; very often, in fact, it wasn't really anything at all, and even when it was something Joan called "marvelous," I knew deep down that it was always, always something bad.

There were evenings too when all I did behind the screen was goof off — read every word of the printing on the inside of a matchbook, say, or all the ads in the back of the *Saturday Review of Literature* — and it was during one of those times, in the fall of the year, that I came across these lines:

> Unusual free-lance opportunity for talented writer. Must have imagination. Bernard Silver.

— and then a phone number with what looked like a Bronx exchange.

I won't bother giving you the dry, witty, Hemingway dialogue that took place when I came out from behind the screen that night and Joan turned around from the sink, with her hands dripping soapsuds on the open magazine, and we can also skip my cordial, unenlightening chat with Bernard Silver on the phone. I'll just move on ahead to a couple of nights later, when I rode the subway for an hour and found my way at last to his apartment.

"Mr. Prentice?" he inquired. "What's your first name again? Bob? Good, Bob, I'm Bernie. Come on in, make yourself comfortable."

And I think both Bernie and his home deserve a little description here. He was in his middle or late forties, a good deal shorter than me and much stockier, wearing an expensive-looking pale blue sport shirt with the tails out. His head must have been half again the size of mine, with thinning black hair washed straight back, as if he'd stood face-up in the shower; and his face was one of the most guileless and self-confident faces I've ever seen.

The apartment was very clean, spacious and cream-colored, full of carpeting and archways. In the narrow alcove near the coat closet ("Take your coat and hat; good. Let's put this on a hanger here and we'll be all set; good"), I saw a cluster of framed photographs showing World War I soldiers in various groupings, but on the walls of the living room there were no pictures of any kind, only a few wrought-iron lamp brackets and a couple of mirrors. Once inside the room you weren't apt to notice the lack of pictures, though, because all your attention was drawn to a single, amazing piece of furniture. I don't know what you'd call it — a credenza? — but whatever it was it seemed to go on forever, chest-high in some places and waist-high in others, made of at least three different shades of polished brown veneer. Part of it was a television set, part of it was a radio-phonograph; part of it thinned out into shelves that held potted plants and little figurines; part of it, full of chromium knobs and tricky sliding panels, was a bar.

"Ginger ale?" he asked. "My wife and I don't drink, but I can offer you a glass of ginger ale."

I think Bernie's wife must always have gone out to the movies on nights when he interviewed his writing applicants; I did meet her later, though, and we'll come to that. Anyway, there were just the two of us that first evening, settling down in slippery leatherette chairs with our ginger ale, and it was strictly business.

"First of all," he said, "tell me, Bob. Do you know *My Flag Is Down?*" And before I could ask what he was talking about he pulled it out of some recess in the credenza and handed it over — a paperback book that you still see around the drugstores, purporting to be the memoirs of a New York taxicab driver. Then he began to fill me in, while I looked at the book and nodded and wished I'd never left home.

Bernard Silver was a cab driver too. He had been one for twenty-two years, as long as the span of my life, and in the last two or three of these years he had begun to see no reason why a slightly fictionalized version of his own experiences shouldn't be worth a fortune. "I'd like you to take a look at this," he said, and this time the credenza yielded up a neat little box of three-by-five-inch file cards. Hundreds of experiences, he told me; all different; and while he gave me to understand that they might not all be strictly true, he could assure me there was at least a kernel of truth in every last one of them. Could I imagine what a really good ghost-writer might do with a wealth of material like that? Or how much that same writer might expect to salt away when his own fat share of the magazine sales, the book royalties and the movie rights came in?

"Well, I don't know, Mr. Silver. It's a thing I'd have to think over. I guess I'd have to read this other book first, and see if I thought there was any —"

"No, wait awhile. You're getting way ahead of me here, Bob. In the first place I wouldn't want you to read that book because you wouldn't learn anything. That guy's all gangsters and dames and sex and drinking and that stuff. I'm completely different." And I sat swilling ginger ale as if to slake a gargantuan thirst, in order to be able to leave as soon as possible after he'd finished explaining how completely different he was. Bernie Silver was a warm person, he told me; an ordinary, everyday guy with a heart as big as all outdoors and a real philosophy of life; did I know what he meant?

I have a trick of tuning out on people (it's easy; all you do is fix your eyes on the speaker's mouth and watch the rhythmic, endlessly changing shapes of lips and tongue, and the first thing you know you can't hear a word), and I was about to start doing that when he said:

"And don't misunderstand me, Bob. I never yet asked a

writer to do a single word for me on spec. You write for me, you'll be paid for everything you do. Naturally it can't be very big dough at this stage of the game, but you'll be paid. Fair enough? Here, let me fill up your glass."

This was the proposition. He'd give me an idea out of the file; I'd develop it into a first-person short story by Bernie Silver, between one and two thousand words in length, for which immediate payment was guaranteed. If he liked the job I did, there would be plenty of others where it came from — an assignment a week, if I could handle that much — and in addition to my initial payment, of course, I could look forward to a generous percentage of whatever subsequent income the material might bring. He chose to be winkingly mysterious about his plans for marketing the stories, though he did manage to hint that the *Reader's Digest* might be interested, and he was frank to admit he didn't yet have a publisher lined up for the ultimate book they would comprise, but he said he could give me a couple of names that would knock my eye out. Had I ever heard, for example, of Manny Weidman?

"Or maybe," he said, breaking into his all-out smile, "maybe you know him better as Wade Manley." And this was the shining name of a movie star, a man about as famous in the thirties and forties as Kirk Douglas or Burt Lancaster today. Wade Manley had been a grammar-school friend of Bernie's right here in the Bronx. Through mutual friends they had managed to remain sentimentally close ever since, and one of the things that kept their friendship green was Wade Manley's oft-repeated desire to play the role of rough, lovable Bernie Silver, New York Hackie, in any film or television series based on his colorful life. "Now I'll give you another name," he said, and this time he squinted cannily at me while pronouncing it, as if my recognizing it or not would be an index of my general educational level. "Dr. Alexander Corvo."

And luckily I was able not to look too blank. It wasn't a celebrity name, exactly, but it was far from obscure. It was one of those *New York Times* names, the kind of which tens of thousands of people are dimly aware because they've been coming across respectful mentions of them in the *Times* for years. Oh, it might have lacked the impact of "Lionel Trilling" or "Reinhold Niebuhr," but it was along that line; you could probably have put it in the same class with "Huntington Hartford" or "Leslie R. Groves," and a good cut or two above "Newbold Morris."

"The whaddyacallit man, you mean?" I said. "The childhood-tensions man?"

Bernie gave me a solemn nod, forgiving this vulgarity, and spoke the name again with its proper identification. "I mean Dr. Alexander Corvo, the eminent child psychologist."

Early in his rise to eminence, you see, Dr. Corvo had been a teacher at the very same grammar school in the Bronx, and two of the most unruly, dearly loved little rascals in his charge there had been Bernie Silver and Manny What's-his-name, the movie star. He still retained an incurable soft spot for both youngsters, and nothing would please him more today than to lend whatever influence he might have in the publishing world to furthering their project. All the three of them needed now, it seemed, was to find that final element, that elusive catalyst, the perfect writer for the job.

"Bob," said Bernie, "I'm telling you the truth. I've had one writer after another working on this, and none of them's been right. Sometimes I don't trust my own judgment; I take their stuff to Dr. Corvo and he shakes his head. He says, 'Bernie, try again.' "

"Look, Bob." He came earnestly forward in his chair. "This isn't any fly-by-night idea here; I'm not stringing anybody along. This thing is building. Manny, Dr. Corvo and myself — we're *building* this thing. Oh, don't worry, Bob, I *know* — what, do I look that stupid? — I know they're not building the way *I'm* building. And why should they? A big movie star? A distinguished scholar and author? You think they haven't got plenty of things of their own to build? A lot more important things than this? Naturally. But Bob, I'm telling you the truth: they're interested. I can show you letters, I can tell you times they've sat around this apartment with their wives, or Manny has anyway, and we've talked about it hours on end. They're interested, nobody has to worry about that. So do you see what I'm telling you, Bob? I'm telling you the truth. This thing is building." And he began a slow, two-handed building gesture, starting from the carpet, setting invisible blocks into place until they'd made a structure of money and fame for him, money and freedom for both of us, that rose to the level of our eyes.

I said it certainly did sound fine, but that if he didn't mind I'd like to know a little more about the immediate payment for the individual stories.

"And now I'll give you the answer to that one," he said. He went to the credenza again — part of it seemed to be a kind of desk — and after sorting out some papers he came up with a personal check. "I won't just tell you," he said. "I'll show you. Fair enough? This was my last writer. Take it and read it."

It was a canceled check, and it said that Bernard Silver had paid, to the order of some name, the sum of twenty-five dollars and no cents. "Read it!" he insisted, as if the check were a prose work of uncommon merit in its own right, and he watched me while I turned it over to read the man's endorsement, which had been signed under some semi-legible words of Bernie's own about this being advance payment in full, and the bank's rubber stamp. "Look all right to you?" he inquired. "So that's the arrangement. All clear now?"

I guessed it was as clear as it would ever be, so I gave him back the check and said that if he'd show me one of the file cards now, or whatever, we might as well get going.

"Way-*hait* a minute, now! Hold your *horses* a minute here." His smile was enormous. "You're a pretty fast guy, you know that, Bob? I mean I like you, but don't you think I'd have to be a little bit of a dope to go around making out checks to everybody walked in here saying they're a writer? I know you're a newspaperman. Fine. Do I know you're a writer yet? Why don't you let me see what you got there in your lap?"

It was a manila envelope containing carbon copies of the only two halfway presentable short stories I had ever managed to produce in my life.

"Well," I said. "Sure. Here. Of course these are a very different kind of thing than what *you're —*"

"Never mind, never mind; naturally they're different," he said, opening the envelope. "You just relax a minute, and let me take a look."

"What I mean is, they're both very kind of — well, literary, I guess you'd say. I don't quite see how they'll give you any real idea of my —"

"Relax, I said."

Rimless glasses were withdrawn from the pocket of his sport shirt and placed laboriously into position as he settled back, frowning, to read. It took him a long time to get through the first page of the first story, and I watched him, wondering if this might turn out to be the very lowest point in my literary career. A *cab* driver, for Christ's sake. At last the first page turned, and the second page followed so closely after it that I could tell he was skipping. Then the third and the fourth — it was a twelve- or fourteen-page story — while I gripped my empty, warming ginger ale glass as if in readiness to haul off and throw it at his head.

A very slight, hesitant, then more and more judicial nodding set in as he made his way toward the end. He finished it, looked puzzled, went back to read over the last page again; then he laid it aside and picked up the second story — not to read it, but only to check it for length. He had clearly had enough reading for one night. Off came the glasses and on came the smile.

"Well, very nice," he said. "I won't take time to read this other one now, but this first one's very nice. Course, naturally, as you said, this is a very different kind of material you got here, so it's a little hard for me to — *you* know —" and he dismissed the rest of this difficult sentence with a wave of the hand. "I'll tell you what, though, Bob. Instead of just reading here, let me ask you a couple of questions about writing. For example." He closed his eyes and delicately touched their lids with his fingers, thinking, or more likely pretending to think, in order to give added weight to his next words. "For example, let me ask you this. Supposing somebody writes you a letter and says, 'Bob, I didn't have time to write you a short letter today, so I had to write you a long one instead.' Would you know what they meant by that?"

Don't worry, I played this part of the evening pretty cool. I wasn't going to let twenty-five bucks get away from me without some kind of struggle; and my answer, whatever sober-sided nonsense it was, could have left no doubt in his mind that this particular writing candidate knew something of the difficulty and the value of compression in prose. He seemed gratified by it, anyway.

"Good. Now let's try a different angle. I mentioned about 'building' a while back; well, look. Do you see where writing a story is building something too? Like building a house?" And he was so pleased with his own creation of this image that he didn't even wait to take in the careful, congratulatory nod I awarded him for it. "I mean a house has got to have a roof, but you're going to be in trouble if you build your roof first, right? Before you build your roof you got to build your walls. Before you build your walls you got to lay your foundation — and I mean all the way down the line. Before you lay your foundation you got to bulldoze and dig yourself the right kind of hole in the ground. Am I right?"

I couldn't have agreed with him more, but he was still ignoring my rapt, toadying gaze. He rubbed the flange of his nose with one wide knuckle; then he turned on me triumphantly again.

"So all right, supposing you build yourself a house like that. Then what? What's the first question you got to ask yourself about it when it's done?"

But I could tell he didn't care if I muffed this one or not. *He* knew what the question was, and he could hardly wait to tell me.

"Where are the windows?" he demanded, spreading his hands. "That's the question. Where does the light come in? Because do you see what I mean about the light coming in, Bob? I mean the — the *philosophy* of your story; the *truth* of it; the —"

"The illumination of it, sort of," I said, and he quit groping for his third noun with a profound and happy snap of the fingers.

"That's it. That's it, Bob. You got it."

It was a deal, and we had another ginger ale to clinch it as he thumbed through the idea file for my trial assignment. The "experience" he chose was the time Bernie Silver had saved a neurotic couple's marriage, right there in the cab, simply by sizing them up in his rear-view mirror as they quarreled and putting in a few well-chosen words of his own. Or at least, that was the general drift of it. All it actually said on the card was something like:

> High class man & wife (Park Ave.) start
> fighting in cab, very upset, lady starts
> yelling divorce. I watch them in rear
> view and put my 2 cents worth in & soon
> we are all laughing. Story about marriage, etc.

But Bernie expressed full confidence in my ability to work the thing out.

In the alcove, as he went through the elaborate business of getting my trench coat out of the closet and helping me on with it, I had time for a better look at the World War I photographs — a long company line-up, a number of framed yellow snapshots showing laughing men with their arms around each other, and one central picture of a lone bugler on a parade ground, with dusty barracks and a flag high in the distance. It could have been on the cover of an old American Legion magazine, with a caption like "Duty" — the perfect soldier, slim and straight at attention, and Gold Star Mothers would have wept over the way his fine young profile was pressed in manly reverence against the mouth of his simple, eloquent horn.

"I see you like my boy there," Bernie said fondly. "I bet you'd never guess who that boy is today."

Wade Manley? Dr. Alexander Corvo? Lionel Trilling? But I suppose I really did know, even before I glanced around at his blushing, beaming presence, that the boy was Bernie himself. And whether it sounds silly or not, I'll have to tell you that I felt a small but honest-to-God admiration for him. "Well, I'll be damned, Bernie. You look — you look pretty great there."

"Lot skinnier in those days, anyway," he said, slapping his silken paunch as he walked me to the door, and I remember looking down into his big, dumb, flabby face and trying to find the bugler's features somewhere inside it.

On my way home, rocking on the subway and faintly belching and tasting ginger ale, I grew increasingly aware that a writer could do a hell of a lot worse than to pull down twenty-five dollars for a couple of thousand words. It was very nearly half what I earned in forty miserable hours among the domestic corporate bonds and the sinking fund debentures; and if Bernie liked this first one, if I could go on doing one a week for him, it would be practically the same as getting a 50 per cent raise. Seventy-nine a week! With that kind of dough coming in, as well as the forty-six Joan brought home from her secretarial job, it would be no time at all before we had enough for Paris (and maybe we wouldn't meet any Gertrude Steins or Ezra Pounds there, maybe I wouldn't produce any *Sun Also Rises*, but the earliest possible expatriation was nothing less than essential to my Hemingway plans). Besides, it might even be fun — or at least, it might be fun to tell people about: I would be the hackie's hack, the builder's builder.

In any case I ran all the way down West Twelfth Street that night, and if I didn't burst in on her, laughing and shouting and clowning around, it was only because I forced myself to stand leaning against the mailboxes downstairs until I'd caught my breath and arranged my face into the urbane, amused expression I planned to use for telling her about it.

"Well, but who do you suppose is putting up all the money?" she asked. "It can't be out of his own pocket, can it? A cab driver couldn't afford to pay out twenty-five a week for any length of time, could he?"

It was one aspect of the thing that hadn't occurred to me — and it was just like her to come up with so dead-logical a question — but I did my best to override her with my own kind of cynical romanticism. "Who knows? Who the hell cares? Maybe Wade Manley's putting up the money. Maybe Dr. Whaddyacallit's putting it up. The point is, it's there."

"Well," she said, "good, then. How long do you think it'll take you to do the story?"

"Oh, hell, no time at all. I'll knock it off in a couple hours over the weekend."

But I didn't. I spent all Saturday afternoon and evening on one false start after another; I kept getting hung up in the dialogue of the quarreling couple, and in technical uncertainties about how much Bernie could really see of them in his rearview mirror, and in doubts about what any cab driver could possibly say at such a time without the man's telling him to shut up and keep his eyes on the road.

By Sunday afternoon I was walking around breaking pencils in half and throwing them into the wastebasket and saying the hell with it; the hell with everything; apparently I couldn't even be a God damn ghost writer for a God damn ignorant slob of a driver of a God damn taxicab.

"You're *trying* too hard," Joan said. "Oh, I knew this would happen. You're being so insufferably *literary* about it, Bob; it's ridiculous. All you have to do is think of every corny, tear-jerking thing you've ever read or heard. Think of Irving Berlin."

And I told her I'd give her Irving Berlin right in the mouth in about a minute, if she didn't lay off me and mind her own God damn business.

But late that night, as Irving Berlin himself might say, something kind of wonderful happened. I took that little bastard of a story and I built the hell out of it. First I bulldozed and dug and laid myself a real good foundation; then I got the lumber out and bang, bang, bang — up went the walls and on went the roof and up went the cute little chimney top. Oh, I put plenty of windows in it too — big, square ones — and when the light came pouring in it left no earthly shadow of a doubt that Bernie Silver was the wisest, gentlest, bravest and most lovable man who ever said "folks."

"It's perfect," Joan told me at breakfast, after she'd read the thing. "Oh, it's just perfect, Bob. I'm sure that's just exactly what he wants."

And it was. I'll never forget the way Bernie sat with his ginger ale in one hand and my trembling manuscript in the other, reading as I'd still be willing to bet he'd never read before, exploring all the snug and tidy wonders of the little home I'd built for him. I watched him discovering each of those windows, one after another, and saw his face made holy with their light. When he was finished he got up — we both got up — and he shook my hand.

"Beautiful," he said. "Bob, I had a feeling you'd do a good one, but I'll tell you the truth. I didn't know you'd do as good a one as this. Now you want your check, and I'll tell you something. You're not getting any check. For this you get cash."

Out came his trusty black cab driver's wallet. He thumbed through its contents, picked out a five-dollar bill and laid it in my hand. He evidently wanted to make a ceremony out of presenting me with one bill after another, so I stood smiling

down at it and waiting for the next one; and I was still standing there with my hand out when I looked up and saw him
putting the wallet away.

Five bucks! And even now I wish I could say that I shouted
this, or at least that I said it with some suggestion of the outrage that gripped my bowels — it might have saved an awful
amount of trouble later — but the truth is that it came out as
a very small, meek question: "Five bucks?"

"Right!" He was rocking happily back on his heels in the
carpet.

"Well, but Bernie, I mean what's the deal? I mean, you
showed me that check, and I —"

As his smile dwindled, his face looked as shocked and hurt
as if I'd spat into it. "Oh, Bob," he said. "Bob, what is this?
Look, let's not play any games here. I know I showed you that
check; I'll show you that check again." And the folds of his
sport shirt quivered in righteous indignation as he rummaged in
the credenza and brought it out.

It was the same check, all right. It still read twenty-five dollars and no cents; but Bernie's cramped scribbling on the other
side, above the other man's signature and all mixed up with the
bank's rubber stamp, was now legible as hell. What it said,
of course, was: "In full advance payment, five write-ups."

So I hadn't really been robbed — conned a little, maybe,
that's all — and therefore my main problem now, the sick,
ginger-ale-flavored feeling that I was certain Ernest Hemingway could never in his life have known, was my own sense of
being a fool.

"Am I right or wrong, Bob?" he was asking. "Am I right or
wrong?" And then he sat me down again and did his smiling
best to set me straight. How could I possibly have thought he
meant twenty-five a time? Did I have any idea what kind of
money a hackie took home? Oh, some of your owner-drivers,
maybe it was a different story; but your average hackie? Your
fleet hackie? Forty, forty-five; maybe sometimes fifty a week

if they were lucky. Even for a man like himself, with no kids and a wife working full time at the telephone company, it was no picnic. I could ask any hackie if I didn't believe him; it was no picnic. "And I mean you don't think anybody *else* is picking up the tab for these write-ups, do you? Do you?" He looked at me incredulously, almost ready to laugh, as if the very idea of my thinking such a thing would remove all reasonable doubt about my having been born yesterday.

"Bob, I'm sorry there was any misunderstanding here," he said, walking me to the door, "but I'm glad we're straight on it now. Because I mean it, that's a beautiful piece you wrote, and I've got a feeling it's going to go places. Tell you what, Bob, I'll be in touch with you later this week, okay?"

And I remember despising myself because I didn't have the guts to tell him not to bother, any more than I could shake off the heavy, fatherly hand that rode on my neck as we walked. In the alcove, out in front of the young bugler again, I had a sudden, disturbing notion that I could foretell an exchange of dialogue that was about to take place. I would say, "Bernie, were you really a bugler in the army, or was that just for the picture?"

And with no trace of embarrassment, without the faintest flickering change in his guileless smile, he would say, "Just for the picture."

Worse still: I knew that the campaign-hatted head of the bugler himself would turn then, that the fine tense profile in the photograph would slowly loosen and turn away from the mouthpiece of a horn through which its dumb, no-talent lips could never have blown a fart, and that it would wink at me. So I didn't risk it. I just said, "See you, Bernie," and got the hell out of there and went home.

Joan's reaction to the news was surprisingly gentle. I don't mean she was "kind" to me about it, which would have damn near killed me in the shape I was in that night; it was more that she was kind to Bernie.

Poor, lost, brave little man, dreaming his huge and unlikely dream — that kind of thing. And could I imagine what it must have cost him over the years? How many of these miserably hard-earned five-dollar payments he must have dropped down the bottomless maw of second- and third- and tenth-rate amateur writers' needs? How lucky for him, then, through whatever dissemblings with his canceled check, to have made contact with a first-rate professional at last. And how touching, and how "sweet," that he had recognized the difference by saying, "For this you get cash."

"Well, but for Christ's sake," I told her, grateful that it could for once be me instead of her who thought in terms of the deadly practicalities, "For Christ's sake, you know *why* he gave me cash, don't you? Because he's going to sell that story to the *Reader's* God damn *Digest* next week for a hundred and fifty thousand dollars, and because if I had a photostated check to prove I wrote it he'd be in trouble, that's why."

"Would you like to bet?" she inquired, looking at me with her lovely, truly unforgettable mixture of pity and pride. "Would you like to bet that if he does sell it, to the *Reader's Digest* or anywhere else, he'll insist on giving you half?"

"Bob Prentice?" said a happy voice on the telephone, three nights later. "Bernie Silver. Bob, I've just come from Dr. Alexander Corvo's home, and listen. I'm not going to tell you *what* he told me, but I'll tell you this. Dr. Alexander Corvo thinks you're pretty good."

Whatever reply I made to this — "Does he really?" or "You mean he really likes it?" — it was something bashful and telling enough to bring Joan instantly to my side, all smiles. I remember the way she plucked at my shirtsleeve as if to say, There — what did I tell you? And I had to brush her away and wag my hand to keep her quiet during the rest of the talk.

"He wants to show it to a couple of his connections in the publishing field," Bernie was saying, "and he wants me to get another copy made up to send out to Manny on the Coast. So listen, Bob, while we're waiting to see what happens on this one, I want to give you some more assignments. Or wait — listen." And his voice became enriched with the dawning of a new idea. "Listen. Maybe you'd be more comfortable working on your own. Would you rather do that? Would you rather just skip the card file, and use your own imagination?"

Late one rainy night, deep in the upper West Side, two thugs got into Bernie Silver's cab. To the casual eye they might have looked like ordinary customers, but Bernie had them spotted right away because "Take it from me, a man doesn't hack the streets of Manhattan for twenty-two years without a little specialized education rubbing off."

One was a hardened-criminal type, of course, and the other was little more than a frightened boy, or rather "just a punk."

"I didn't like the way they were talking," Bernie told his readers through me, "and I didn't like the address they gave me — the lowest dive in town — and most of all I didn't like the fact that they were riding in my automobile."

So do you know what he did? Oh, don't worry, he didn't stop the cab and step around and pull them out of the back seat and kick them one after the other in the groin — none of that *My-Flag-Is-Down* nonsense. For one thing, he could tell from their talk that they weren't making a getaway; not tonight, at least. All they'd done tonight was case the joint (a small liquor store near the corner where he'd picked them up); the job was set for tomorrow night at eleven. Anyway, when they got to the lowest dive in town the hardened criminal gave the punk some money and said, "Here, kid; you keep the cab, go on home and get some sleep. I'll see you tomorow." And that was when Bernie knew what he had to do.

"That punk lived way out in Queens, which gave us plenty of time for conversation, so I asked him who he liked for the National League pennant." And from there on, with deep folk wisdom and consummate skill, Bernie kept up such a steady flow of talk about healthy, clean-living, milk-and-sunshine topics that he'd begun to draw the boy out of his hard delinquent shell even before they hit the Queensboro Bridge. They barreled along Queens Boulevard chattering like a pair of Police Athletic League enthusiasts, and by the time the ride was over, Bernie's fare was practically in tears.

"I saw him swallow a couple of times when he paid me off" was the way I had Bernie put it, "and I had a feeling something had changed in that kid. I had a hope of it, anyway, or maybe just a wish. But I knew I'd done all I could for him." Back in town, Bernie called the police and suggested they put a couple of men around the liquor store the following night.

Sure enough, a job was attempted on that liquor store, only to be foiled by two tough, lovable cops. And sure enough, there was only one thug for them to carry off to the pokey — the hardened-criminal one. "I don't know where the kid was that night," Bernie concluded, "but I like to think he was home in bed with a glass of milk, reading the sports page."

There was the roof and there was the chimney top of it; there were all the windows with the light coming in; there was another approving chuckle from Dr. Alexander Corvo and another submission to the *Reader's Digest*; there was another whisper of a chance for a Simon and Schuster contract and a three-million-dollar production starring Wade Manley; and there was another five in the mail for me.

A small, fragile old gentleman started crying in the cab one day, up around Fifty-ninth and Third, and when Bernie said, "Anything I can help with, sir?" there followed two and a half pages of the most heart-tearing hard-luck story I could imagine. He was a widower; his only daughter had long since married and moved away to Flint, Michigan; his life had been an agony of loneliness for twenty-two years, but he'd always been brave enough about it until now because he'd had a job he loved — tending the geraniums in a big commercial green-house. And now this morning the management had told him he would have to go: too old for that kind of work.

"And only then," according to Bernie Silver, "did I make the connection between all this and the address he'd given me — a corner near the Manhattan side of the Brooklyn Bridge."

Bernie couldn't be sure, of course, that his fare planned to hobble right on out to the middle of the bridge and ease his old bones over the railing; but he couldn't take any chances, either. "I figured it was time for me to do some talking" (and he was right about that: another heavy half-page of that tire-some old man's lament and the story would have ruptured the hell out of its foundation). What came next was a brisk page and a half of dialogue in which Bernie discreetly inquired why the old man didn't go and live with his daughter in Michigan, or at least write her a letter so that maybe she'd invite him; but oh, no, he only keened that he couldn't possibly be a bur-den on his daughter and her family.

" 'Burden?' I said, acting like I didn't know what he meant. 'Burden? How could a nice old gentleman like you be a burden on anybody?' "

" 'But what else would I be? What can *I* offer them?' "

"Luckily we were stopped at a red light when he asked me that, so I turned around and looked him straight in the eye. 'Mister,' I said, 'don't you think that family'd like having some-body around the place that knows a thing or two about growing geraniums?' "

Well, by the time they got to the bridge the old man had decided to have Bernie let him off at a nearby Automat instead, because he said he felt like having a cup of tea, and so much for the walls of the damn thing. This was the roof: Six months later, Bernie received a small, heavy package with a Flint, Michigan, postmark, addressed to his taxi fleet garage. And do you know what was in that package? Of course you do. A potted geranium. And here's your chimney top: There was also a little note, written in what I'm afraid I really did describe as a fine old spidery hand, and it read, simply, "Thank you."

Personally, I thought this one was loathsome, and Joan wasn't sure about it either; but we mailed it off anyway and Bernie loved it. And so, he told me over the phone, did his wife Rose.

"Which reminds me, Bob, the other reason I called; Rose wants me to find out what evening you and your wife could come up for a little get-together here. Nothing fancy, just the four of us, have a little drink and a chat. You think you might enjoy that?"

"Well, that's very nice of you, Bernie, and of course we'd enjoy it very much. It's just that offhand I don't quite know when we could arrange to — hold on a second." And I covered the mouthpiece and had an urgent conference about it with Joan in the hope that she'd supply me with a graceful excuse.

But she wanted to go, and she had just the right evening in mind, so all four of us were hooked.

"Oh, good," she said when I'd hung up. "I'm glad we're going. They sound sweet."

"Now, *look.*" And I aimed my index finger straight at her face. "We're not going at all if you plan to sit around up there making them both aware of how 'sweet' they are. I'm not spending any evenings as gracious Lady Bountiful's consort among the lower classes, and that's final. If you want to turn this thing into some goddamn Bennington girls' garden party for the servants, you can forget about it right now. You hear me?"

Then she asked me if I wanted to know something, and without waiting to find out whether I did or not, she told me. She told me I was just about the biggest snob and biggest bully and biggest all-around loud-mouthed jerk she'd ever come across in her life.

One thing led to another after that; by the time we were on

the subway for our enjoyable get-together with the Silvers we were only barely on speaking terms, and I can't tell you how grateful I was to find that the Silvers, while staying on ginger ale themselves, had broken out a bottle of rye for their guests.

Bernie's wife turned out to be a quick, spike-heeled, girdled and bobby-pinned woman whose telephone operator's voice was chillingly expert at the social graces ("How do you do? So nice to meet you; do come in; please sit down; Bernie, help her, she can't get her coat off"); and God knows who started it, or why, but the evening began uncomfortably with a discussion of politics. Joan and I were torn between Truman, Wallace, and not voting at all that year; the Silvers were Dewey people. And what made it all the worse, for our tender liberal sensibilities, was that Rose sought common ground by telling us one bleak tale after another, each with a more elaborate shudder, about the inexorable, menacing encroachment of colored and Puerto Rican elements in this part of the Bronx.

But things got jollier after a while. For one thing they were both delighted with Joan — and I'll have to admit I never met anyone who wasn't — and for another the talk soon turned to the marvelous fact of their knowing Wade Manley, which gave rise to a series of proud reminiscences. "Bernie never takes nothing off him, though, don't worry," Rose assured us. "Bernie, tell them what you did that time he was here and you told him to sit down and shut up. He did! He did! He kind of gave him a push in the chest — this *movie* star! — and he said, 'Ah, siddown and sheddep, Manny. *We* know who you are!' Tell them, Bernie."

And Bernie, convulsed with pleasure, got up to reenact the scene. "Oh, we were just kind of kidding around, you understand," he said, "but anyway, that's what I did. I gave him a shove like this, and I said, 'Ah, siddown and sheddep, Manny. *We* know who you are!'"

"He did! That's the God's truth! Pushed him right down in that chair over there! Wade Manley!"

A little later, when Bernie and I had paired off for a man-to-man talk over the freshening of drinks, and Rose and Joan were cozily settled in the love seat, Rose directed a roguish glance at me. "I wouldn't want to give this husband of yours a swelled head, Joanie, but do you know what Dr. Corvo told Bernie? Shall I tell her, Bernie?"

"Sure, tell her! Tell her!" And Bernie waved the bottle of ginger ale in one hand and the bottle of rye in the other, to show how openly all secrets could be bared tonight.

"Well," she said. "Dr. Corvo said your husband is the finest writer Bernie's ever had."

Later still, when Bernie and I were in the love seat and the ladies were at the credenza, I began to see that Rose was a builder too. Maybe she hadn't built that credenza with her own hands, but she'd clearly done more than her share of building whatever heartfelt convictions were needed to sustain the hundreds on hundreds of dollars its purchase must be costing them on the installment plan. A piece of furniture like that was an investment in the future; and now, as she stood fussing over it and wiping off little parts of it while she talked to Joan, I could have sworn I saw her arranging a future party in her mind. Joan and I would be among those present, that much was certain ("This is Mr. Robert Prentice, my husband's assistant, and Mrs. Prentice"), and the rest of the guest list was almost a foregone conclusion too: Wade Manley and his wife, of course, along with a careful selection of their Hollywood friends; Walter Winchell would be there, and Earl Wilson and Toots Shor and all that crowd; but far more important, for any person of refinement, would be the presence of Dr. and Mrs. Alexander Corvo and some of the people who comprised their set. People like the Lionel Trillings and the Reinhold Niebuhrs, the Huntington Hartfords and the Leslie R. Groveses — and if anybody on the order of Mr. and Mrs. Newbold Morris wanted to come, you could be damn sure they'd have to do some pretty fancy jockeying for an invitation.

It was, as Joan admitted later, stifling hot in the Silver's apartment that night; and I cite this as a presentable excuse for the fact that what I did next — and it took me a hell of a lot less time to do it in 1948 than it does now, believe me — was to get roaring drunk. Soon I was not only the most vociferous but the only talker in the room; I was explaining that, by Jesus God, we'd all four of us be millionaires yet.

And wouldn't we have a ball? Oh, we'd be slapping Lionel Trilling around and pushing him down into every chair in this room and telling him to shut up — "And you too, Reinhold Niebuhr, you pompous, sanctimonious old fool! Where's *your* money? Why don't you put your money where your mouth is?"

Bernie was chuckling and looking sleepy, and Joan was looking humiliated for me, and Rose was smiling in cool but infinite understanding of how tiresome husbands could sometimes be. Then we were all out in the alcove trying on at least a half a dozen coats apiece, and I was looking at the bugler's photograph again wondering if I dared to ask my burning question about it. But this time I wasn't sure which I feared more: that Bernie might say, "Just for the picture," or that he might say, "Sure I was!" and go rummaging in the closet or in some part of the credenza until he'd come up with the tarnished old bugle itself, and we'd all have to go back and sit down again while Bernie put his heels together, drew himself erect, and sounded the pure, sad melody of Taps for us all.

That was in October. I'm a little vague on how many "By Bernie Silver" stories I turned out during the rest of the fall. I do remember a comic-relief one about a fat tourist who got stuck at the waist when he tried to climb up through the skyview window of the cab for better sight-seeing, and a very solemn one in which Bernie delivered a lecture on racial tolerance (which struck a sour note with me, considering the way he'd chimed in with Rose's views on the brown hordes advancing over the Bronx); but mostly what I remember about him during that period is that Joan and I could never seem to mention him without getting into some kind of an argument.

When she said we really ought to return his and Rose's invitation, for example, I told her not to be silly. I said I was sure they wouldn't expect it, and when she said "Why?" I gave her a crisp, impatient briefing on the hopelessness of trying to ignore class barriers, of pretending that the Silvers could ever really become our friends, or that they'd ever really want to.

Another time, toward the end of a curiously dull evening when we'd gone to our favorite premarital restaurant and failed for an hour to find anything to talk about, she tried to get the conversation going by leaning romantically toward me across the table and holding up her wineglass. "Here's to Bernie's selling your last one to the *Reader's Digest*."

"Yeah," I said. "Sure. Big deal."

"Oh, don't be so gruff. You know perfectly well it could happen any day. We might make a lot of money and go to Europe and everything."

"Are you kidding?" It suddenly annoyed me that any intelligent, well-educated girl in the twentieth century could be so gullible; and that such a girl should actually be my wife, that I would be expected to go on playing along with this kind of simple-minded innocence for years and years to come, seemed, for the moment, an intolerable situation. "Why don't you grow up a little? You don't really think there's ever been a chance of his selling that junk, do you?" And I looked at her in a way that must have been very much like Bernie's own way of looking at me, the night he asked if I'd really thought he meant twenty-five a time. "Do you?"

"Yes, I do," she said, putting her glass down. "Or at least, I did. I thought you did too. If you don't, it seems sort of cynical and dishonest to go on working for him, doesn't it?" And she wouldn't talk to me all the way home.

The real trouble, I guess, was that we were both preoccupied with two far more serious matters by this time. One was our recent discovery that Joan was pregnant, and the other was that my position at the United Press had begun to sink as steadily as any sinking fund debenture.

My time on the financial desk had become a slow ordeal of waiting for my superiors to discover more and more of how little I knew about what I was doing; and now however pathetically willing I might be to learn all the things I was supposed to know, it had become much too ludicrously late to ask. I was hunching lower and lower over my clattering typewriter there all day and sweating out the ax — the kind, sad dropping of the assistant financial editor's hand on my shoulder ("Can I speak to you inside a minute, Bob?") — and each day that it didn't happen was a kind of shabby victory.

Early in December I was walking home from the subway after one of those days, dragging myself down West Twelfth Street like a seventy-year-old, when I discovered that a taxicab had been moving beside me at a snail's pace for a block and a half. It was one of the green-and-white kind, and behind its windshield flashed an enormous smile.

"Bob! What's the matter, there, Bob? You lost in thought or something? This where you live?"

When he parked the cab at the curb and got out, it was the first time I'd even seen him in his working clothes: a twill cap, a buttoned sweater and one of those columnar change-making gadgets strapped to his waist; and when we shook hands it was the first time I'd seen his fingertips stained a shiny gray from handling other people's coins and dollar bills all day. Close up, smiling or not, he looked as worn out as I felt.

"Come on in, Bernie." He seemed surprised by the crumbling doorway and dirty stairs of the house, and also by the whitewashed, poster-decorated austerity of our big single room, whose rent was probably less than half of what he and Rose were paying uptown, and I remember taking a dim Bohemian's pride in letting him notice these things; I guess I had some snobbish notion that it wouldn't do Bernie Silver any harm to learn that people could be smart and poor at the same time.

We couldn't offer him any ginger ale and he said a glass of plain water would be fine, so it wasn't much of a social occasion. It troubled me afterwards to remember how constrained he was with Joan — I don't think he looked her full in the face once during the whole visit — and I wondered if this was because of our failure to return that invitation. Why is it that wives are nearly always blamed for what must at least as often as not be their husbands' fault in matters like that? But maybe it was just that he was more conscious of his cab driver's costume in her presence than in mine. Or maybe he had never imagined that such a pretty and cultivated girl could live in such stark surroundings, and was embarrassed for her.

"I'll tell you what I dropped by about, Bob. I'm trying a new angle." And as he talked I began to suspect, more from his eyes than his words, that something had gone very wrong with the long-range building program. Maybe a publishing friend of Dr. Corvo's had laid it on the line at last about the poor possibilities of our material; maybe Dr. Corvo himself had grown snappish; maybe there had been some crushing final communication from Wade Manley, or, more crushingly, from Wade Manley's agency representative. Or it might have been simply that Bernie was tired after his day's work in a way that no glass of plain water would help; in any case he was trying a new angle.

Had I ever heard of Vincent J. Poletti? But he gave me this name as if he knew perfectly well it wouldn't knock my eye out, and he followed it right up with the information that Vincent J. Poletti was a Democratic State Assemblyman from Bernie's own district in the Bronx.

"Now, this man," he said, "is a man that goes out of his way to help people. Believe me, Bob, he's not just one of your cheap vote-getters. He's a real public servant. What's more, he's a comer in the Party. He's going to be our next Congressman. So here's the idea, Bob. We get a photograph of me — I have this friend of mine'll do it for nothing — we get it taken from the back seat of the cab, with me at the wheel kind of turning around and smiling like this, get it?" He turned his body away from his smiling head to show me how it would look. "And we print this picture on the cover of a booklet. The title of the booklet —" and here he sketched a suggestion of block lettering in the air — "the title of the booklet is 'Take It from Bernie.' Okay? Now. Inside the booklet we have a story — just exactly like the others you wrote except this time it's a little different. This time I'm telling a story about why Vincent J. Poletti is the man we need for Congress. I don't mean just a bunch of political talk, either, Bob. I mean a real little story."

"Bernie, I don't see how this is going to work. You can't have a 'story' about why anybody is the man we need for Congress."

"Who says you can't?"

"And anyway I thought you and Rose were Republicans."

"On the national level, yes. On the local level, no."

"Well, but hell, Bernie, we just had an election. There won't be another election for two years."

But he only tapped his head and made a faraway gesture to show that in politics it paid a man to think ahead.

Joan was over in the kitchen area of the room, cleaning up the breakfast dishes and getting the dinner started, and I looked to her for help, but her back was turned.

"It just doesn't sound right, Bernie. I don't know anything about politics."

"So? Know, schmow. What's to know? Do you know anything about driving a cab?"

No; and I sure as hell didn't know anything about Wall Street, either — Wall Street, Schmall Street! — but that was another depressing little story. "I don't know, Bernie; things are very unsettled right now. I don't think I'd better take on any more assignments for the time being. I mean for one thing I may be about to —" but I couldn't bring myself to tell him about my

UP problem, so I said, "For one thing Joan's having a baby now, and everything's sort of —"

"Wow! Well, isn't that something!" He was on his feet and shaking my hand. "Isn't — that — something! Congratulations, Bob, I think this is — I think this is really wonderful. Congratulations, there, Joanie!" And it seemed a little excessive to me at the time, but maybe that's the way such news will always strike a middle-aged, childless man.

"Oh, listen, Bob," he said when we settled down again. "This Poletti thing'll be duck soup for you; and I'll tell you what. Seeing as this is just a one-shot and there won't be any royalties, we'll make it ten instead of five. Is that a deal?"

"Well, but wait a second, Bernie. I'm going to need some more information. I mean what exactly does this guy do for people?"

And it soon became clear that Bernie knew very little more about Vincent J. Poletti than I did. He was a real public servant, that was all; he went out of his way to help people. "Oh, Bob, listen. What's the difference? Where's your imagination? You never needed any help before. Listen. What you just told me gives me one idea right off the bat. I'm driving along; these two kids hail me out in front of the maternity hospital, this young veteran and his wife. They got this little-biddy baby, three days old, and they're happy as larks. Only here's the trouble. This boy's got no job or anything. They only just moved here, they don't know anybody, maybe they're Puerto Ricans or something, they got a week's rent on their room and that's it. Then they're broke. So I'm taking them home, they live right in my neighborhood, and we're chatting away, and I say, 'Listen, kids. I think I'll take you to see a friend of mine.'"

"Assemblyman Vincent J. Poletti."

"Naturally. Only I don't tell them his name yet. I just say, 'this friend of mine.' So we get there and I go in and tell Poletti about it and he comes out and talks to the kids and gives them money or something. See? You got a good share of your story right there."

"Hey, yeah, and wait a minute, Bernie." I got up and began dramatically pacing the floor, the way people in Hollywood story conferences are supposed to do. "Wait a minute. After he gives them money, he gets into your cab and you take off with him down the Grand Concourse, and those two Puerto Rican kids are standing there on the sidewalk kind of looking at each other, and the girl says, 'Who *was* that man?' And the boy looks very serious and he says, 'Honey, don't you know? Didn't you notice he was wearing a mask?' And she says, 'Oh no, it couldn't be the —' And he says 'Yes, yes, it was. Honey, that was the Lone Assemblyman.' And then listen! You know what happens next? Listen! Way off down the block they hear this voice, and you know what the voice is calling?" I sank to the floor on one trembling knee to deliver the punch line. "It's calling 'Hi-yo, Bernie *Silver* — away!' "

And it may not look very funny written down, but it almost killed me. I must have laughed for at least a minute, until I went into a coughing fit and Joan had to come and pound me on the back; only very gradually, coming out of it, did I realize that Bernie was not amused. He had chuckled in bewildered politeness during my seizure, but now he was looking down at his hands and there were embarrassing blotches of pink in his sober cheeks. I had hurt his feelings. I remember resenting it that his feelings could be hurt so easily, and resenting it that Joan had gone back to the kitchen instead of staying to help me out of this awkward situation, and then beginning to feel very guilty and sorry, as the silence continued, until I finally decided that the only decent way of making it up to him was to accept the assignment. And sure enough, he brightened instantly when I told him I'd give it a try.

"I mean you don't necessarily have to use that about the Puerto Rican kids," he assured me. "That's just one idea. Or maybe you could start it off that way and then go on to other things, the more the better. You work it out any way you like."

At the door, shaking hands again (and it seemed that we'd been shaking hands all afternoon), I said, "So that's ten for this one, right, Bernie?"

"Right, Bob."

"Do you really think you should have told him you'd do it?" Joan asked me the minute he'd gone.

"Why not?"

"Well, because it *is* going to be practically impossible, isn't it?"

"Look, will you do me a favor? Will you please get off my back?"

She put her hands on her hips. "I just don't understand you, Bob. Why *did* you say you'd do it?"

"Why the hell do you think? Because we're going to need the ten bucks, that's why."

In the end I built — oh, built, schmilt. I put page one and then page two and then page three into the old machine and I *wrote* the son of a bitch. It did start off with the Puerto Rican kids, but for some reason I couldn't get more than a couple of pages out of them; then I had to find other ways for Vincent J. Poletti to demonstrate his giant goodness.

What does a public servant do when he really wants to go out of his way to help people? Gives them money, that's what he does; and pretty soon I had Poletti forking over more than he could count. It got so that anybody in the Bronx who was even faintly up against it had only to climb into Bernie Silver's cab and say, "The Poletti place," and their troubles were over. And the worst part of it was my own grim conviction that it was the best I could do.

Joan never saw the thing, because she was asleep when I finally managed to get it into an envelope and into the mail. And there was no word from Bernie — or about him, between the two of us — for nearly a week. Then, at the same hour as his last visit, the frayed-out end of the day, our doorbell rang. I knew there was going to be trouble as soon as I opened the door and found him smiling there, with spatters of rain on his sweater, and I knew I wasn't going to stand for any nonsense.

"Bob," he said, sitting down, "I hate to say it, but I'm disappointed in you this time." He pulled my folded manuscript out of his sweater. "This thing is — Bob, this is nothing."

"It's six and a half pages. That's not nothing, Bernie."

"Bob, please don't give me six and a half pages. I know it's six and a half pages, but it's nothing. You made this man into a fool, Bob. You got him giving his dough away all the time."

"You told me he gave dough, Bernie."

"To the Puerto Rican kids I said yes, sure, maybe he could give a little, fine. And now you come along and you got him going around spending here like some kind of — some kind of drunken sailor or something."

I thought I might be going to cry, but my voice came out very low and controlled. "Bernie, I did ask you what else he could do. I did tell you I didn't know what the hell else he could do. If you wanted him to do something else, you should've made that clear."

"But *Bob*," he said, standing up for emphasis, and his next words have often come back to me as the final, despairing, everlasting cry of the Philistine. "Bob, *you're* the one with the imagination!"

I stood up too, so that I could look down at him. I knew I was the one with the imagination. I also knew I was twenty-two years old and as tired as an old man, that I was about to lose my job, that I had a baby on the way and wasn't even getting along very well with my wife; and now every cab driver, every two-bit politician's pimp and phony bugler in the city of New York was walking into my house and trying to steal my money.

"Ten bucks, Bernie."

He made a helpless gesture, smiling. Then he looked over

into the kitchen area, where Joan was, and although I meant to keep my eyes on him, I must have looked there too, because I remember what she was doing. She was twisting a dish towel in her hands and looking down at it.

"Listen, Bob," he said. "I shouldn't of said it was nothing. You're right! Who could take a thing six and a half pages long and say it's nothing? Probably a lot of good stuff in this thing, Bob. You want your ten bucks; all right, fine, you'll get your ten bucks. All I'm asking is this. First take this thing back and change it a little, that's all. Then we can —"

"Ten bucks, Bernie. Now."

His smile had lost its life, but it stayed right there on his face while he took the bill out of his wallet and handed it over, and while I went through a miserable little show of examining it to make God damn sure it was a ten.

"Okay, Bob," he said. "We're all square, then. Right?"

"Right."

Then he was gone, and Joan went swiftly to the door and opened it and called, "Goodnight, Bernie!"

I thought I heard his footsteps pause on the stairs, but I didn't hear any answering "Goodnight" from him, so I guessed that all he'd done was to turn around and wave to her, or blow her a kiss. Then from the window I saw him move out across the sidewalk and get into his taxicab and drive away. All this time I was folding and refolding his money, and I don't believe I've ever held anything in my hand that I wanted less.

The room was very quiet with only the two of us moving around in it, while the kitchen area steamed and crackled with the savory smells of a dinner that I don't think either of us felt like eating. "Well," I said. "That's that."

"Was it really necessary," she inquired, "to be so dreadfully unpleasant to him?"

And this, at the time, seemed clearly to be the least loyal possible thing she could have said, the unkindest cut of all. "Un*pleasant* to him! Un*pleasant* to him! Would you mind telling me just what the hell I'm supposed to do? Am I supposed to sit around being 'pleasant' while some cheap, lying little parasitic leech of a *cab* driver comes in here and bleeds me *white*? Is that what you want? Huh? Is *that* what you want?"

Then she did what she often used to do at moments like that, what I sometimes think I'd give anything in life never to have seen her do: she turned away from me and closed her eyes and covered her ears with both hands.

Less than a week later the assistant financial editor's hand did fall on my shoulder at last, right in the middle of a paragraph about domestic corporate bonds in moderately active trading.

It was still well before Christmas, and I got a job to tide us over as a demonstrator of mechanical toys in a Fifth Avenue dimestore. And I think it must have been during that dimestore period — possibly while winding up a little tin-and-cotton kitten that went "Mew!" and rolled over, "Mew!" and rolled over, "Mew!" and rolled over — it was along in there sometime, anyway, that I gave up whatever was left of the idea of building my life on the pattern of Ernest Hemingway's. Some construction projects are just plain out of the question.

After New Year's I got some other idiot job; then in April, with all the abruptness and surprise of spring, I was hired for eighty dollars a week as a writer in an industrial public-relations office, where the question of whether or not I knew what I was doing never mattered very much because hardly any of the other employees knew what they were doing either.

It was a remarkably easy job, and it allowed me to save a remarkable amount of energy each day for my own work, which all at once began to go well. With Hemingway safely abandoned, I had moved on to an F. Scott Fitzgerald phase; then, the best of all, I had begun to find what seemed to give every indication of being my own style. The winter was over, and things seemed to be growing easier between Joan and me too, and in the early summer our first daughter was born.

She caused a one- or two-month interruption in my writing schedule, but before long I was back at work and convinced that I was going from strength to strength: I had begun to bulldoze and dig and lay the foundation for a big, ambitious, tragic novel. I never did finish the book — it was the first in a series of more unfinished novels than I like to think about now — but in those early stages it was fascinating work, and the fact that it went slowly seemed only to add to its promise of eventual magnificence. I was spending more and more time each night behind my writing screen, emerging only to pace the floor with a headful of serene and majestic daydreams. And it was late in the year, all the way around to fall again, one evening when Joan had gone out to the movies, leaving me as baby-sitter, when I came out from behind the screen to pick up a ringing phone and heard: "Bob Prentice? Bernie Silver."

I won't pretend that I'd forgotten who he was, but it's not too much to say that for a second or two I did have trouble realizing that I'd ever really worked for him — that I could ever really have been involved, at first hand, in the pathetic delusions of a taxicab driver. It gave me pause, which is to say that it caused me to wince and then to sheepishly grin at the phone, to duck my head and smooth my hair with my free hand in a bashful demonstration of *noblesse oblige* — this accompanied by a silent, humble vow that whatever Bernie Silver might want from me now, I would go out of my way to avoid any chance of hurting his feelings. I remember wishing Joan were home, so that she could witness my kindness.

But the first thing he wanted to know about was the baby. Was it a boy or a girl? Wonderful! And who did she look like? Well, of course, naturally, they never did look like anybody much at that age. And how did it feel to be a father? Huh? Feel pretty good? Good! Then he took on what struck me as a strangely formal, cap-holding tone, like that of a long-discharged servant inquiring after the lady of the house. "And how's Mrs. Prentice?"

She had been "Joan" and "Joanie" and "Sweetheart" to him in his own home, and I somehow couldn't believe he'd forgotten her name; I could only guess that he hadn't heard her call out to him on the stairs that night after all — that maybe, remembering only the way she'd stood there with her dish towel, he had even blamed her as the instigator of my own intransigence over the damned ten bucks. But all I could do now was to tell him she was fine. "And how've you people been, Bernie?"

"Well," he said, "*I've* been all right," and here his voice fell to the shocked sobriety of hospital-room conferences. "But I almost lost Rose, a couple of months back."

Oh, it was okay now, he assured me, she was much better and home from the hospital and feeling well; but when he started talking about "tests" and "radiology" I had the awful sense of doom that comes when the unmentionable name of cancer hangs in the air.

"Well, Bernie," I said, "I'm terribly sorry she's been ill, and please be sure to give her our —"

Give here our what? Regards? Best wishes? Either one, it suddenly seemed to me, would carry the unforgivable taint of condecension. "Give her our love," I said, and immediately chewed my lip in fear that this might sound the most condescending of all.

"I will! I will! I'll certainly do that for you, Bob," he said, and so I was glad I'd put it that way. "And now, what I called you about is this." And he chuckled. "Oh, don't worry, no politics. Here's the thing. I've got this really terrifically talented boy working for me now, Bob. This boy's an artist."

And great God, what a sickly, intricate thing a writer's heart is! Because do you know what I felt when he said that? I felt a twinge of jealousy. "Artist," was he? I'd show them who the hell the artist was around *this* little writing establishment.

But right away Bernie started talking about "strips" and

"layouts," so I was able to retire my competitive zeal in favor of the old, reliable ironic detachment. What a relief!

"Oh, an *artist*, you mean. A *comic*-strip artist."

"Right. Bob, you ought to see the way this boy can draw. You know what he does? He makes me look like me, but he makes me look a little bit like Wade Manley too. Do you get the picture?"

"It sounds fine, Bernie." And now that the old detachment was working again, I could see that I'd have to be on my guard. Maybe he wouldn't be needing any more stories — by now he probably had a whole credenzaful of manuscripts for the artist to work from — but he'd still be needing a writer to do the "continuity," or whatever it's called, and the words for the artist's speech balloons, and I would now have to tell him, as gently and gracefully as possible, that it wasn't going to be me.

"Bob," he said, "this thing is really building. Dr. Corvo took one look at these strips and he said to me, 'Bernie, forget the magazine business, forget the book business. You've found the solution.'"

"Well. It certainly does sound good, Bernie."

"And Bob, here's why I called. I know they keep you pretty busy down there at the UP, but I was wondering if you might have time to do a little —"

"I'm not working for the UP any more, Bernie." And I told him about the publicity job.

"Well," he said. "That sounds like you're really coming up in the world there, Bob. Congratulations."

"Thanks. Anyway, Bernie, the point is I really don't think I'd have time to do any writing for you just now. I mean I'd certainly like to, it isn't that; it's just that the baby does take up a lot of time here, and then I've got my own work going — I'm doing a novel now, you see — and I really don't think I'd better take on anything else."

"Oh. Well, okay, then, Bob; don't worry about it. All I meant, you see, is that it really would've been a break for us if we could of made use of your — *you* know, your writing talent in this thing."

"I'm sorry too, Bernie, and I certainly do wish you luck with it."

You may well have guessed by now what didn't occur to me, I swear, until at least an hour after I'd said goodbye to him: that this time Bernie hadn't wanted me as a writer at all. He'd thought I was still at the UP, and might therefore be a valuable contact close to the heart of the syndicated comic-strip business.

I can remember exactly what I was doing when this knowledge came over me. I was changing the baby's diaper, looking down into her round, beautiful eyes as if I expected her to congratulate me, or thank me, for having once more managed to avoid the terrible possibility of touching her skin with the point of the safety pin — I was doing that, when I thought of the way his voice had paused in saying, "We could of made use of your —"

During that pause he must have abandoned whatever elaborate building plans might still have lain in saying, "your connections there at the UP" (and he didn't know I'd been fired; for all he knew I might still have as many solid connections in the newspaper business as Dr. Corvo had in the child psychology field or Wade Manley had in the movies), and had chosen to finish it off with "your writing talent" instead. And so I knew that for all my finicking concern over the sparing of Bernie's feelings in that telephone conversation, it was Bernie, in the end, who had gone out of his way to spare mine.

I can't honestly say that I've thought very much about him over the years. It might be a nice touch to tell you that I never get into a taxicab without taking a close look at the driver's neck and profile, but it wouldn't be true. One thing that is true, though, and it's just now occurred to me, is that very often in trying to hit on the right wording for some touchy personal letter, I've thought of: "I didn't have time to write you a short letter today, so I had to write you a long one instead."

Whether I meant it or not when I wished him luck with his comic strip, I think I started meaning it an hour later. I mean it now, wholeheartedly, and the funny part is that he might still be able to build it into something, connections or not. Sillier things than that have built empires in America. At any rate I hope he hasn't lost his interest in the project, in one form or another; but more than anything I hope to God — and I'm not swearing this time — I hope to whatever God there may be that he hasn't lost Rose.

Reading all this over, I can see that it hasn't been built very well. Its beams and joists, its very walls are somehow out of kilter; its foundation feels weak; possibly I failed to dig the right kind of hole in the ground in the first place. But there's no point in worrying about such things now, because it's time to put the roof on it — to bring you up to date on what happened to the rest of us builders.

Everybody knows what happened to Wade Manley. He died unexpectedly a few years later, in bed; and the fact that it was the bed of a young woman not his wife was considered racy enough to keep the tabloids busy for weeks. You can still see reruns of his old movies on television, and whenever I see one I'm surprised all over again to find that he was a good actor — much too good, I expect, ever to have gotten caught in any cornball role as a cab driver with a heart as big as all outdoors.

As for Dr. Corvo, there was a time when everybody knew what happened to him, too. It happened in the very early fifties, whichever year it was that the television companies built and launched their most massive advertising campaigns. One of the most massive of all was built around a signed statement by Dr. Alexander Corvo, eminent child psychologist, to the effect that any boy or girl in our time whose home lacked a television set would quite possibly grow up emotionally deprived. Every other child psychologist, every articulate liberal, and very nearly every parent in the United States came down on Alexander Corvo like a plague of locusts, and when they were done with him there wasn't an awful lot of eminence left. Since then, I'd say offhand that the *New York Times* would give you half a dozen Alexander Corvos for a single Newbold Morris any day of the week.

That takes the story right on up to Joan and me, and now I'll have to give you the chimney top. I'll have to tell you that what she and I were building collapsed too, a couple of years ago. Oh, we're still friendly — no legal battles over alimony, or custody, or anything like that — but there you are.

And where are the windows? Where does the light come in?

Bernie, old friend, forgive me, but I haven't got the answer to that one. I'm not even sure if there *are* any windows in this particular house. Maybe the light is just going to have to come in as best it can, through whatever chinks and cracks have been left in the builder's faulty craftsmanship, and if that's the case you can be sure that nobody feels worse about it than I do. God knows, Bernie; God knows there certainly ought to be a window around here somewhere, for all of us.

— 1961